Karl heard gunfire below him. The guards must have rushed the stairs. He had very little time left. He emptied his lungs. Waited for his heart to calm then, before his muscles started to shake, he fired.

Karl could have lived and died twice over in the split second between making the shot and the bullet finding its target. That's how long it felt. There was no way he could have seen the bullet slice through the two wires. There was no way he could have missed the resulting explosion.

He seemed to feel it before he saw it. It rattled through him, shaking his innards. There was an immense roar that increased in volume until it was agonising to hear.

The walls of the silo crumbled and flew apart like they were made of sugar paste. The roof dissolved into tatters and was flung miles up into the air with the force of the blast.

An Abaddon Books™ Publication
www.abaddonbooks.com
abaddon@rebellion.co.uk

First published in 2006 by Abaddon Books™, Rebellion Intellectual
Property Limited, The Studio, Brewer Street, Oxford, OX1 1QN, UK.

Distributed in the US and Canada by SCB Distributors,15608 South
Century New Drive, Gardena, CA 90248, USA.

10 9 8 7 6 5 4 3 2 1

Editor: Jonathan Oliver
Cover: Mark Harrison
Design: Simon Parr
Series Advisor: Andy Boot
Marketing and PR: Keith Richardson
Creative Director and CEO: Jason Kingsley
Chief Technical Officer: Chris Kingsley

ISBN 13: 978-1-905437-04-7
ISBN 10: 1-905437-04-8
A CIP record for this book is available from the British Library

Printed in the UK by Bookmarque, Surrey

SPEAR OF DESTINY

Jaspre Bark

Abaddon
Books

WWW.ABADDONBOOKS.COM

CHAPTER ONE

Konig Strasse shook with the leaden drone of the Russian Katyushas. The rockets had been bombarding Berlin for weeks. Karl Fairburne felt the impact of each one vibrate through the floor of the ruined building where he was lying.

He had a cramp in his left side that he had been ignoring for the last 20 minutes. He turned slowly to stretch the muscles without moving too much. He had to remain as still as possible in his vantage point, otherwise he could give away his position, even when he wasn't firing. As with so much of his job, it was a matter of patience and discipline.

Karl put his binoculars carefully up to his eyes so as not to reflect any light off the lenses and surveyed the warehouse 500 yards away. Ten years ago, when Karl had walked this same street as a young man, it would have been impossible to see so far, even with a good pair of binoculars and from the high vantage point he had chosen. That was before Allied bombs had reduced most of the centre of Berlin to rubble.

Karl could remember when the street had teemed with respectable families going about their everyday business. Young men and women, who were now very probably dead, had flirted in doorways and on street corners that no longer existed. Children had chased hoops, swapped marbles and played war, pretending to shoot one another on the same spot where real soldiers now fell to real bullets.

Karl didn't let any of this trouble his thoughts though. He couldn't let anything distract him from his designated task. The slightest lapse in his concentration could cost not only his life, but those of many others fighting to protect the free world.

The warehouse was itself a ruin. The walls were still standing, but most of the roof was missing and few of its windows were intact. His mission was to provide covering fire for a fellow OSS operative who was holed up there on the top floor and needed to escape. Karl and the man he was helping to escape were waiting for the arrival of a jeep so the man could make his getaway.

The jeep was late. There could have been many reasons for that. The main reason being that it had to get close enough to the warehouse for the trapped operative to reach it on foot without being spotted by the NKVD troops stationed around the building.

Karl took stock of the men and where they were stationed. There were two posted at all four of the ground floor exits, hugging the wall so they couldn't be picked off by the OSS operative they aimed to capture. A group of five were stationed on the south-east corner where they were out of the line of fire and Karl presumed another four or five would also be waiting on the northwest corner. This made seventeen or eighteen, by his count, all within range and with little cover.

Karl did not know the name of the operative whose flight he had been ordered to assist. He did know that the man was armed with two Russian issue rifles, a pistol and a good stock of ammunition. This had stood him in good stead for the past six hours. Judging from the type of building he was holed up in, and the way the NKVD troops were reacting to the situation, Karl guessed he had stationed himself near to both the stair well and the fire escape. The stairwells were narrow, as was the fire escape, so any troops storming the building would have to go in single file, making them sitting targets for a good shot.

So long as he had enough nerve, ammunition and food, the man could last several days with relative impunity.

Karl was also aware that the man must be in possession of extremely valuable intelligence. Otherwise Karl's superiors at the Office of Strategic Services would not have gone to so much trouble to rescue and retrieve him. Nor would the NKVD expend so many men on his apprehension.

Karl studied the men stationed around the warehouse, carefully assessing each soldier. Much of Karl's job as a sniper involved observing and evaluating the German and Russian strategic outposts. He had learned a lot about human nature and how a man reacts when under fire. The average soldier has no idea how much he gives away just from the way he stands and holds his weapon. Karl had a fair idea how each of them would react when the conflict began. Where they would shoot, and what they would try and use for cover.

This knowledge was vitally important to the survival of a sniper in the field. As much as he had to understand about the effects of wind speed, gravity and distance on the bullets he was firing, he also had to know all about the possible responses and likely retaliations of the men he was firing at.

Karl could tell the Russian soldiers stationed around the warehouse were angry about the comrades they had lost to the OSS operative, but they were confident that they had the building surrounded and that it was only a matter of time until they caught the man. This confidence had made them complacent though. They weren't expecting anyone to come to the man's aid. They had secured the building but not the surrounding area, and they had not made any provisions for a sniper attack.

The purpose of Karl's fire would be to cause fear and

confusion amongst the men as much as to pick them off. The effect of a single sniper's bullet, appearing out of nowhere to strike down a comrade, had a singular effect on a fighting man. It made him feel exceptionally vulnerable.

When a man comes towards you with his weapon drawn, or shoots at you from a position where he can be seen, a trained soldier knows how to react. When instant death strikes without warning, and you have no idea where it came from, even the hardiest veteran is unnerved. Panic sets in and a man's normal judgement and courage under fire is forgotten. Some men go to pieces altogether.

This was the power that a well trained sniper held in his hands. Karl could still remember what his training instructor had said that first day on the sharpshooters programme at Westpoint. "Son, when you hold the power of life and death in your hands. When you get to decide who lives and who dies, you ain't gonna wonder what it's like to be God. God is gonna wonder what it's like to be you."

The soldiers manning the Katyushas took a welcome break and silence settled on the ruined streets. In the far distance Karl heard the 'put-put' of a jeep approaching. He hoped the man driving was sensible enough not to give his position away too soon.

Karl scanned the streets through his binoculars and picked out the jeep. It wasn't hard to spot as there was a plume of black smoke escaping from the exhaust. He cursed the driver for not choosing a better vehicle and for being sloppy about maintaining it. Karl picked up his rifle. A Geweher 43, German issue, like his uniform and the rest of his kit. He preferred the American M1 Garand, the weapon he'd been trained on, but that would have compromised his cover. Karl was posing as a German soldier from the SS, so he could move around Berlin and operate behind enemy lines without much impediment.

He looked through his scope and drew a bead on his first target. The NKVD soldier in question was a large, burly man with a broad moustache, standing on the southeast corner of the warehouse. The man was grinning and making obscene gestures. The other four men around him were laughing and nodding their heads. He was either telling a dirty joke or relating a sexual incident for the amusement of his comrades.

Karl fixed the man dead in his sights and squeezed the trigger. It was a perfect shot. The bullet entered the man's open mouth, as he was roaring with laughter, and went out through his neck, severing his spinal column. He took two steps backwards, hit the wall behind him and then his legs gave out and he slid to the floor.

The four other men didn't react at first. They probably thought their comrade's actions were all part of the joke. When they realised what had happened there was a lot of shouting and commotion. Two men hit the ground. One of them curled into a foetal position out of sheer fright. One of the two men standing started firing his rifle indiscriminately in a wild, defensive reaction. Only one of the men tried to find proper cover and to scan the surrounding streets to find the direction from which Karl's shot had come.

Karl targeted the wildly firing soldier next. He focused on the man's midriff and let off another shot. The bullet shot through his stomach and blew his guts out of the hole it tore in his back. He bent double and staggered backwards as his innards escaped in a crimson spray. He hit the ground and screamed for help. The shot had undoubtedly sealed his fate, but he would take a good few hours to die. This was just what Karl wanted.

The gutshot soldier's cries brought his comrades running to his aid. The two soldiers guarding the nearest exit raced around the corner to help their comrade, a reckless and misinformed manoeuvre that cost them both their lives. Karl judged the speed and direction at which they were running and made allowances for the air currents around the corner of the building then fixed his sight and waited for the men to move into range. He caught the first with a well aimed head shot, taking the top of the soldier's skull clean off in a fountain of blood and brain tissue. The man dropped on the spot.

Karl's second shot wasn't quite so accurate. He hit the running man in the throat, tearing it clean out. The man kept running and his hands went up to the bloody mess under his chin. He tripped over the soldier he had been running to help and fell directly on top of him. The soldier he landed on screamed in pain at the collision and started beating his fists against the corpse slumped over him.

Karl had now cleared an exit for his fellow operative to escape. He had also sewn fear and confusion among the troops guarding the warehouse. The time was right for the operative to make a run for the waiting jeep. Karl was assuming that he would have stolen a pair of binoculars, when his cover was blown and he had to flee. He would have been watching the jeep pull up from his vantage point and would also have seen that an exit was now clear for him.

The soldier from the southeast corner started shouting that one of the warehouse exits was unsecured. Karl let off a shot in his direction, but the man was a seasoned soldier and new how to find cover. Two soldiers appeared at the northeast corner and levelled their submachine guns at it, intending to catch the man they had under siege as he came through it.

Karl took careful aim. Only one of the soldiers was in range. He got the man level in his crosshairs then fractionally adjusted his aim to accommodate for wind and gravity. The man had his metal helmet pulled down low over his eyes, limiting the target. Karl let off a shot, the soldier's head snapped back and he slumped over sideways.

The shot could not have been timelier, for a fraction of a second later the operative burst through doors of the unguarded exit. He was carrying a shotgun in his left hand, modified by the looks of things, and had a Russian issue pistol in his right. The exit was right in the middle of the warehouse wall. The operative fired shots at both corners to cover himself the minute he left the door. Karl could tell the man was well trained and had been prepared for this sort of outcome.

The operative raced across the open yard in front of the warehouse towards a gate in the broken metal fence. This was when he was most vulnerable and most reliant on Karl's covering fire. The operative was zigzagging to make himself less of a target, and trying to stay out of range of the soldiers posted around the building.

There was a small alley opposite the gate and the operative charged towards it. As he was about to leave the yard, eight of the NKVD guard came after him around the warehouse in a pincer movement, four on each side. Two of the eight NKVD soldiers were firing pistols at the fleeing man. Karl quickly aimed and fired at the nearest of them. The bullet went through the man's shoulder and out his chest. The arm firing the pistol went limp and he dropped to the ground. The soldier directly behind him tripped over his body and sprawled on the ground, dropping his weapon.

Karl aimed at the other pistol-firing soldier. He allowed for the speed at which the man was running and fired at the point the man ought to hit. Unfortunately the soldier doubled back at the last minute, as though some sixth sense had made him anticipate Karl's shot. The bullet bit into the dirt on the ground beside him.

Karl cursed under his breath. He had to change the magazine on his semi-automatic rifle. This left the operative without cover for several seconds at a crucial moment in the operation. He hoped the man could cope. Karl rammed the magazine into place and checked out what was happening with his binoculars.

The pistol firing soldier levelled his weapon at the operative just as the man was rushing through the gate. The soldier fired and the bullet glanced off the top of the operative's shoulder. The operative swung round and unloaded both barrels of the shotgun into the soldier. The soldier flew backwards with a raw, smoking hole in his chest and collided with the man behind him.

The operative turned and made for the alley. Karl took aim at the lead soldier chasing him. He let out his breath, steadied his grip and pulled the trigger. It was an excellent headshot. The Russian soldier crumpled as soon as the bullet pierced his skull. The remaining five NKVD men halted and gave up the chase, heading for cover. Something was not quite right though. They didn't seem unnerved, they appeared to have some knowledge that neither Karl nor the operative had.

Karl shifted his binoculars to check the operative's progress. The man was racing up the alley as fast as he could. As he got halfway up, a Russian vehicle pulled up and blocked his exit. There were three armed men and a driver aboard. They opened fire and the operative turned tail and ran back down the alley with bullets ricocheting all around him. He ducked into an open doorway and took cover behind a ruined wall, pinned down by fire.

Karl realised that drastic action was in order. He scanned the vehicle through his binoculars and broke into a smile as he saw that it had a prominent exterior fuel tank. He picked his rifle up and found the tank in his sights. He estimated the vehicle to be around 1,170 to 1,190 metres away, which was at the far end of the rifle's range. The alley was like a wind tunnel, which would have a severe influence on the shot.

Karl let out a slow breath as he adjusted his aim to compensate for the effects of wind. He probably had one shot at the fuel tank. If he missed, the soldiers on the vehicle would realise what he was doing and simply move out of his range and carry on with their offensive. He steadied the rifle and squeezed the trigger. Time seemed to slow down and almost pause for a second as he made the shot. He felt a part of himself leave and travel with the bullet as it left the muzzle and covered the distance between him and the vehicle.

Karl's aim was dead on. A giant red and orange fireball exploded out from underneath the truck engulfing the vehicle. Even from his vantage point, Karl could hear the roar of the explosion. The back of the truck flipped up and the vehicle landed to one side of the alley, un-blocking the entrance. No survivors stumbled from the wreckage.

The operative peered out from the doorway and raced back up the alley. He had to cross a broad road to get to the side street where the Jeep was parked. As he was halfway across, an NKVD soldier appeared out of a doorway and opened fire with a sub-machine gun. The bullets sent plumes of shrapnel up as they tore into the road. Only one found its mark, nipping the operative's leg. He halted, shifted his weight to his other leg and emptied his pistol into the soldier. He threw the spent weapon at the twitching corpse of his attacker and limped off with blood trickling down his leg.

Karl waited until he was certain that the operative had reached the jeep and that they had gotten away without any problem, before he started to plan his own withdrawal. The NKVD would be angry now. They would have to report to their superiors that they had let a spy carrying valuable information escape during what should have been a simple retrieval operation. Locating Karl would be their top priority, to compensate for losing the operative. If they did find him, it would mean certain death.

No sniper who fell into enemy hands could expect to survive. The fear a sniper instils in enemy soldiers will eventually turn to anger. The soldiers he had terrified would want payback, for the friends and comrades they had lost, and for the powerlessness they had been made to feel. The Geneva Convention wouldn't count for a thing.

Karl had seen the type of treatment he could expect first hand. Before his undercover work for the OSS he had been briefly posted to France to help with the Allied campaign to liberate the country. He was called to flush a German sniper from an abandoned farmhouse who had inflicted severe casualties on American troops. By the time Karl got there though, the sniper had run out of ammunition.

The German threw his rifle out of the window and walked out with his hands up. An officer, whose men had suffered serious losses thanks to the sniper's sharp shooting, walked up to the defenceless man, pulled out his pistol and shot him in the crotch. The German doubled over with pain and was dragged off by the officer's men who made sport with him for the rest of the day. The sniper took a long time to die and his screams and curses still haunted Karl. No soldier was ever reprimanded for the incident. In fact most commanding officers on all sides lent their tacit, but unspoken, support to such treatment of snipers.

Karl decided there and then that he was never going to let that happen to him. He kept a P-38 pistol with him at all times, in case he could not avoid falling into enemy hands, to ensure a quick and painless death by his own hand.

CHAPTER TWO

As Karl was making ready to leave a rifle bullet struck the wall about twenty inches above his head. He froze; someone had worked out his position. From the size of the hole Karl estimated it was a 7.62mm calibre bullet which meant it would have come from either a Tokarev SVT-40 or more likely a Mosin-Nagant M91, both Russian rifles. The NKVD patently had its own sniper, someone good enough to flush Karl out.

Karl knew the remaining troops would be making their way directly over to the ruined tenement building where he was camped out. If he waited around too long they would undoubtedly catch up with him. If he panicked and ran now he would be easy game for the Russian sniper.

Another bullet hit the wall above him, this one a few feet away. This meant the sniper had worked out his approximate position from the shots Karl had taken, but hadn't seen him yet. These shots were experimental, to see if Karl would lose his nerve and bolt. The Russian sniper was feeling him out. Karl's first action had to be to take out the other sniper before he made his escape, but he didn't have long before the NKVD guards would be on him.

Another bullet struck the wall just below him and Karl now had enough information to work out the sniper's approximate position and return fire. The sniper couldn't be more than five hundred metres away or he would be out of range, he would probably be closer. He wouldn't have had time to get very far away from where the NKVD guards were posted either. From the impact the bullets were making Karl could tell he was shooting from a slightly higher vantage point.

This left only one option, the building twenty metes away from the warehouse. It was relatively unscathed and was three storeys higher than the building Karl was in. From the directions at which the bullets had struck the wall around Karl, he surmised that the Russian sniper must be firing from one of three windows.

He zeroed in on the position through his binoculars. At first glance he couldn't see a thing. The Russian was good at his job and had remained well hidden. Karl noticed that one of the windows had a pane of glass that was entirely missing, not just cracked like the others, or smashed with a few jagged edges. All the glass had been removed. He looked closer and saw the end of a bayonet mount and a muzzle in the gloom. This meant the sniper was firing a Mosin-Nagant M91, the Russian army still issued them with bayonets. It also meant Karl had the upper hand, he knew the Russian sniper's exact position, but was still hidden himself.

Karl had one shot. After that the Russian sniper would know his exact position and he would have lost the upper hand. The scope on his rifle was not as powerful as his binoculars so it was more difficult to pick out the muzzle of the rifle. He could remember where it was though and chose his shot accordingly.

Just as Karl was levelling his rifle the sniper sent off another shot. The bullet landed alarmingly close to Karl but he saw the flash. He aimed and pulled the trigger. Karl saw the Russian's head jerk upwards as the bullet entered it, putting an end to his sniping days forever.

He checked the streets outside and saw six NKVD guards charging towards him, less than two minutes away. He could have picked off one, maybe two of them, but by that time they would have reached the building and he had six flights of stairs to get down. He grabbed his kit and left the room.

Four flights down he heard the door of the tenement fly open as one of the guards put his boot through it. Karl checked the back window on the second floor landing. There was a small roof that looked strong enough to support a man's weight about half a storey below. He jimmied open the window as the Russian guards' heavy boots sounded on the stairs.

He climbed out, hung on to the sill and dropped to the roof below. Karl staggered a few steps as he landed and hit a loose tile. His feet flew out from under him and he skidded down on his back. Reaching out a hand as he slid he caught hold of the guttering in time to stop his fall.

As he came to a halt he heard footsteps in the alleyway just to the side of the tenement building. Karl rolled on to his stomach and crawled up to the edge of the roof to investigate, making certain to stay well hidden. Two of the guards were doubling round to the rear of the building.

Karl pulled out his P-38, with silencer attached, and shot both men in the head from behind. They fell without making a sound. Karl swung himself over the wall and dropped. Without any warning, he felt a pair of arms encircle his shoulders from behind, and the cold steel of a rifle barrel was pressed against his throat, cutting off his air supply.

Karl had been caught off guard by a third NKVD soldier he hadn't spotted. The man called out in Russian to his comrades at the top of his voice. Karl struggled but the man held him tight. Red blotches appeared in front of his bulging eyes as his empty lungs burned. Karl lifted his right foot and grabbed the knife he kept in his boot. The handle caught on his sock and he nearly dropped it. For a second he thought this was where it all ended. Then he regained his grip.

He buried the blade deep in his captor's left armpit. The Russian's grip relaxed and Karl pushed the rifle away from his throat with his left hand then swung round and thrust the knife at the Russian's chest. The man caught Karl's wrist with his right hand and they fought for the knife. The Russian called out again. Karl lunged forward and head butted him. Blood streamed from the soldier's nose and he reeled back, dazed.

Karl took the opportunity to wrest the knife free from the Russian's grip and ram it into his throat. Blood frothed up into the Russian's mouth, Karl took hold of the knife's handle with both hands and drove it diagonally downwards, severing the artery. Blood sprayed out in a fine jet, covering the walls and Karl. The Russian's legs gave out and he keeled over.

Karl could hear the other three NKVD guards approaching the alley. He bent down and searched the Russian's still twitching corpse. There were two grenades on his belt. He took one of them off, armed it and waited until all three men turned the corner at the top of the alley. Karl was crouching in the gloom and they didn't see him until he stood up and threw the grenade into the centre of all three. The explosion tore the men apart and lit-up the darkened alley with its bright orange flare.

Karl took stock of the situation. He was covered in blood with the smell of burning flesh in his nostrils. The still warm corpses of the six men he had just killed lay at his feet and in the last hour he had been directly responsible for the deaths of ten more. His work was done. It was time to go get breakfast.

CHAPTER THREE

The whining roar of a fighter plane broke the silence of the street. The women and children dropped the rubble they'd been using to build a barricade and quickly found what shelter they could.

Karl hugged a half-demolished wall and glanced up at the plane as it buzzed the street, flying low enough to see every join in its fuselage. It was a British Spitfire, designed for aerial combat. It was not carrying any bombs. The women and children, who comprised the Citizens Militia for this section of the city, came out from their makeshift hiding places and carried on with their business.

Their faces showed that they were now completely resigned to the constant threat of death. Human beings will adapt quickly to any situation and death had long since ceased to frighten them. They had lived with it so long it was almost a member of the family. When it did finally strike, whether it was in an Allied bombing raid or from an enemy bullet, they would simply be welcoming an old friend who had come to bring their suffering to an end.

Karl had seen many types of soldier in his tour of duty, but these were without doubt the most miserable. Women, children and old or crippled men, most of whom had lost their homes, their possessions and much of their family, were now forced to defend the outskirts of the city from the invading Allied armies.

They were armed with the most rudimentary weapons; spades sharpened to become axes and broom handles whittled into spears, antique hunting rifles and whatever else they could scavenge off the corpses of fallen enemy soldiers. They were the last line of defence of a former super-power, reduced to relying on women and children to do its dirty work.

In a way Karl had to admire the indomitability of the German spirit, fighting on to the very last citizen even when defeat was imminent. On the other hand, the citizens pressed into service didn't care about the honour of the Third Reich. They were just trying to stay alive, trapped between the threat of their Nazi leaders and the Russian forces bearing down on the city, eager to avenge the slaughter at Stalingrad.

Karl leant on his crutch and hobbled off. He was disguised as a crippled soldier. His right leg was bound up and the trouser leg was pinned below the knee. He looked like an invalid, sent back from the front to defend his home city. It was the perfect cover for this part of town.

Gathering intelligence behind enemy lines is all about hiding right out in the open. Twenty minute ago Karl had passed an Autowagen full of SS officers, none of whom had batted an eyelid. They had no idea he was on his way to a briefing with his commanding officer in the OSS.

A small boy of no more than ten was standing on top of a hastily erected barricade as Karl hobbled past. He spotted the rifle slung over Karl's shoulder and mimed the action of firing it.

"Shoot a little piggy for me," the boy called out in German.

"I will," Karl replied, in a perfect Berliner accent, even though the little piggies the boy had in mind were on Karl's side.

Karl continued past a row of abandoned shop fronts, in what used to be a picturesque suburban district, until he came to an old Bierkeller. He hopped down the steps and banged on the old wooden door. "Wer ist das?" A voice called out from within.

"Fritz," Karl shouted back.

"Haben Sie meine Kartoffeln?" the voice asked.

"Nein," replied Karl. "Ich habe nur zweibel." This was the correct answer, Karl heard the thick bolts being unlocked and the door swung open.

He stepped into a large cellar with a low ceiling. There were no windows, no electric power and the whole place was lit with candles. A fire hissed and popped in the grate, two men sat in front of it on rickety wooden chairs, a large leather attaché case between them.

Karl turned to Hank, the man who had opened the door to him, a tall burly man with an eye patch and a thick black beard. He looked like a simple peasant who had been dragged out of the fields, wounded in war, and then sent back to die on the home front. Like all the best agents, his appearance belied that he was a highly trained and deadly security operative. Karl knew the briefing was in safe hands the minute he heard Hank's flawless German.

Karl put his hand on Hank's shoulder to support himself and began to unstrap his right leg. Hank's eye patch was as false as Karl's leg. There was a capsule of cyanide gas sewn into it potent enough to kill ten men in an open space and twenty in a confined area like the cellar. Hank turned his back to the door as Karl walked over to the fire.

Karl didn't recognise the younger of the two men sitting there. The older man rose to greet him. He was tall and slender with a slight stoop. He had piercing blue eyes and his bald head was ringed with close cut steel grey hair. "Karl," he said. "Pull up a stool." Karl had known Max Avery since before he was a teenager. Max had been Special Assistant to Karl's father at the Embassy in Berlin.

Karl's father was a high-ranking US diplomat, and between the wars he had been posted to Berlin. Karl had grown up in the city, walked its streets as a boy, played softball in its parks, made out in its cinemas. Uncle Max had been part of his life during a good part of this time.

Karl's father, like all great leaders, inspired huge amounts of respect and devotion in those who had worked under him. No one had been more devoted to Karl's father than Max. Karl's father had repaid that devotion by welcoming Max into his family. Max was always a feature at Thanksgiving, dressing up as a Native American, to the complete bemusement of the German staff. He had taught Karl how to throw a curve ball and how to steal a base.

The whole family were disappointed when Max was reassigned back to the States. Karl's father probably felt the loss the worst. He said nothing when his wife asked him if he could do something about it, and she knew better than to push the subject.

Max never did find a nice American girl to settle down with, though he did find a new career when President Roosevelt approached 'Wild Bill' Donovan to establish the Office of Strategic Services. Donovan personally recruited Max who had worked in the Co-ordinator of Information, the predecessor to the OSS. Max's experience made him the ideal candidate to head up the OSS's operation in Berlin. It was a choice position. Berlin was key to American post-war policy.

Max had been keeping a careful eye on Karl's military career. Karl was one of the first operatives he had recruited upon being posted back to Germany. Not only did Karl know the city as intimately as Max, he had also graduated from Westpoint with the second highest ranking in marksmanship on record. This made him ideal for the elite team of snipers that Max wanted to put together.

To Karl's surprise his father had been against him working for Max. He had tried to find Karl a safe job in the War Department, but Karl could simply not countenance sitting out the war behind some desk when his country, not to mention the rest of the free world, needed his skills. Max was delighted with Karl's decision.

Karl was the only operative whom Max briefed personally. Every other agent, including the elite sniper unit – which was Max's little baby – received their orders from one of Max's subordinates. The honour Max did him was not lost on Karl. He had seen and done many things in his tour of duty that tested, and even shattered, his concepts of morality, integrity and honour, but his personal faith in Max had never wavered. The older man was a rock in Karl's life. Proof that he was doing right by his country, no matter how dirty things got.

Karl pulled up the proffered stool.

It had three uneven legs and put him a head lower than the other two. This meant the younger man was extremely important to the OSS. He was around five-foot nine. He wore his dark brown hair in a buzz cut and gave the impression that he knew how to handle himself.

"I don't believe you've met Chuck Fleischer, though you saved his life yesterday," Max said.

"That was you?" Karl said in surprise.

"It certainly was," Chuck affirmed. "That was some pretty fancy shooting too. When the truck pulled up at the top the alley I thought I was a goner for sure. I still can't believe how easily you took out the gas tank."

"Oh, our Karl here certainly knows his way around a rifle," said Max. "You couldn't have been in safer hands. We needed you home, so I sent the best."

"I have to say Chuck," Karl said. "You didn't seem to need much help getting out. I thought you carried yourself pretty well."

"But not so well that I didn't get caught in the first place."

"Yeah, what happened there?" said Karl. He glanced at Max. "If it's not 'need to know'." Chuck looked at Max.

"That's okay," said Max. "It won't hurt to hear your story again. Karl and Hank here are briefed at the highest levels."

"I was assigned to go undercover in the NKVD here in Berlin. I had to go to a bit of trouble to get inside the organisation, but we had a spot of luck. A supervisor was sent out from Moscow, travelling with only one bodyguard. We took the man and his bodyguard out then I replaced him. My cover story was that I was attacked by assassins. We even planted two dead bodies to corroborate the tale. The NKVD here in Berlin had no visual record of the man I replaced and all my papers were in order so they bought it."

"They weren't at all suspicious?" Karl asked.

"Not of the USA. We're still supposed to be their allies. They watch us quite closely but they don't have any respect for our intelligence operations. They've been at this sort of thing for hundreds of years. You know what these Europeans are like. We've only had an operation the size of the OSS for just over three years. They think we're rank amateurs, they didn't believe we would have the initiative to pull off something like this."

"So what happened?"

"Well it turns out the man I replaced was a bit of a philanderer. Couldn't keep it in his pants. He had a wife and several girlfriends, one of whom he got pregnant just before he left. Turns out this girl's father has influential friends in the Kremlin. So he tracks down my whereabouts and travels out here with his daughter, who's eight months pregnant, to confront me with my sins. Only when he gets here and surprises me I'm not the man he expected to find. I tried to deny everything of course. To convince him and his daughter that there had been a big mix up, but he wouldn't let it go. He got back to his contacts in Moscow and I was rumbled. They came to arrest me but I got the drop on the guards, raided the arsenal and fled. I managed to get word to Max before I ended up holed up in that warehouse and he sent you to help me. You know the rest."

"That's a tough break," said Karl.

Chuck shrugged nonchalantly. "It happens in this game"

"I don't want to jump the gun or anything," Karl said. "But the NKVD sent eighteen men to retrieve you. Now I know you're good, I've seen you in action, but they wouldn't have sent that many men if you didn't have something that they didn't want to fall into our hands. I'm guessing that *something* is the purpose of this briefing."

"Astute as ever Karl," said Max. "What do you know about the A-bomb?"

"I know we got some guys back home working on one," Karl said. "If you split an atom it releases a lot of energy right? Enough of a bang to take out a lot of buildings."

"Worse than that," said Max. "Enough of a bang to take out a whole city, maybe more. This weapon will change the face of warfare forever. But we're not the only ones working on it. The Nazis have beaten us to the draw."

Max bent forward and picked up the attaché case at his feet. He pulled out a photograph and handed it to Karl. It showed a pudgy, middle-aged man, with a stern expression in an SS officer's uniform.

"That's General Friedrich Helmstadt. A close confidant

of SS Reichsführer Heinrich Himmler and a member of the powerful inner circle at Castle Wewelsburg, the SS Headquarters."

"I hear they got all kinds of weird stuff happening there," said Karl. "Is that true?"

"As weird as it gets," said Chuck. "Black rites, magic circles, the works."

"But we're dealing with something a lot more serious than a few grown men dressing up and biting the heads off chickens," Max said. "Helmstadt is the head of the Nazi's nuclear programme. He was the one who first brought the possibility of splitting the atom to Hitler's attention."

"But I thought Hitler was against nuclear power. I didn't even know the Nazi's had a nuclear programme."

"Neither did we until a little while ago," said Max. "And Hitler *was* against nuclear power at the beginning of the war. It was dirty Jew science as far as he saw it. Einstein, a Jew, came up with the idea and other Jewish scientists developed it. Therefore it was as good as a lie. Helmstadt changed his mind though. He convinced the Nazi's that it was an Aryan idea all along. He dug up a small-time research assistant of Einstein's called Hans Durenmatt, a mediocre talent with blond hair and blue eyes, who also happened to be a member of the Nazi party. He told everyone that nuclear fission, in fact most of Einstein's theories, originated with Durenmatt. Einstein stole those ideas off him and passed them off as his own, and the international Jewish conspiracy had conspired to keep Durenmatt from enjoying the rewards of his true brilliance.

"Durenmatt was put in charge of research and development for the nuclear programme. He and Helmstadt were smart enough not to believe their own hype though. They used captured Polish and Jewish scientists as slave labour to work on the project and push it forward. Nuclear power is a dangerous business. You've got to work with all sorts of unstable materials. Our guys on the Manhattan Project are hidebound by all kinds of safety regulations that the Nazis just didn't care about. That's how they stole a march on us."

"The supervising German scientists all took precautions," said Chuck. "But hundreds of great Jewish and Polish minds perished to make the Nazi's A-bomb."

"So, if this weapon is as powerful and important as you say it is," said Karl. "How come the Germans haven't used it yet?"

"That's a complicated issue," said Max. "For one thing Germany's air force is in ruins and they might not have the means to deploy it. Also an operation like that would need clearance at the very highest level. No one would dare stick their neck out without it."

"The Nazi party is torn apart by factional in-fighting at the moment," said Chuck. "The Führer's retreated to his bunker and no-one knows who's running the asylum."

"If you don't mind me saying," Karl said to Chuck. "You seem to know a lot about this."

"I should do," said Chuck. "It was my job in the NKVD. I was in charge of identifying and locating key personnel in the Nazi nuclear programme who were ripe for turning."

"You mean going over to the Soviets?"

"That's right," said Chuck. "About four months ago I received word that Helmstadt has lost some serious ground to his rival in the SS, Gruppenführer Hans Kammler, the head of the V2 programme. Kammler has always seen the nuclear programme as his by right. He's coveted it since it was founded. Recent events meant the Nazi high command have been looking for scapegoats to blame for the failure of the German war effort. Kammler had his project up and running in time to do some damage to the Allied war machine, but Helmstadt didn't provide them with the super weapon they were promised in time."

"So Helmstadt wants to get out of the country before he finds himself on the wrong end of a Luger, and you arranged his defection, is that it?" said Karl.

"It's not quite that simple," said Chuck. "Helmstadt knows how to play the game. He wields great power in one of the most cut throat organisations there is and he's very good at hanging on to it. He wants to defect, but he knows the price of what he can bring with him. He's cut some kind of deal with Kammler that gets him out of the corner he was in. This means if he's going to go over to the Soviets, with all the Nazi nuclear secrets he can do so at leisure, and on his own terms."

"What sort of deal has he cut with Kammler?" Karl asked.

"I can't tell you the full details but I know that they're bringing a nuclear warhead into Berlin. My last order, before I was rumbled, was to detail a lot of reinforcements to guard it."

"Is there any way we can get to Helmstadt," Karl asked. "Make him tell us what's going on?"

"That won't be possible," said Max, reaching into the attaché case again. He handed Karl a file with a set of photos in it.

"What's this?" said Karl.

"Those are pictures of a reinforced steel case that Helmstadt carries with him at all times," said Max. "Treat them carefully, they cost us the lives of two operatives. The case contains sole copies of practically every nuclear secret the Nazi's have, along with a built in thermo-nuclear device. Helmstadt had a surgeon wire his heart up to a radio controlled detonation device. If his heart stops, or that case gets more than ten feet away from him then the device is triggered and he could wipe out half a city. It's his security against apprehension or theft of the secrets. The only way to open the case is with a twelve-part combination that only Helmstadt knows. Use the wrong combination and..."

"Boom," said Karl.

"Exactly," said Max, he leaned in close. His manner became avuncular and an affectionate tone crept into his voice. "Now you understand Karl that we're telling you all this as a courtesy. This information could compromise the safety of a lot of agents if it fell into the wrong hands. We want you to be briefed to the very height of your clearance. It's important to me that you know exactly what kind of stakes we're playing for here."

"Well I'm honoured that you have taken me into your confidence," said Karl.

"Don't be honoured," said Max. "Just be careful."

"So what's my part in all this?" Karl asked.

Max handed him a map of central Berlin and some notes. "We've got quite a few plans for you," he said. "To begin with, we want you to find out where the NKVD reinforcements detailed to help guard the warhead are coming into the city, and take out at least one full team. Do as much damage as you possibly can. It's vital for us that this operation is as undermanned as we can make it. That will make any other sabotage operations run a lot more smoothly and will swing the odds in our favour when we have to use ground troops.

"We have a mobile operation in the centre of Berlin intercepting broadcasts on every known frequency that the Russians are using. They move around as much as possible to avoid detection. It's a three-man team, an engineer, a radio operator and one of our best code-breakers. This map shows you where they're going to be tomorrow from noon onwards. Rendezvous with them and see what you can find out about Russian troop movements."

"Do I contact you once I know something?"

"Use your initiative on this mission," Max said. "But send word to me at all key stages of its development, so I'm kept up to date. If anything alters, or I need you to change course, I'll get word to you through the usual channels. Now memorise the map and throw it into the fire."

Karl scanned the streets and landmarks. It was a part of town he knew. Although he hadn't been to the street in question he was fairly certain he could find it. Once he'd burned the picture of the map into his mind, he threw the paper into the fire and burned the original.

Hank turned quickly and motioned for them to be quiet. All three men froze. Outside there was the sound of foot fall on the stairs. It sounded like four or more men. Karl couldn't be entirely certain. A fist rapped on the door.

"Open up!" An officious voice said in German.

"There's no other exit is there?" Karl whispered.

"None," Max said under his breath. Hank looked to Max. Max signalled him to open the door. An officer and four soldiers from the Gestapo stood on the steps outside.

CHAPTER FOUR

"What's this?" said the Gestapo officer as he led his men into the cellar. "An unlicensed Bierkeller? I didn't know this place was still open." He walked up to the fire, two of his men followed him and stood either side of Karl, Max and Chuck. The other two men flanked Hank at the door. The officer warmed his hands for a moment and smiled. He turned to address one of his men. "You remember Commandant Mann don't you Heinz? He and I used to drink in this very establishment, just after the Polish campaign. Of course the decor was a lot better then." Karl sat very still, giving nothing away in his expression or posture. He knew the officer's familiar tone was meant to catch them off guard, and so did the others.

"Aren't you going to offer your guests a drink?" said the officer. "I remember this place used to have one of the finest selections of schnapps in the city."

"Please Herr Officer," said Max in perfect German.

"That's Herr Capitan to you," the officer snapped, suddenly becoming officious.

"Please Herr Capitan," Max continued. "We're not here to drink, we're simple soldiers from the Citizen's Militia."

"From the Militia are we?" said the officer. "So you men have deserted your posts."

"Oh-no, Herr Capitan. We were investigating reports of unauthorised activity here in the cellar."

"But you had time to light a fire and lock the door," said the officer.

"The fire was lit when we got here. Whoever was in the place must have just left. I'm told there are spies and saboteurs operating in the area and you can't be too careful. We locked the door to make certain they couldn't escape if they were still hiding in the building. We only sat down for a moment to warm our bones."

Karl, Hank and Chuck were watching Max very carefully. They trusted his management of the situation and were waiting to follow his lead. For the moment Max was assessing whether they could bluff their way out of the predicament, but all three men were readying themselves for action.

"Ridiculous," sneered the officer. "You suspect this place is being used for unauthorised purposes, so rather than conduct a thorough search of the cellar and surrounding streets you shut the door and settle yourself down by the fire. In case you gentlemen haven't noticed this city is under siege and you're supposed to be engaged in its defence. Not sitting by a fire warming your useless bones. Bones that would be better employed if they were melted down for glue to use in the war effort."

Chuck looked over at Karl and signalled with his eyes that he would take the man on the left and that Karl should jump the one on the right. Karl blinked his assent without anyone noticing. Max caught Hank's eye to tell him to be ready to move on his signal.

The officer was working himself into a fit of self-righteous fury. He spotted the attaché case at Max's feet. "What's in that case?" he demanded.

"Nothing," said Max. "Just some old newspapers."

"Doesn't look like newspapers to me. Then again, what would an illiterate old dolt like you know. That's far too good an attaché case to waste on old newspapers. Give it here."

Max picked up the case and stood very slowly. Karl and the other two watched him intently. On the surface they all appeared calm but inside they were coiled like springs straining to be released. Max fumbled the case and dropped it at the officer's feet. He shot Hank a glance that meant go. Then he gave Karl and Chuck the same glance as he bent apologetically to pick up the case.

Karl's adrenaline levels shot up, as they always did in close combat situations. Time seemed to slow down in those moments. Or at least he seemed to take so much more in.

Karl pulled a hidden knife from his belt. It had a short double-sided blade that was scalpel sharp. In one single movement he got up from his chair, swivelled round and drove the blade into the chest of the man in back of him, right between the sixth and seventh ribs and straight into his heart. The soldier pushed Karl backwards without realising what had happened, and reached involuntarily for his gun. Then he saw the knife in Karl's hand and the torrent of blood gushing from the hole in his chest. His eyes rolled up into his head and he hit the floor.

At the edge of his peripheral vision Karl took in what the other three were doing simultaneously. Max stooped down to grab the attaché, and as the officer loomed over him, he brought his head up sharp into the man's chin, grabbing the officer's pistol as he did so.

The soldier behind Chuck trained his weapon on Karl. Chuck doubled round behind him, grabbed the hair at the back of his head then rammed a broad, thin knife into the back of the soldier's neck, just below the fourth vertebrae. Thick clear liquid gushed out as his spinal column was severed. Death was instantaneous and he hit the floor like a belt of spent ammo.

On getting the signal from Max, Hank had fallen upon the two soldiers flanking him. He slammed the heel of his palm into the base of the right hand soldier's nose, breaking it at the bridge and driving the shard of shattered bone up into the front of his brain. He was dead before he hit the cold stone floor.

At the same time, Hank smashed his left forearm into the back of the other soldier's neck then swung his right arm around the front of the man's throat. Hank grasped his left elbow, lifted the man off the floor and flexed his muscles. The pressure snapped the soldier's neck, his body jerked a few times and his legs kicked, then he went limp and Hank dropped him.

Karl turned back to Max who had a pistol trained at the temple of the terrified officer. "Now," Max said. "If you value your miserable life in the slightest you'll answer everything I ask you as truthfully and succinctly as you can. All three men in front of you are experts in interrogation. If you lie to me they will know and I will kill you. Do you understand?" The officer swallowed hard and nodded.

"Are you the only men on patrol around here?" Max said. The officer nodded and licked his lips, his throat was hoarse when he spoke.

"We were inspecting the barricades the militia are building and someone mentioned they had seen a couple of men go in here. We were just checking it out."

"Who told you about us?"

"One of the militia. An old woman, too feeble to fire a gun, she was carrying dirt to the barricade in the front of her apron. She saw a couple of you go in here, she thought you were shirking your duties."

"How did you and your men get here?"

"We have an armoured car parked just around the corner from here."

"Perfect," said Max in English. "Karl you keep our guest here covered. Hank and Chuck you switch clothes with these soldiers. Try to keep the blood off the uniforms."

Max, Hank and Chuck chose a soldier closest to their size and weight and swapped clothes with him. They stripped the fourth body as well and took all the weaponry and any identification the men had. Then Max relieved Karl, sticking the pistol in the base of the officer's back.

"We're going to leave here now," he said. "You're going to walk us slowly to your car and we're going to drive away. If I even suspect you're going to call out or try to double cross us you'll be dead before you can draw your next breath. Is that clear?"

"Clear," said the officer.

"Karl," said Max, "put your hands on your head and walk in front of us. Hank, train your rifle on him. Chuck, you take up the rear." Karl led the way out of the cellar and up the steps. They walked steadily to the end of the street and turned the corner. The officer directed them to the car and Max climbed in along with Hank, Chuck and the officer.

"This is where we part company Karl," said Max, when he'd made sure they weren't being watched. "You have your orders and you know where you're going. I'll be in touch soon." He turned to Hank, who was sitting behind the wheel, and motioned for him to leave.

Karl watched them depart then ducked into an alley. He was already planning a route back into the city centre that would draw the least attention.

CHAPTER FIVE

Karl stopped and surveyed the half demolished streets. The ruined state of the city centre did not match up with the map he had memorised. He knew the area from his childhood, but he was having a hard time locating the address where he was supposed to meet the other agents.

The streets of central Berlin were labyrinthine at the best of times. With rubble covering many intersections and whole rows of buildings levelled by Allied bombs, it became impossible in places to decipher how the roads had looked before the war. Karl was progressing towards his destination by means of memory and deduction.

He knew he was in the right area; he needed to find a building with enough height to mount an aerial and enough shelter to hide from detection. Karl had narrowed it down to two possible buildings. He scanned them both with a trained military eye to determine which would be most likely.

As he was checking them out he noticed a slight movement in the far building. It was in a window on the third floor. Karl pulled the binoculars out of his pack. He saw the tops of two German infantry helmets and the lenses of a set of standard issue German army binoculars. They were monitoring activity in the building opposite. Karl now knew he had found the radio-monitoring outfit; it was in the building closest to him. More importantly, the operation was under enemy surveillance and thereby in serious jeopardy.

To make contact with the outfit now would endanger all their lives. Karl had to find out what the Germans knew about the activities of the mobile radio surveillance unit and what they intended to do about it. He walked slowly up to the building where he had seen the two German soldiers, making certain to choose a path that was out of their field of vision.

This area of town had been a red-light district before the war. The building where the German soldiers were staked out had probably been a brothel as had the building they were watching. These buildings always had several entrances and exits, to allow for the discretion of their clients and to provide a quick getaway if the place was raided. Karl chose the most secluded entrance and made his way soundlessly up to the third floor.

The two German soldiers were lying flat on the ground staring out of the window. They did not hear Karl as he approached the doorway and he paused to watch them for a minute. The fatter of the soldiers broke wind loudly. "Ach, not again," said his companion. "You've got foulest backside in the whole regiment."

"Well it's not my fault. Blame the cabbage and potato soup they've been feeding us this past week. What I wouldn't give for a proper Wiener schnitzel, or a good Bratwurst."

"There was more than a few Bratwurst swallowed in this place before the war."

His companion broke into a dirty belly laugh at this. "Ja. And I bet your mother swallowed half of them."

"Heil Hitler!" Karl barked from the doorway, catching both men off guard. They swivelled round and pointed their weapons at him, then relaxed when they saw his uniform.

"Ach man, you made us jump," said the fat one.

"Did you have to creep up on us like that?" said the other. "What are you doing here?"

"I might ask you the same question," Karl said, and

indicated his rifle. "There have been reports of enemy movements near here. I came to pick a few of them off."

"Oh, you're a scharfenschützer," said the fat soldier with a scowl. The attitude of the two cooled towards him then. Snipers were not popular with the ordinary infantry. Even if they were on the same side they were a hated breed. Most men had lost friends and comrades to a sniper at this point in the war and felt hostility to snipers in general.

All snipers, like Karl, acted alone and apart from the common troops, so they were seen as distant, aloof at best, and cold hearted killers at worst. They didn't socialise or mix with their own troops and they were ordered not to talk about what they did, most didn't care to anyway. This only heightened the antipathy the other soldiers felt towards them.

Whatever the average soldier does in wartime he can blame on the fact that he was only doing what he was told. Orders are orders and it's kill or be killed, so he doesn't really have a choice about taking another life. A sniper does have a choice, he determines the fate of every man who comes into his crosshairs, and many front-line soldiers, on all sides, see him as little better than a murderer.

"You men are scouts I take it," Karl said. "What have you seen across the way?"

"What makes you think we were looking across the way?" said the thin soldier.

"The position you're lying in, the direction you're pointing your binoculars," said Karl. "I've been out on the street so I know there's nothing down there. It stands to reason, then, that you've got to be checking out the building across from us."

The two men were guarded in their response. "There's

something we're monitoring," said the thin one. "We think they're British or Russian, it's hard to tell without hearing them speak."

"How many of them are there?" asked Karl.

"We can't tell. We've seen two, there's probably more."

"Do you want me to take a shot at one, or do you have different orders

"Which division did you say you were with again?" asked the fat soldier suspiciously.

"I'm sorry," said Karl breaking into a smile. "I ask a lot of questions. I like to know as much as possible about an area I'm working in. I thought we could trade info."

"I don't hear you volunteering anything," said the thin soldier. The men were wary of Karl. As a scout, you don't stay alive as long as they had, this far into the war, without being very wary.

"I just told you I was down in the street didn't I, and that I didn't see anything."

The two soldiers regarded Karl for a moment then the thin one broke out laughing. "Hey what is this?" he said. "A staring match. You know we'll never win one of those with a scharfenschütze." He motioned for Karl to crawl over and join them at the window. "Come, we'll show you what we've seen," he said. The two soldiers exchanged a look. Their faces were as relaxed and genial as they could make them, but their bodies were tensed and ready for action. Karl knew they were trying to lure him to the window so they could jump him.

He pretended to play along, crouching down and making as though he were about to crawl over. The he began to scratch himself vigorously. "Damn these fleas," Karl said. "I don't know what's worse, the fleas or the pox that regimental whore gave me." He reached inside his jacket and pretended to continue scratching as he un-holstered his P-38.

He pulled it out and put one bullet right between the eyes of the thin soldier. His face registered surprise as his body went rigid and his brains spattered the window behind him. Without giving the other soldier time to react Karl turned and put two in his stomach. He doubled over and retched with the pain.

Karl walked over and kicked away the man's weapons, then knelt beside him. "You're a seasoned soldier," Karl said. "You know how long it takes to die from a bullet to your gut, and how painful that is. Tell me everything I need to know and I'll end your suffering straight away."

"Go screw your... mother!" the fat soldier heaved, spraying blood and spittle.

He was a tough one, Karl could see that but he tried again. "Have you reported your position and what you've seen to your command post? Or were you posted here to observe the men across the way? Who else knows about this?" The fat soldier tried to mouth another obscenity but was in too much pain to speak. "I could make this a lot easier on you if you'd co-operate," Karl said.

The soldier made an obscene gesture then rolled over and curled up into a foetal position, whimpering like a child. "Mutter," was all he would say, "oh Mutti..." Karl could see that it was pointless to try any further interrogation. From the state of the room the men had not been here long and there was no communication equipment about, so it was safe to assume that they had not reported anything. They were probably on a reconnaissance mission when they spotted the OSS outfit and decided to investigate. The communications team wouldn't have been there long anyway.

Karl stood over the fat soldier and put one last bullet in his brain. He was not a sadist and saw no reason why the man should suffer any further.

CHAPTER SIX

After climbing to the top of the whorehouse and scanning the area with his binoculars to check for any other troops, Karl crossed the rubble-strewn street to the other building.

He walked up the first flight of steps and whistled a refrain from a popular tune. There was a slight pause and someone within the building whistled a few more bars. Karl responded with the next part of the song and a door opened on the floor above him. "Up here."

Through the door Karl could just make out the face of an operative. "You're late," he said.

"There was something I had to sort out across the way. I'll explain inside." The door swung open and Karl stepped into the room.

The place was bare apart from a wooden table and three chairs. Tatters of the once luxurious wallpaper still clung to the walls and an old kerosene stove burned in the corner. "You must be Karl," said the man who let him in. He was of average height with sandy brown hair and a thick brown moustache. "I'm John," he said. He turned to a slightly younger man sitting at the table, who was tall and thin with wispy blond hair. "This is Robert," he said, "and this is Gary." John indicated a heavy set man with glasses and an intelligent, yet sardonic, set to his features. He wore a long leather coat and looked like he knew how to carry himself. "Howdy," said Robert, Gary just nodded.

"Good to meet you," said Karl.

"We received word from command that you'd be coming," said John. "What can we do for you?"

"I'll come to that in a minute. How long have you been

set up at this location?"

"About two or three hours," said John. "We move around regularly between a set of safe bases. We were obliged to give a location for our next foray last time we checked in to command to make our report, so we chose here."

"Is something wrong?" asked Robert. "It's just that you seem kinda agitated."

"You were being watched by two German soldiers. I took care of them for you, that's why I'm late, but I didn't get anything out of them before they died."

Robert and John blanched at this. Karl could tell they were worried by how close they had come to being captured, and were perturbed by the matter of fact way Karl had spoken of taking human life. They were typical Communications Branch operatives, college graduates – probably Ivy League – recruited for their knowledge and expertise in languages, engineering or local know-how. They were not soldiers and had probably not seen any form of active service. This was a grand caper to them. A 'Boys Own' adventure full of intrigue and information gathering. Although they had to be careful, they were rarely called on to get their hands dirty.

"How did they know we were here?" said John.

"I checked and there were no other troops around," said Karl. "So my guess is that they just got lucky while they were on a routine patrol and saw you as you approached the place. However... " He broke off as he thought matters over.

"Uh oh," said Robert, anticipating bad news.

"If we're unlucky then they know this is one of your regular bases and they've been staking it out waiting for you to return, so they can set a trap."

"What can we do?" said Robert. He was worried and

the geniality and contrived flippancy had gone from his voice.

"We keep our cool," said Karl. "Stay alert and stay away from any of the windows. We don't have much time if they are on to us so we need to do this quickly. How many ways are there out of this place?"

"Two," said John, "your standard front and back exits."

"Three," said Gary, speaking for the first time. "There's a toilet down in the basement at the back that's been destroyed. The soil pipe is the old fashioned German kind. It's large enough for a man to fit through and it goes straight down to the sewers. The tunnels down there are well built and intact in this part of the city."

"How in God's name do you know that?" said Robert incredulously.

"It's my job to know these things," Gary told him, in a manner that would brook no further discussion.

"Well we better find out what you need to know and quickly," John said to Karl.

"There are two sets of NKVD troops coming into Berlin. One by road, the other by rail. They're reinforcements that are to meet a German platoon and provide extra security for their operation."

"Wait a minute," said Robert. "Russians providing security for a German operation? I thought they hated the fascists."

"They do. That doesn't stop them protecting their own interests though."

"I don't know," said Robert. "This war just keeps on getting weirder the longer we're out here. Sometimes I'm not certain who I'm working for."

"You'll have to forgive Robert," said John. "He's our resident pinko. He hates fascists and has a hard on for the commies. He can't see what a threat to US interests they're shaping up to be."

"They're our allies," Robert said.

"They're as bad as the Nazis," John replied. "The only difference is that the Soviets aren't finished as a military empire. They've only just started down that route."

"We don't have time to have this discussion now," Karl said cutting in. "I need you to find out where the NKVD troops are coming in to the city and what their eventual destination will be. I need as much information as you can give me regarding routes that they'll take and points at which they'll meet up with the Nazi soldiers."

"We'll have to monitor a lot of broadcasts," said Robert. "German, Russian and British, just for good measure."

"You get a broader picture that way," said John. "It won't take as long as it sounds though. Over half of the job is deduction, once we pick out the few threads we need it'll be easier to chase down what you want to know."

"How long will that take?" asked Karl.

"How long is a piece of string?" John shrugged.

Karl looked around the room, there were several cases and a box or two filled with maps, books and other paper work. "Where's the radio equipment?" Karl wanted to know.

"Right here," said Robert, patting two large cases. He unhooked the catches and opened them to reveal compact radios. "Meet the SSTR-1."

"That stands for Strategic Services Transmitter Receiver," said John. "Sometimes known as 'suitcase radios'."

"We might have been late into the international cloak and dagger business," said Robert. "But when we do get in, boy do we get in with a vengeance. You've got to admire good ol' US ingenuity. Not only does the combined power of these little beauties allow us to monitor every radio broadcast on every frequency within practically the whole country, we can also send messages as far abroad as France and Switzerland."

"Really," said Karl politely.

"Absolutely," Robert continued, warming to his theme as he warmed the two radio sets up, flicking switches and turning dials. "This is what you get when the best minds in the most industrialised nation in the world get involved in national security. This is nothing compared to what the guys in Research and Development have cooked up though. Spy cameras, miniature bombs, time fuses; do you know they've even got an explosive with properties so similar to flour you can bake a loaf of bread with it? No kidding. 'Aunt Jemima' is its codename. Oh wait a minute here's something..."

For the next hour Karl watched as John, Robert and Gary surfed every radio frequency coming into and out of Berlin. They chased down leads, translating and decoding messages on the hoof. Picked at scraps of information then cross referenced them with a whole array of facts they'd gleaned monitoring German and Russian broadcasts. This way they built up a plausible picture of the combined movements of both Russian and German troops.

They knew many of their Russian counterparts by name, rank and serial number. They knew who they worked for, what frequencies they used and what codes they customarily used on them. This insider knowledge allowed them to zoom in and focus on the most pertinent intelligence they picked up.

Some radio frequencies and codes were used by Russia and Germany to stop operatives from other countries listening in, and some were used to stop agents from their own country picking up on what they were saying. With this information it was then easy to determine which troop movements the Nazis and the NKVD wanted to hide from their own people.

"Given the current situation, an operation of this sort is going to be highly contentious with most of the military on both the German and Russian sides," explained John. "They're going to want to keep it as secret as possible. That brings us to these six messages." He stabbed at six scraps of paper with his pencil. Each of them contained a hastily scrawled message that they'd plucked out of the airwaves. They'd narrowed it down to six out of the hundreds of messages they'd picked up, decoded and written down in the last hour and a half. Karl's initial opinion of the men as intelligence operatives had not been high, but he had to admit he was impressed with their encyclopaedic knowledge of codes, ciphers and secret broadcasts.

"Okay," said Robert. "We know they were all encrypted by agents who wanted to make sure their own side didn't pick up this information and they're all about troop movements of one kind or another in and out of Berlin. What do each of the messages tell us about the others though?"

"There's a message here in Russian stating that British agents have detonated two of the tracks on the eastern branch lines into Berlin with plastic explosive. It recommends a detour along a north-eastern line," said John.

"That means there's one of two stations on the outskirts of Berlin that they could call at," said Robert.

"Now," said John. "There's a strange message in German ordering a stores manager to deliver a consignment of uniform rain capes to just one of those stations."

"That cape is not dissimilar to one worn by NKVD troops," said Gary.

"Which would make it a good way to camouflage both Russian and German troops and make them blend in more easily with each other," said Robert. "An outsider wouldn't be able to tell what side the different soldiers were on."

"So it's a safe bet to say that they'll be arriving at Ostbhanhof station at sixteen hundred hours tomorrow," said John.

"Okay," said Karl, unable to hide the admiration in his voice. "So what road is the truck load of reinforcements coming in on?"

"Now that's more interesting," said John. "There's a further broadcast from the German stores manager we mentioned before. He's contacting the source of the original broadcast. He's asking what he's supposed to do with the extra box of capes that are to be kept aside from the main consignment. So it's a safe to say our truck of reinforcements is going to be swinging by the same station. This narrows down the number of roads they're going to use into the city."

"Then there's this one," said Robert, unable to contain his excitement. "It went out on a secret Russian frequency but it's in English and the agent was a Russian adopting a fake English accent."

"How in hell do you know that?" asked Karl.

"It's all in the vowels," said Robert with a smile of self-congratulation. "That's where everyone gives themselves away. Unless someone was brought up bilingual, like you were, which before you ask I can tell from the way you speak, they will always get their vowel sounds slightly wrong. Russians adopting an English accent will always be a fraction off with their 'O's and their 'U's, no matter how good they are."

Karl looked at the scrap of paper. All it contained was a list of familiar names and numbers. "It's just famous baseball players," he said. "And their batting average."

"Not all," said Robert. "Look at this one under Mickey Mantle."

"Donald Mouse," Karl read out.

"And this one," Robert pointed to another.

"Mickey Duck," Karl read.

"And here's Elmer Bunny and second to last there's Bugs Fudd." Robert picked up a German map of Berlin. "If you take the initials of those names and the number of the false batting average and cross reference them with a map of Berlin what do you find?"

"Co-ordinates?" said Karl.

"Exactly," said Robert. "Co-ordinates of the road into Berlin that leads to the station where the NKVD troops, coming in by train and truck, will rendezvous, pick up the capes to camouflage their activities and head on to their destination."

Karl gazed in wonder at the map. "That's brilliant," he said. He felt for a moment like a bumbling sidekick in the presence of master detectives.

Robert adopted a modest tone that did not sound sincere. "Just doing our bit to smash the fascists," he said.

"And the commies," John added, not to be outdone.

There was the sound of an engine outside. Karl pressed himself up against the front wall, so he couldn't be seen outside, and glanced through the window. Two canvas topped military vehicles carrying Gestapo soldiers pulled up across the street.

"We've been compromised," said Karl, "It's the Gestapo."

"What." said Robert turning white. "I thought you said we were safe."

"Looks like I was wrong."

"Can't you just shoot them?" said Robert. "You're supposed to be a sniper aren't you?"

"There's too many. By the time I'd shot two the rest would be on us."

"What can we do?" said Robert. He looked on the verge of hysterics. He had obviously never been this close to danger. Not everyone stood up to it well.

Karl scanned the room. "Set light to the two radios, using the kerosene from the stove and throw them out the back window," Karl said.

"What!" exclaimed Robert. "Do you know how much one of those costs to make? There's only about ten in existence!"

"That's why we don't want them falling into enemy hands," said Karl. "Plus it'll cause enough of a diversion to give us time to get away."

Gary was already screwing up all the documents and maps to make tapers. "What are you doing?" asked Robert. "We might need that... " Gary shot Robert a look that shut him up mid-sentence.

Karl watched the vehicles outside while Gary poured kerosene over the radio equipment. "Give me one of those and a match," Karl said having a sudden brain wave. Gary handed him one of the cases, being careful not to get kerosene on either himself or Karl.

Karl waited as Gary set light to one radio and flung it out of the back window. It fell like a comet to the ground with a huge tail of flames that lit up the whole building and was clearly visible from the front. There was a large crash as it hit the floor. Four Gestapo soldiers, already off the first truck, charged around to the rear of the building to investigate.

The soldiers hadn't yet gotten off the second truck to arrive. Karl set a match to the kerosene soaked suitcase radio and threw it through the front window. It soared across the street and landed on the canvas top of the truck, instantly setting it alight. Soldiers began to leap off, covered in flames. They were screaming, beating themselves and rolling on the ground in an attempt to extinguish the flames.

"Quick," said Karl. "Show us this exit that leads to the sewer."

Gary opened a connecting door to the room behind them and ushered everyone through. At the end of the room on the other side was a small broom closet. At the back of the broom closet Gary pushed open a false wall and revealed a hidden back staircase. "A lot of these places have a staircase like this," he said. "For important clients to make a quick exit in a raid."

"We've only been to this base three times in the last four months," said Robert. "How did you find even find out this was here?"

"Like I said, it's my business to know these things." And the matter was closed.

As Karl and the other three moved swiftly but silently down the stairs they heard the sound of German boot leather beating down the front and back doors. The doors splintered and burst open as Gary took Karl and the other two to the toilet stall. When they got there they discovered part of the ceiling had dislodged and had covered the pipe that led to the sewer. "Seems you didn't know about this though did you Gary?" said John.

"It must have happened since we were last here," Gary replied.

"You two start uncovering the rubble while we cover

you," said Karl. "I take it you're armed Gary?"

"Very," Gary replied.

Karl pulled out his P-38, and from under his leather great coat Gary produced a PP-40 SMG sub-machine gun. "I'm impressed," said Karl. Gary simply nodded. They stood either side of the door, aiming their weapons at the bottom of the main staircase as John and Robert began pulling chunks of ceiling out of the exposed soil pipe.

The pipe was practically clear when the first German soldiers, having searched the rest of the building, finally came down the stairs. Karl levelled his pistol and shot the first man down. Gary let rip and took out the second two with a blast from his sub-machine gun. All three tumbled down the remaining steps and lay at the bottom in a blood soaked heap.

The two soldiers behind them backed up sharply, taking cover at the top but not before one let off a shot. By sheer chance it nicked Gary's ear and hit John in the back of his head, blowing his Harvard educated brains out of the front of his face and all over Robert.

Karl took his attention off the stairs momentarily and turned to see Robert staring at John's body and breathing heavily with the shock. "Pull yourself together," he barked at Robert. "Move that body and finish digging, now!" Robert slowly rolled John's body off the rubble and started clearing it in a daze.

Karl turned back to the stairs. From the snatches of whispered conversation he caught, he could tell the soldiers knew that they had shot someone but didn't know how many of them were still alive. The sound of footsteps over their heads told Karl that the German soldiers were trying to find another way into the basement to either catch them off guard or trap them in a pincer movement.

"How's that exit coming?" Karl said over his shoulder.

"Nearly there," said Robert, who seemed to have picked up a bit of speed. There was a hint of panic in his voice and he was probably driven by hysteria at the prospect of imminent death.

There was a flurry of movement at the top of the stairs. Karl heard someone shout "Jetz, jetz, gehen Sie". Then he heard footsteps coming down the hidden back staircase. One of their number had obviously forgotten to close the door of the broom closet and the Germans had found their way down. They were going to attack from both sides. "Hurry it up back there," said Karl. "We need to leave right now."

Karl turned to cover the other door while Gary kept watch on the main stairs. He listened as the footsteps of the soldiers came to the bottom and clattered across the flagstones of the basement floor. He could make three out in the darkened gloom of the room adjacent. He aimed and fired at each of them in turn, hearing but not seeing them drop. Fire was returned even as he was shooting. Karl heard a gasp behind him and swivelled round to see that Gary had been shot in the right shoulder. He fell to his knees. It was not a fatal wound but it had knocked the wind out of him. Karl holstered his pistol and grabbed the sub machine gun. Two more men ran through the doorway from the back stairs. Karl cut them down in a spray of bullets.

More soldiers came down the main staircase. "It's clear," called Robert. "We're through." Before Karl could provide covering fire Robert rushed over to help Gary to his feet. A German bullet caught him in the throat and he was thrown backwards, jerking spasmodically as his life ebbed out of him.

Karl covered the bottom of the stairs in a spray of bullets, cutting down a couple of Germans and sending the rest towards cover. He lifted Gary to his feet and slung an arm over his shoulder. Gary hobbled with him to the open soil pipe. It was just about wide enough for a man to squeeze down.

"You'll have to go first," said Karl to Gary. "Do you think you can make it?"

"Help me get this coat off," he replied. Under his great coat he was wearing a holster for the sub machine gun and another holster for a pistol, in addition he had a belt full of ammo from which hung a couple of grenades. Gary lowered himself into the pipe with some pain and difficulty as Karl let off a few blasts of gunfire to ward off any German soldiers.

Once he heard the splash of Gary landing in the sewer below, Karl lowered himself into the pipe feet first. He wriggled his way down through the tight space, which was not easy as he was very restricted and even had difficulty breathing. The pipe was longer than he thought and seemed to get tighter towards the end. For a moment he thought himself stuck as he couldn't go any further no matter how much he moved. Then he felt Gary's hands on his ankles, pulling him down.

He landed next to Gary with a great splash that soaked him through. The sewer stunk worse than Karl could have imagined and he had difficulty controlling his gag reflex. Gary handed him a grenade. "Use this to seal the exit," he said.

Karl pulled the pin and threw it back up the pipe. There was a muffled explosion and they heard masonry fall and block the pipe once again. For the time being, they were safe.

CHAPTER SEVEN

The journey through the sewers of Berlin was long and arduous. Gary had sustained a serious injury. The hole in his shoulder was large and there was nothing he or Karl could do to stem the bleeding.

They could only guess at a route out of the sewer. They didn't see any manholes overhead and they hit several dead ends, forcing them to turn back and retrace their steps. Gary was getting weaker all the time, leaning on Karl more and more.

Eventually they came to a spot where daylight broke through. A bomb had landed in the road over their heads and caused a big enough crater to crack the ceiling of the sewer tunnel below. A large mound of rubble had fallen through the crack which they could both scramble up. Karl went ahead to scope out the area above.

The crack in the ceiling was just large enough for him to push through. He recognised the area of Berlin straight away. It was the industrial docks right by the River Spree. Karl went back for Gary and helped him climb the mound and the steep walls of the crater above it.

Out in the sunlight for the first time, Karl could see that Gary's wound was a lot more serious than either had realised. He must have kept going by sheer will-power alone. "I can't go any further with you," Gary said. "We both know I'm just holding you back."

Karl surveyed the area quickly. "There's a harbour master's office a few hundred metres from here. You can hide there safely until I get the word out to someone who can come and help you." Gary nodded. Karl was all too aware how much pain he was blocking out to stay focused.

They hobbled over to the office and pushed open the heavy wooden door. In the downstairs back room Karl found a couple of chairs and propped Gary up in them. Gary unholstered his pistol with his good hand. The hole in his shoulder had rendered his right arm useless.

"There's a hip flask in my right pocket," Gary said. "Will you join me in one last drink?"

"I'd be honoured," Karl said. Gary took a long drink from the flask and handed it to him. He took a mouthful and smiled. "Bourbon, haven't tasted that in years."

"Kentucky's finest," Gary said. "A taste of home in a foreign land."

"Southerner, huh?" said Karl.

"By the grace of God."

"Figures."

"How so?"

"Only a good ol' boy would have too much poison in his veins not to know when it was time to lay down and die."

"And only a Yankee would let so little liquor loosen his tongue," Gary shot back. Karl smiled at this.

"How'd you know I was a Yankee?"

"I know quite a bit about you actually Fairburne. But I'm going to need a little more liquor inside me if I'm going to get my tongue loose enough to tell you what I mean to." Karl handed him back the flask and he took a good swallow. "This here shoulder's infected from the sewer and we both know it. I doubt you'd be able to get anyone back here in time to help me, even if you forgot about your mission to do so. And we both know you ain't gonna do that. Reckon I'll have a smoke, get a little drunk and finish this the honourable way." He held up his pistol to illustrate what he meant. "You're a stand up guy though Fairburn and I think you deserve the truth."

"Truth," said Karl "Should I be worried?"

"From what I've seen of you, you should be wary, but you don't need to worry. You've probably guessed I'm not a typical C branch operative."

"You've got the brains and the knowledge of a typical C branch operative but none that I've met have got your obvious combat experience."

"That's because I got my education on the GI Bill. Didn't have no rich daddy to pay for it. So I've had quite a bit of combat experience. You could also say I have two paymasters at the OSS."

"Should I be hearing about this?" Karl asked.

"Probably not, but sometimes a soldier has to do what he thinks is right even if it breaks orders. I'm not gonna be around to face the consequences anyway." Gary coughed, his whole body shook and for the first time Karl saw how much pain he was in. He had been hiding it successfully until now, but Karl saw flecks of blood at the corner of Gary's mouth. The wound in his shoulder was discharging equal amounts of blood and pus. It didn't look healthy. Gary took a deep breath and bit back on his discomfort, regaining a semblance of composure. "I'm part of the security wing of C branch, and I operate on their behalf in the field, but I answer to X-2."

"The counter espionage branch," said Karl, surprised. "You guys root out double agents."

"We keep an eye on the men who work for the OSS. This is a dangerous business, the lives of a lot of people in the field are in constant danger from traitors and informants. The problem with these Ivy League types who work for Research and Analysis or C branch is that they read so much they get confused about where their allegiances lie. So men like me have to keep an eye on them."

"Were Robert or John double agents?" asked Karl.

"Robert was a blowhard and a bit too liberal for his own good, but he was a patriot."

"So why are you telling me this? Do you want to make a final confession before you're done here?"

"Don't flatter yourself brother. If I wanted to clear my conscience I'd corner a priest. You stepped up for us back there, you didn't just save your own skin. There are things I know that you ought to. See, we've been keeping an eye on you for a while now."

"Me?" said Karl, rising quickly to anger. "I love my country. How else do you think I can do all the things I do in the name of democracy?" Karl's fists were balled and only Gary's fatal condition stopped Karl from laying one on him. "Where do you get off accusing me of..."

"I ain't accusing you of anything," Gary cut in. "I'm telling you that folks back in Washington have their suspicions."

"Oh," said Karl, settling down as the anger drained out of him and incomprehension replaced it. "But why?"

"It stems from your father. He left Berlin under a cloud. Seems he had some dealings with certain parties among the Nazis that put his loyalties in question."

"What sort of dealings? I've got a right to know."

"I'm not briefed at that level. As far as I know there was an exchange of favours that got your father out of a difficult corner."

"That sort of thing is par for the course when you're a diplomat. Of course he had dealings with the Nazis. He was stationed in their country."

"It's not that transparent. It only came to light after he returned to the US, there's no official record of the meeting or the deal he struck. No-one's sure how much your father was compromised and when they asked him he refused to give up any of the goods. That's why they pensioned him off."

"So they think my old man's a Nazi collaborator," said Karl. "That's crazy!"

"Nothing was ever proved. But it wasn't disproved either."

"And they think I'm involved too. Is that it?"

"You can't be too suspicious in this business. You grew up in this city, you know the culture. Back in Washington they've gotta be sure where your sympathies lie. You got some highly placed friends though, in spite of this. They're willing to go to bat for you, that's why you're still in the field."

Good old Max, thought Karl. "So how do I clear myself completely?"

"Find out the truth. I can't tell you any more than I know, except that the name Hans Kammler kept cropping up. He must be one of the men your father met with."

"SS Gruppenführer Kammler?"

"The very same. If you can get near to Kammler you'll be near to the truth."

Gary started coughing again. He didn't look good. "I'm gonna need to be alone now."

Karl nodded. "I owe you a big debt of gratitude," he said.

"Then repay me by making your mission a success. Three good men died to get you that Intel. Don't forget that."

"I won't. Believe me, I won't." He'd left the river far behind and was crossing a completely demolished square when he heard the shot from Gary's pistol ring out in the distance.

CHAPTER EIGHT

Berlin was divided into 20 districts, or Bezirke as the locals called them. The NKVD troop on the truck was coming into Berlin through the far eastern district of Hellersdorf. From there they were bound for Ostbahnhof where they would pick up their capes before proceeding to the central Mitte district.

Karl had memorised the route from the map Robert and John had shown him. He knew that there was a perfect spot for an ambush just as the truck came into the Pankow district which would be far enough away from the station they were bound for, so that they couldn't call for help.

He stationed himself in an abandoned hut at the top of a railway bridge that spanned the road and settled down to wait for the truck. The spot had the advantage of over-looking the only road the troop could take to the station.

Karl couldn't help but feel a pang of guilt about the death of the three C branch operatives. It was irrational to think he was responsible, but he couldn't shake the feeling. Perhaps he'd drawn attention to the operatives by despatching the two scouts. Maybe he should have tried harder to get them out safely or have moved them away from a location he knew was compromised before they got him the info he wanted.

Maybe that was all pointless conjecture. If the Gestapo had the place under surveillance already then they would have attempted to capture the outfit even if Karl hadn't been there. Maybe Gary would have got them out alive if he hadn't been there, maybe he wouldn't.

Then there was the matter of Gary's deathbed revelation. Karl felt numb about the whole business; like he couldn't process his real feelings about his father being a possible traitor, so he wasn't even going to go there.

It couldn't be true. It had to be a mistake. Karl had never known a man with as much integrity as his father. He was a stickler for doing the right thing by everyone, especially those he worked for. He was a patriot to his very core. The love Karl himself felt for his country was inspired by his father, every bit of it. Something had to be wrong and Karl was going to get to the bottom of it.

No sooner had Karl made this promise to himself than the truck he was waiting for pulled into view. They must have made good time, they were twenty minutes earlier than he expected. He looked though his scope and got the front tires in his crosshairs. Then he realised his breathing was all wrong.

He had been too distracted by the things Gary had told him, a fatal mistake in his profession. The ability to maintain a constant and fixed concentration was central to the role of a sniper. There were times when he had to remain in the same position for days on end, without once taking his eye off the ball.

Karl had been expecting the truck to arrive a lot later and he had not regained his composure. Now he wasn't properly prepared. He banished all other thoughts from his mind, as though wiping chalk from a black board and fixed his intent solely on the job in hand.

He monitored his heartbeat, making certain it had the right rhythm. He synchronised his breathing with his heart, emptying his lungs every time he breathed out. Then he focused his attention, without wavering, on the right front tire in his crosshairs. He let out one long breath and when there was no more air in his lungs, his muscles relaxed.

It was a moment of perfect clarity when his whole

consciousness was directed towards one single task. He made the necessary allowance for wind speed across the road and for the movement caused by the uneven surface, and the second he knew he had the perfect shot he squeezed the trigger.

The tire exploded and the driver lost control of the truck. It skidded across the road and came to a halt. The driver opened his door, stepped down and inspected the tire. Three more soldiers jumped off the back of the truck and came around to help. From the way he was giving orders, the tallest of the three appeared to be a sergeant.

There was a heated exchange as all four men checked the tire over and tried to decide what had happened. Karl took careful aim on all of them, waiting for the best moment to strike. When the sergeant sent one of the soldiers off for a spare tire and the man returned with another soldier Karl knew the moment was right.

He drew a bead on the sergeant first. He was obviously in command and the men depended on him. To lose him would cause them the most confusion. Two of the soldiers were using a jack to lift the truck while the other two fitted the spare tire. The sergeant was standing over all four, supervising.

Karl fired and the sergeant's head jerked back sharply. He collapsed against the canvas covering of the truck, already wet with his blood and brain tissue, and slumped to the ground. Only then did the men stop what they were doing and register what had happened to their NCO.

By that point Karl already had the driver in his sights. Before the men could properly react to the death of the sergeant he fired again. At the very last second the driver moved back a fraction. What should have been another perfect headshot entered the driver's skull just above the jaw instead. This shattered the jawbone and the bottom of the driver's face fell off in a torrent of blood, teeth and bone cartilage.

The three remaining men finally realised what was happening and ran for cover. The man who had been working the jack rolled under the truck. The other two ran in opposite directions. The soldier on the left ran around the front of the vehicle. He would be under cover quickest so Karl aimed at him next, carefully judging his shot so that the man would run straight into it. Less than a second before the soldier would have been safely behind the truck his hands jerked to his throat as Karl's bullet bored through it. Blood gushed between the man's fingers and he dropped to the floor.

The other soldier was sprinting around the back of the truck calling out frantically to his comrades. Karl aimed low and took out the man's kneecap, an exceptional shot considering how fast he was moving. Karl was very pleased with his handiwork. He left the man rolling on the floor, screaming in agony. This was a psychological tactic, the soldier's wails of pain would impact negatively on the morale of his comrades, raising their levels of terror and thereby affecting their ability to do their jobs properly.

With that accomplished, Karl turned his attention to the jack holding up the truck. He aimed at the central ratchet and shot it out. The jack collapsed, taking the truck with it and crushing the man taking shelter beneath. There must have been too many soldiers standing over that side of the truck when the jack collapsed, because the whole vehicle started to over-balance then keeled over on its side.

Soldiers began to clamber out of the back of the fallen vehicle, scrambling desperately over one another in their effort to get under cover. Several were unlucky enough to give Karl a clear shot and he despatched each with cold ruthlessness.

Once the remaining soldiers had taken cover Karl waited for their next move. The soldier with the shattered kneecap lay screaming on the ground. In spite of his pleas for help none of his comrades would come to his aid. They knew that would mean certain death at Karl's hands and they weren't taking the bait, preferring to grit their teeth and leave the man to die.

Several men were trying to remove the canvas cover from the back of the truck. Karl couldn't tell why and the men managed to remain out of sight enough to stop him picking them off. Finally the canvas cover slipped off its metal frame and Karl saw what they were up to.

There were two soldiers still inside. They had set up and were sitting behind an MG42 machine gun. What's more they had made his position. They opened fire. Karl hit the floor as a wave of bullets tore into the corrugated iron walls, shattering the remaining glass in the window from which he'd been firing. Shards rained down on him as he crawled, face down, to the door.

Karl made it out of the hut and commando crawled across the loose stones at the side of the track. He was hidden by the knee-high wall at the side of the bridge. The machine gunners kept firing at the hut, completely obliterating the whole structure.

Karl set up in the fall back position he had picked out on the opposite end of the bridge. He set his sights at 300 metres, aimed at the soldier operating the machine gun and fired. The machine gunner continued his work. It was as if Karl had fired a blank.

His mind raced, trying to come up with the reason he had missed so badly. Did he jerk the trigger when he fired? Was his breathing pattern broken? Maybe the sights had been knocked as he crawled across the bridge and needed to be re-calibrated.

Then Karl swore under his breath as the answer came to him. He hadn't allowed for the fact that he was shooting at a much steeper downward angle in his new position and was still aiming according to his last. He would need to raise his sights by one eighth of the total distance. He reset them to 337.5 metres and fired again. He missed this time as well. His shot was close enough to his target to let the soldiers know he had changed position though and they turned the machine gun and began firing in his general direction.

Karl knew he had judged the angle correctly so the problem must lie elsewhere. Then he saw the air rippling as heat currents rose in the crisp April atmosphere. The endless firing had heated the air and the haze made his target look nearer than it was, an optical illusion. He shifted his target two points lower on the vertical bar of his sights and pulled the trigger one final time. The machine gunner was thrust backwards with the impact of the bullet but his finger was caught in the trigger and the gun continued to fire as it swung round, letting off a wild stream of bullets that peppered the street.

The second soldier, who had been feeding the belt of ammunition into the gun, grabbed his dead comrade and pulled his body free from the gun. Karl's last shot gave the man a decent idea of his location and he trained the weapon in Karl's vicinity, resuming the bombardment.

Karl ducked under cover instinctively and the involuntary action saved his life. He saw a movement out of the corner of his eye. He swung round and saw a Russian soldier climbing on to the bridge over the other side. Karl had been so distracted by the machine gun fire the man had taken the opportunity to sneak round and climb up the same metal ladder that Karl had used to get on to the bridge.

The Russian's bayonet was fixed and he charged. Karl pulled out his pistol and let off two shots. Both bullets found their mark but the Russian didn't even slow his pace. He twitched slightly as each bullet struck him and kept on bearing down. He was a big bear of a man raised on the Russian steppes. It would take more than Karl's small calibre bullets to stop him.

Karl fired twice more at the Russian's head but neither shot found its mark. It was hard to be a crack shot at this range with a pistol and a moving target. Karl couldn't move far because the machine gun fire had him pinned down. It inadvertently came to his rescue though.

The Russian was nearly upon him when a stray bullet from the machine gun caught the man square between the eyes. His face twisted in surprise at the ironic betrayal of his comrade's 'friendly fire', and he sank to his knees and fell forward.

Karl was thankful to the machine gunner for saving his life, but that didn't stop him fixing the man in his sights as soon as he got under cover from the hail of bullets. This time he made the necessary adjustments to accommodate for the angle of his shot and the disturbance to the air.

The machine gunner was crouching low behind the guard on his weapon and was wearing a steel helmet. This gave Karl a very limited target. He focused on the man's left shoulder, which was the most exposed part of his body, and fired. The gunner was hit but he wasn't killed. He simply adjusted his aim and shot straight at Karl's position. Karl ducked down, then aimed and fired again. The machine gunner fell backwards as the shot hit home then got back up and resumed firing.

Undeterred Karl fired again, this time at the gunner's

right arm. The bullet tore a bloody hole in the man's arm but he kept firing. Then he stopped a second as the pain overtook him. Karl thought the man was finished but he pulled himself together and resumed firing with renewed ferocity.

Karl ducked back under cover, wondering what on earth was going to stop the Russian soldier. Then, without any warning, the firing stopped. Karl took the chance of peering through his binoculars. The Russian gunner was still alive but he looked worse the wear for the three bullets he had stopped. He was sitting slumped against the truck, calling out to his comrades to come and help him.

One foolish soldier poked his head around the truck and crawled over to the wounded man. Karl took aim and shot the man. The bullet went in the back of the man's ribs and straight through his heart. Karl was pleased with the shot. Death would have been instantaneous. Next Karl got the wounded machine gunner in his sights and put the man out of his misery.

The street was suddenly still and quiet now that the ferocious roar of the machine gun had been silenced. Karl listened for any activity from the Russian troops then he heard the sound of multiple feet clanking on the steel ladder to the bridge. More of the men from the truck must have sneaked round while the machine gunner bought them time.

Crouching low, so as not to be seen, Karl snuck over to the other side of the bridge and peered over. He saw three NKVD soldiers climbing the ladder. The range was too close for him to use his rifle as the sights were set for a much farther distance. He pulled out his P-38 again and shot twice at the soldier who was furthest up. The man went rigid, let go of the ladder and plummeted to the street below.

Karl aimed at the next soldier down and pulled the trigger. Nothing happened. The pistol mechanism had jammed and wouldn't come free. The other two soldiers were rapidly making their way up. Karl holstered his pistol while he thought what to do. He remembered the dead Russian lying on the other side of the bridge and raced over to him.

The huge Russian had nothing of value on his body that Karl could find. He picked up the man's rifle, with the bayonet still fixed, and charged back to the top.

He met the NKVD soldier at the top and thrust the steel blade between his ribs and right into the man's heart. The Russian reached and out wrapped his fingers around Karl's throat, dragging Karl towards him. Karl could smell the man's stale sweat and see into his eyes as blood bubbled out of his mouth and sprayed Karl's face.

Karl tried to push the man off with the rifle. He keeled over backwards but didn't relax his grip. Karl lost his footing and fell forwards as the Russian soldier toppled backwards off the bridge.

His stomach turned over and time seemed to slow right down. He went off the edge then stopped falling as his left leg was jerked violently back. He hung upside down and watched as the Russian soldier fell away from him with the bayonet still in his chest. Karl's rifle slipped from his back and fell too.

He swivelled round as he hung upside down and saw that his left ankle had miraculously caught in some broken telephone cable. He swung himself over to the ladder and caught hold. Then he tried to pull his left foot free but it was stuck fast. He was as good as immobilised as the last Russian soldier climbed towards him. He kicked at the wall with his right foot and wriggled his left. The cable bit into skin and drew blood as he tugged.

Finally something gave and his foot came free, but his boot fell off and tumbled to the ground. He swung on to the ladder and his feet scrambled to find a rung as the Russian soldier reached him.

Karl brought his right, booted foot hard down into the Russian's face. The man turned his head and caught the impact on the side of his skull. He grabbed at Karl's leg and tried to pull him off the ladder. Karl slammed the heel of his boot into the man's face again and connected with his nose this time. Blood spilled from the Russian's nostrils as he let go of Karl's leg and slipped down a few rungs.

The Russian reached into his jacket and tried to pull out a pistol that got caught in the jacket lining. Karl saw his chance. He took hold of a lower rung, planted both his feet on the Russian's shoulders and pushed down hard.

The Russian only had one hand on the ladder and it came free. He grasped at Karl's trouser legs and hung on. Karl pushed the man away with his feet and kicked his legs free. The Russian made a desperate attempt to get hold of the ladder and failed. He let out a shriek of terror as he realised he was plummeting to his death.

Karl heard the man's skull split open as he hit the ground. It echoed off the bottom of the railway arch as the soldier stared upwards out of unmoving eyes.

He listened for any more activity below him but couldn't hear a thing. There was total silence. For a rare moment the streets of Berlin did not ring with the sounds of warfare. He was so used to the constant backdrop of gunfire, bombs going off and planes screaming overhead that the silence was almost eerie.

He clambered down the rusted steel ladder, fighting the urge to wince at the pain in his left ankle. Half way down his muscles began to shake. He stopped and a wave of relief tore through him. It was followed by an overwhelming elation at having survived a kill or be killed situation. He had succeeded, he was alive and all the men who were coming to kill him were dead. He bit back on the primal impulse to roar out his delight, like a hunter after a successful kill.

As he reached the bottom and stepped on to the street his ecstatic mood faded, to be replaced by a creeping sorrow. Surrounded by the broken bodies of the Russian soldiers he was overcome by the inescapable pity of war.

He could just as easily have been lying on this street, breathing his last. Only luck, and a little training, had saved him from that fate.

These men all had mothers, or lovers or even children that would never see them again. Neither they nor Karl had a personal stake in the battle they had just fought and that was the saddest thing of all. The impersonal brutality of what their lives now amounted to.

Then Karl's survival instinct woke up. Like a drill sergeant screaming in his ear – 'Right that's enough of that, pull yourself together man, get your ass into gear and stop moping about like a freaking faggot!' Karl shook off the malaise and went to look for his rifle.

Quite by chance his weapon had survived the fall completely intact. Even the sight was unharmed. It must have had a soft landing on one of the corpses. Karl couldn't find his left boot anywhere so he took a strong, comfortable pair from one of the Russians. Fine leather boots built to withstand a long march across the snows of a Russian winter.

CHAPTER NINE

Karl climbed back up onto the bridge and followed the tracks to the station. He changed lines several times when the tracks split and around two kilometres from Ostbahnhof station, on the line the train would be coming in on, he came across a water tower.

As Karl walked up to the tower he felt the tracks vibrate with the approach of a train. Trains into Berlin were rare at this late stage in the war. According to Karl's information the train carrying the NKVD troops wasn't due for another two and half hours, giving him time to get to Ostbahnhof on foot.

Maybe his information was wrong though. The truck had been a lot earlier than he'd expected so perhaps the train was too. It was plausible that there had been a last minute change in the schedule that Karl couldn't have known about.

He hid himself at the base of the tower and watched as the train pulled into view. It slowed to a stop with a wrenching shriek of brakes and a great hiss of steam. Three guards got off along with four soldiers. By the way the soldiers were treating them the guards were patently German.

The train was of German design too. Rather than requisition a train to travel all the way from Russia the NKVD must simply have captured a working German train near the border and ordered it to take them into Berlin. Karl saw that this might give him an opening.

The three German train guards went about the business of taking on water from the tower while the four Russian soldiers smoked and lounged with their weapons trained on the Germans. They weren't particularly vigilant and no one aboard was paying much attention, so Karl was able to sneak past them and make his way up to the front of the train.

He made his way up to the engine. A single Russian was guarding the driver and his two helpers. The man had his back to Karl and didn't catch sight of him but the driver did. Karl put his finger up to his lips to caution the man not to give him away. The driver clocked Karl's uniform, nodded and glanced over at the Russian, who was not paying attention.

Karl hugged the side of the train and snuck up to the doorway where the Russian was standing. He was about to hop up into the cabin and jump the Russian when he leaned out of the train to see how the guards were getting on with the water. Karl ducked out of view and the driver knocked a set of shovels over on to the Russian's feet.

The Russian shouted and cursed at them in broken German. While the man was distracted Karl slipped into the cabin behind him, grabbed his chin and the back of his head and wrenched his head hard, snapping his neck. The Russian stopped shouting, let out a choked gurgling and dropped to the floor.

The driver and his two assistants stared at Karl with a mixture of admiration and apprehension. "Many thanks for your help," said Karl in German.

"You are welcome," said the driver. "I have a brother in the SS still fighting these communist scum. May they roast in the fires of hell." He spat on the Russian corpse and the two assistants started kicking it viciously.

"Enough, enough," said Karl, for fear their exuberance would give them all away.

Just then the other guards called out that the train was ready to continue. "Quickly check and tell me what the Russian soldiers are doing," Karl told one of the assistants.

The man stole a surreptitious glance out of the cabin.

"It's okay," he said. "They are just getting back on the train with our men." Karl relaxed a little as the driver took off the brakes and started up the engine.

"What do we do now?" the driver asked once the train got going again. All three men looked worried now that the fervour of their hatred had cooled and turned to fear.

"If the Communists find him here and find out what you've done, they'll kill us all," the younger assistant said, starting to panic. "What are we going to do? What are we going to do?"

Karl put a hand over the young man's mouth and looked around the cabin. There were some shovels and tools and in the coal store was a pile of logs. Coal was in short supply so the men must have been forced to use whatever fuel came to hand. On top of the wood pile was a medium size axe. Karl smiled. "We're going to roast him in the fires of our own little hell. Help me undress him." The men stripped the Russian corpse pocketing whatever valuables they found, which included an expensive Swiss pocket watch. They offered his two pistols to Karl. "Keep them," he said. "You may need them."

When the corpse was down to its stained, woollen undergarments Karl lifted the axe and brought it down on the arm. It bit into the still warm flesh and cracked the bone. Karl swung again, slicing through muscle and tendon, then took hold of the wrist and wrenched the arm free. "Open the furnace," he said and the driver complied. Karl threw the arm into the fire and the men smiled as it sizzled and popped in the flames.

Karl hacked the other limbs off the corpse and also disposed of them in the furnace. Then he and one of the assistants picked up the torso and shoved that head first into the flames, which rose hungrily to greet it. The whole cabin filled with the smell of roasting human flesh.

"What about the blood?" The younger assistant asked. "Won't that give us away?"

Karl reached into the coal store and picked up a large handful of dust. "We'll cover it with this," he said. The porous coal dust absorbed the blood turning the red liquid to black sludge.

When all the blood was covered, they ground it in with their feet and spread it around the floor of the cabin. "This is where the Russians belong," said the older assistant. "Beneath the soles of German boots." He laughed a short, hard laugh and looked about the cabin for the other men's approval. The driver and the young assistant smiled nervously and Karl simply nodded. He was distracted by the sight of the station coming up ahead of them.

"Can you drop me off before we get to the station?" Karl said to the driver.

"There's an old shack that the linesmen used to use before the war. It's on the opposite side of the tracks, a few metres from the station. I'll slow down enough for you to jump off. The hut's covered by undergrowth so you shouldn't be seen," the driver said.

Karl put on the dead Russian's overcoat and stuffed the rest of the uniform in his pack in case he might need it. The driver slowed the train by degrees and pointed out the shack. "Gentlemen, you have done the Fatherland a great service," said Karl. "Heil Hitler!"

"Heil Hitler!" all three men replied.

Karl leaped from the train and ran down the embankment into the bushes. He beat the branches and brambles to one side and slipped into the wood and tar paper shack. Once inside he glanced back through the cracked window to make certain that he had not been observed leaving the train.

He wondered briefly about the fate of the three Germans who helped him. The Russians had little regard for German life, soldier or civilian, especially after the siege of Stalingrad. Many soldiers took it as a point of personal honour to reek as much, if not more, chaos and disorder in Berlin as the German's wreaked in the mother country. There were many scores to be settled.

The train driver and his two assistants would probably survive as long as they proved useful. There was no telling how long that would be. At least two of them were now armed, which put them in a better position than they had previously been. Karl thought it strange that he should give the men's safety any thought; they were the enemy after all. The war in Berlin was a strange war at this late stage, however, and allegiances changed with alarming rapidity.

CHAPTER TEN

The train pulled up at the platform and the NKVD troops began to alight. Karl couldn't see very much at all from where he was stationed though. He decided that he would need to move to make a proper observation of the impending operation.

Karl crossed over the line and made for a wooded copse right next to the station. He found a good tall cedar tree and climbed to the top. From this vantage point he could observe everything happening both on the platform and outside the station through his binoculars.

The NKVD troops disembarked from the train and made their way in an orderly fashion out to the large parking lot at the front of the station. In the lot they lined up as though on a parade ground. A platoon of SS troopers were overseeing the distribution of rain capes to disguise the NKVD troops. Officers from the NKVD and the SS were fraternising awkwardly outside the station. Some of them apparently spoke the other's language.

Troop carriers began pulling up and the NKVD started to climb aboard. The bulk of the troops were going in one party while a smaller number were waiting behind for some other purpose. Karl guessed it was linked in some way to the soldiers in the truck that he had dispatched.

Karl realised that it would not be possible for him to track the movements of the troops on foot. He would have to infiltrate them and follow their progress from within. He shimmied down the tree and raced around the front of the station. Once there he slowed his pace and caught his breath as he approached an SS officer chatting with an NKVD captain.

"Heil Hitler!" said Karl saluting.

"Heil Hitler" replied the officer returning the salute only perfunctorily, in consideration of the Russian officers surrounding him.

"Sir," said Karl. "I've been detailed at the last minute to accompany Gruppen B of the NKVD." He was taking a risk on the name of the smaller group of NKVD soldiers. He guessed that with typical German lack of imagination they would name the smaller group after the second letter of the alphabet and not give it any other codename. If he was wrong he would have blown his cover.

"Gruppen B, eh?" said the officer, looking Karl over and tapping his SS insignia. "You're from the SS Panzer Leibstandarte division eh, first amongst equals." The officer was referring to the fact that the SS Leibstandarte had originally been the Führer's personal bodyguard, back when the SS was an elite force and not the military machine it had become of late. As such they had a special prestige amongst their fellow Waffen SS members. This was one of the reasons Karl wore the uniform he did. "It's simply an honour to serve the Fatherland sir," he replied. It seemed his gamble about the name of the smaller group had paid off as no-one was challenging him over it.

"You're a sharfenshützer also I see," said the officer, pointing to Karl's rifle. "And who ordered you to accompany Gruppen B then?"

"SS Gruppenführer Kammler sir." It was another reckless bluff. Karl was counting on the fact that Kammler would currently be in Berlin, would be directly involved in this operation and that the officer would be aware of all this. He was also hoping that Kammler was so high-ranking, the officer wouldn't dare question, or even check, an order that came from him.

Luckily his assumption seemed to be correct because the officer quite visibly blanched at the mention of Kammler's name. The Russian officers noticed the German's reaction and wanted to know what the matter was. The officer exchanged a few words with them in Russian then turned back to Karl.

"Why have you been detailed to this operation?"

"Security may have been compromised," said Karl. "The NKVD troop you are waiting for were met by a sniper. They were all killed."

"All killed! Impossible."

"Sir I can show you if you wish. Command thought it wise to send someone with my abilities to accompany you."

"Do we know who is responsible?"

"Sir, it could be someone from our side, this operation is highly confidential and few even in the SS know about it. It could be the British or Americans, their relations with Russia become more strained every month. Whoever it is we don't know, but they are still at large and pose a threat to the whole operation."

The German officer turned back to his Russian counterparts and explained what had happened. There was a flurry of debate then the German turned back to Karl again. "You're to join Gruppen B as ordered," he said. "Take them to see the murdered group so that they can verify your story and identify the dead. After that you're to accompany them to their destination and await further orders. Is that clear?"

"That's clear sir," Karl replied.

Gruppen B began to ready itself and board the vehicle that had come for them. Karl was introduced to a Russian lieutenant, who spoke German, called Sergei. "We will ride together, yes?" he said. "And I will be translating what others say."

"Okay," said Karl and climbed into the back of the

vehicle with him.

As they pulled away Karl could feel the hatred emanating from the men in the back with him. It came off them in waves and they didn't bother to hide it, either in the way they looked at or treated him. "I don't feel too popular at the moment."

"Please to not take it personally," Sergei replied. "You are fascist and sniper. This is not popular combination. Even our own snipers are not liked greatly by the men. You are killers by choice and you don't mix much with other soldiers. Also we have been brought up since children to hate fascists like you."

"We had a treaty a few years ago," said Karl. "We were allies."

"Yes. And look how you treat us. All of the men here lost comrades and even family members when you invaded our country. Many fell to German snipers. They are thinking maybe you are responsible."

"I wasn't part of that campaign. I've never even been to Russia."

Sergei smiled. "But you would say that wouldn't you?"

Karl couldn't help smiling back. Sergei was definitely charming. Behind his geniality Karl could sense tension though. He didn't trust Karl and his joviality was a mask to put him at ease in case he needed to catch him off guard.

Karl gave directions to the railway bridge, where the dead NKVD troop lay, and Sergei shouted them to the driver. He nearly got lost on a couple of occasions as his memory of Berlin's roads, gleaned from the maps he had seen and his childhood in the city, failed to mesh with the bombed out streets that the vehicle traversed. On each occasion that this happened he was able to rectify the mistake and find his way back to the planned route before he was discovered.

A little while later they pulled up alongside the overturned truck. The men climbed out and surveyed the scene. The driver remained in the truck as did the front passenger, whom Karl caught sight of for the first time.

As the Russians began collecting identifying items from the corpses, there was a weak cry from under the capsized truck. The men lifted the canvas cover and they could see a leg underneath. It was the soldier Karl had shot in the knee cap. He was pinned under the metal frame of the vehicle.

Moved by his plaintive cries for help the men took hold of the corners of the frame and lifted the truck enough for one of them to crawl under and pull the man free. He was pretty beaten up and did not look as though he would live much longer.

The knee Karl had shot had gone septic, most probably from lead poisoning. It was swollen and oozing puss. From the way he was breathing the man seemed to have many broken ribs, one of which had probably punctured a lung. In between sobs and groans of pain, the man repeated something over and over again like a litany.

"What is he saying?" Karl asked Sergei.

"He is praying."

"But I thought you were all atheists."

"Atheism is hard stance to maintain in face of impending death."

Karl wasn't used to seeing his victims suffer up close like this. He tried to separate the man's suffering from the consequences of his actions in his mind, but he wasn't entirely successful. The dying soldier's cries and the corpses of their fallen comrades cast a long shadow over the moods of all the NKVD soldiers. Even with everything they had seen in the war so far it was hard for them not to be affected.

The men had a brief consultation about what to do with the dying soldier and all seemed to reach an agreement. The officer in the group stood over the dying man and drew his pistol. He put the gun to the forehead of his fallen comrade. The soldier grabbed his hand and kissed it. Everyone, including Karl turned away as the trigger was pulled.

The officer barked a question at Sergei and he turned to Karl. "They want to know where rest of soldiers are," said Sergei.

"Follow me," said Karl and he took them 300 metres down the road to the bridge where he had hidden in the hut. They walked in silence. Karl pretended to be wary, scanning the shadows and surrounding buildings for possible snipers. The NKVD soldiers were on edge, waiting for a bullet to come from the sniper that had killed their comrades, little realising that he was walking right beside them.

Karl led them under the bridge and showed them the other corpses. One of the Russians suddenly broke down and wailed his dismay as he saw the corpse of the man Karl had pushed off the top of the ladder. He knelt beside the man and scooped him into his arms, weeping openly. The dead soldier's head lolled and the weeping Russian was smeared with the congealed blood on the back of his skull.

"What's the matter with him?" Karl asked.

"That man was his brother," said Sergei. "They had been right through war together, since five years ago. He has lost whole family in battle for Stalingrad. That man was only relative still living."

The Russian sobbed out his grief for a whole lost

family, the floodgates of long suppressed feeling, finally opening. The other men waited for him to finish. Karl turned his back, not wanting to intrude on the grieving man's moment.

He waited until the Russian's sobs had subsided into painful, rapid sighs, and began to walk back to the NKVD vehicle. He heard footsteps charging up behind him and instinctively braced himself, swinging round to face his attacker and bending his knees for impact. The grieving Russian screamed with new found rage as he lunged, arms outstretched, for Karl's throat. His eyes were wild and maddened by hatred for every German left alive. As the only apparent Nazi in sight, Karl bore the brunt of his desperate need for revenge.

Without thinking Karl's training and experience kicked in. He caught hold of the Russian's wrist and turned his shoulder to catch the man full in the chest, knocking the wind out of him. Then he tugged the man's arm towards him, twisted his hips and bent forwards pulling the Russian over his shoulder to land on his back at Karl's feet. He twisted the Russian's arm and put his foot on the man's throat to immobilise him.

Karl heard guns cocking and looked up to see seven of the NKVD, including Sergei, pointing their pistols at him. "Please to be taking your jackboot off our comrade, fascist!" Sergei demanded. Karl released his attacker and stepped back with his hands clearly at his sides.

The grieving Russian got to his feet, brushed himself down, and then sprang at Karl again. This time he was caught by two of his comrades who pulled him away before he reached Karl. The man's mood seemed to calm, he held up his hands to signal he was okay and that his comrades should take their hands off him. Then as soon as they had stepped far enough away he jumped at Karl again.

This time the grief stricken Russian came in with his fists, and Karl didn't stop him. The right fist hit Karl on the cheek and the left on the side of the nose. He bowed to take the brunt of the attack on the top of his head and his shoulders. The Russian swung wildly with little precision. He was simply working out his rage.

Karl let him. He needed the pain. He was losing focus. The revelation about his father still had him on the back foot and his mission had become complicated. He wasn't certain whom to trust on his own side, who apparently suspected he was working with the Nazis. He was posing as a Nazi and an enemy of the Russians with whom he was supposed to be allied and pretending he was secretly working as their ally. This was because he had been ordered to treat the Russians as the enemy and had to infiltrate them.

Sergei stepped in and put his hand on the grieving man's shoulder, telling him that was enough. Karl looked up and stretched his neck. The pain had cleared his head.

His main purpose was to find out what was happening with the Russians and the Germans. Why were two mortal enemies working together? He needed to report his findings back to Max. Good old Max, the only person in the whole of Berlin who was fighting his corner. When that was accomplished he would track down the truth about his father.

"I think we should ride up in front of vehicle," said Sergei and led Karl away from the other NKVD men.

"So how did you know about location of our missing troop?" Sergei asked as they bounced along the Berlin streets in the front of the troop carrier, next to the driver and the other passenger, Isaac. Isaac said nothing the whole journey, just stared ahead.

"I'm not at liberty to say anything about the intelligence I'm given or where it comes from," said Karl.

"You are briefed at highest levels yes," said Sergei. "Snipers always are. You told your officer your orders came from Kammler himself, did he give you them personally?"

"I've said I can't tell you."

"I think you are playing game with me. You think I am in dark about your Waffen SS? You forget I work for finest secret service in world. We taught rest of world how to spy. You think I don't know all about your Kammler. I know more than your men know."

Sergei was playing a game. He was trying to trip Karl up and to shame him into revealing something to prove Sergei wrong. Though Karl knew this, he still played along in order to learn something more about the man with whom his father was accused of betraying the USA.

"Let me tell you something about Herr Kammler," Sergei continued. "You know how he came to be head of the V2 programme of course?" Karl said nothing. "I think maybe you don't. Your SS Reichsführer Himmler coveted rocket programme for long time. Head scientist Werner Von Braun is captain in SS and Himmler thought he should bring his project to SS. For some reason Von Braun resists Himmler though. So you know what Kammler does? He has Von Braun arrested on charges of treason. Von Braun is pilot and Von Braun is also developing rocket, not as he see it, to launch missiles but to reach stars. Kammler say he trick Nazis, say Von Braun plan to fly with secrets to US. Only Albert Speer's intervention saved his life. Von Braun learns his lesson and Himmler seizes control of component manufacture, missile assembly and military deployment from military. Kammler takes over programme from General Dornberger. I am right so far yes?"

Karl shrugged, hoping to draw more information from Sergei with his apparent indifference. "You see what type of man you work for?" said Sergei. "Nothing stand in his way. He want something, he go get it. You think your General Helmstadt will keep hold of his nuclear secrets? Kammler wants those too, no? That is what Spear of Destiny is really all about is it not? You know all about this secret weapon which will turn tide of war, of course?"

"Far more than you do," said Karl, bluffing.

Sergei laughed and wagged his finger at Karl. "Now I think you play me at my own game," he said. The conversation moved on to other matters of a more trivial nature. The tactic Sergei had been employing to get Karl to talk had not gained him any important intel, so he abandoned it.

Karl had learned much though. Not least of which was how little he actually knew about the game in which he was caught up. Many questions raced through his mind. What was his father's connection to Kammler? Did it have anything to do with the mysterious Spear of Destiny project to which Sergei referred? And could the Russians and Germans really be working on a secret weapon that could change the course of the war?

CHAPTER ELEVEN

They travelled south for a while leaving the centre of Berlin and the contested battle grounds behind them. From the scenery passing the window Karl recognised that they were in the district of Neukölln.

Eventually the vehicle drove into the ruins of Hafen Neukölln, the smallest of Berlin's ports. As far as Karl could remember it had mainly been used to ship building materials before the war. It had not fared well in the Allied bombing campaign and all that remained were a series of warehouses where goods had once been stored for shipping.

They pulled up outside one of the warehouses. The building had looked deserted as they approached it, but now Karl could see two German sentries posted at the entrance. Karl, Sergei and Isaac hopped down from the front of the vehicle and were joined by the NKVD men who had ridden in the back. The men provided the three of them with an armed guard as they walked up to the front of the warehouse.

"Heil Hitler!" one of the sentries said to Karl as they reached the entrance.

"Heil Hitler!" Karl replied.

"State your business here," the sentry demanded. He was very wary. Both sentries had their hands on their weapons.

Before Karl could answer Sergei stepped in. "We are here to view contents of building. You have received order to expect us, no?"

The sentry who addressed them nodded to his colleague who went inside the building. There was a tense pause while the remaining sentry blocked their way then his colleague returned and ushered Karl and the Russian party through the door.

Inside, a platoon of technicians were busy at work. The place resembled an air hangar. Lying on their sides, on a series of huge metal racks against one wall, were four fifty-foot rockets. In the centre of the building, in a special hoist, was another rocket undergoing a whole battery of tests.

Against the far wall were a series of large containers about a third of which contained liquid oxygen with the other two thirds containing ethyl alcohol. Right at the back of the building were two lorries side by side. Each had trailers at the rear, which were at least fifty-five foot in length and had a large mechanised arm fitted, along with other specialised loading equipment.

Karl exhaled in surprise at the sheer scale of the operation. All this had been successfully hidden in a city that was under siege from three different armed forces. The ingenuity and the sheer audacity it must have taken to set it up staggered him.

The NKVD men were hemmed into a corner by an armed guard of Wehrmacht soldiers. Isaac and Sergei were escorted over to the rocket that was undergoing tests and Karl was left to wander where he liked. He walked over to the rack where the four rockets were stacked.

A commotion erupted behind him. He turned to see one of the Wehrmacht soldiers shouting at an NKVD man. "Rauchen sind verboten!" The NKVD agent was holding an unlit cigarette and shouting right back in the soldier's face. The German called the Russian an idiot and asked if he wanted to have them all killed. The Russian reached for his pistol and all the Wehrmacht soldiers levelled their weapons on the NKVD agents.

Sergei raced over to his men to see what the problem

was. The Wehrmacht soldier told Sergei that one of his men had tried to light a cigarette. Sergei was livid. He stepped past the German soldiers as if they weren't there and made a bee line for his own man. He snatched the pistol from the agent's hand and beat him about the head with it.

Sergei sternly reiterated what the Wehrmacht soldier said. A single spark could send the whole building up and kill everyone. Then he turned to the Wehrmacht soldier and apologised briskly for the idiocy of his man. The soldier acknowledged Sergei's apology but demanded that he now stay with his men. Sergei began to forcefully argue against this.

Karl turned to see that Isaac was still chatting with the German technicians around the rocket. His German appeared very fluent and the technicians were responding respectfully to his precise and insightful questions. Karl had supposed that Isaac needed Sergei to translate for him. Especially as he had not said a thing to Karl, but he must have understood everything Karl had discussed on the way over. Sergei either trusted Isaac implicitly or he had something big to hold over him.

Karl turned back to look at the rockets. He was no expert on rocket science but he had never seen a design like it. "She's really beautiful is she not," said a voice behind him. "A shining testament to the brilliance of German engineering."

Karl looked over and saw a German technician gazing at the rockets with unbridled admiration. He was a short stocky man with a large moustache

"No-one has ever built a rocket capable of travelling so far at such incredible velocity. It can cover distances larger than most oceans and might very well break out of the planet's atmosphere with a little more development.

There are less than twenty of them in existence."

"I thought I had never seen anything like it," said Karl. "It is not a V2 obviously."

"She's a V10. The most accomplished missile ever built by man. You wouldn't believe the breakthroughs we've made in aerodynamics, in forging lighter alloys for the shell, not to mention the advances in fuel consumption and acceleration after lift off. You've no idea how much further we could have gone had we but been given more time."

"You don't think the SS will give you any more time to develop rockets?" said Karl.

The technician's approach to Karl became a little more considered and apologetic. "My friend, I have a brother who is an officer in the SS." He pointed to Karl's rifle. "He is also a marksman like you. Like me he is inspired by the things that German technical ingenuity can achieve. This is why I talked to you. I hoped that you were inspired too when you laid eyes on these rockets. They command awe in their construction do they not?"

"They are quite something."

"I do not mean any disrespect to the SS when I say that it isn't a matter of them giving us any more time, I don't think the SS have very much time left. This war, it does not look good for Germany. The Fatherland will endure in the hearts of all her sons and daughters but I don't think the SS will. Nor do I think the V10 rocket programme will survive the passing of the SS."

"Why do you continue to make weapons then," said Karl. "When you know that Germany will not win this war?"

"To show what can be accomplished in the field of rocketry. To prove to future generations that it can be done. So that when people look upon this watershed in modern engineering, they won't be able say that nothing good came out of Germany under the Nazis. Maybe a change is coming for Germany, and perhaps it is needed in some areas, but this is the legacy we will leave for the future. It could be that the Earth is too small for all its different races. One day this technology will be used to explore the stars. Out there in the vastness of space we might just find enough room to live together in peace, do you not think?"

"I think you're one hell of an idealist," said Karl.

"But this rocket inspires idealism does she not?"

Before Karl could answer, Sergei interrupted. "We need to go. You are to come with me now."

"Who are you to be giving me orders here?" snapped Karl.

Sergei's manner became more authoritarian. "You were detailed to provide security to our unit until ordered to do otherwise. Isaac must leave and join the rest of our troops at another location. He has expressly requested that you accompany him should he be in need of a counter sniper. In light of atrocity you just showed us I think that his request should be authorised, don't you?"

Karl wanted to check out the other location to which the majority of the NKVD troops were posted. He would not receive a better opportunity so he complied with Sergei and said goodbye to the technician. "Until we meet again," said the technician. "In the frontier of the stars."

Karl followed the NKVD soldiers out of the makeshift missile silo. A jeep was waiting to take him, Isaac and one other NKVD man onto the next location. Sergei and the rest of the group got back into their vehicle and drove off elsewhere.

Isaac chatted with the other NKVD man in Russian as the three of them bumped along in the back of the jeep. Isaac nodded his head towards Karl and he and the other Russian laughed. Isaac then turned to Karl and addressed him in perfect German. He spoke as though he were jeering at him but what he said in no way matched his tone of voice.

"I have told our friend that for the sake of amusement I am going to ask you an impertinent question about your mother. Please answer me as though you were enraged by this."

"Why would I want to do that?" said Karl raising his voice and playing along with Isaac's request. For the sake of the guard Isaac made to sneer at Karl's supposed riposte. "There are things I need to tell you and I do not want our escorts to know of this. At the next junction pretend to spot a sniper. Under the pretence of running for cover we can lose these two long enough to talk."

"What would impel me to do that?"

"I know many secrets which will be of use to your commanders. In return there is something I need you to help me with." Isaac then burst out laughing and said something to the NKVD soldier in Russian. The two of them laughed heartily and Karl pretended to glower.

The jeep crossed an intersection with several tall buildings still standing by the side of the road. Karl stood up in the jeep and pointed to one of the buildings. "Sharpshooter!" he cried in alarm. "There, in that window across the way. Stop the jeep and get out!" Isaac translated what he said to the other men who slammed on the brakes and leaped out. Karl and Isaac ran for cover in a nearby building, away from the other men.

To add authenticity to his claim Karl knelt and fired

at the building across the street as soon as he and Isaac were out of sight of the other men. The shot ricocheted off the building and landed near the jeep. The Russian driver and soldier dived for cover.

Karl turned to Isaac. "What are you offering?"

"There are many secrets about the Spear of Destiny project of which all but a handful of men on your side are aware. Such information will be of great use to your superiors in the SS. What I offer will advance you no-end in their eyes."

"What do you want in return?"

Isaac pulled out a slim leather wallet and produced a photograph. "These are my daughters, Ruth and Sarah. I have not seen them for eight months. My country does not take risks when it wants to assure your loyalty. Last year someone denounced my wife. It came as a shock to us all but she was sent to a labour camp in Siberia. That was the last I ever saw of her. An epidemic of killer influenza swept the camp and killed nearly everyone, inmates and guards alike. My daughters are all I have left." Karl looked at the crumpled photograph. It showed two little girls aged eight and ten. They were dressed in traditional Jewish garb and were smiling shyly at the camera. The edges of the photo were worn and creased. Karl could not guess how many times Isaac had pulled it out of his wallet to look at over the last eight months.

"When I was first recruited to work for the Soviet missile programme, I was not considered entirely trustworthy, but my knowledge and abilities were too valuable for my country to waste. So to guarantee that I would be totally loyal and obedient they took both my daughters."

"Why were you not considered trustworthy?"

"For a start I am an orthodox Jew. This is nearly as frowned on in my country as it is in yours. Secondly I was a member of the International Interplanetary Society. This is why I speak such good German. Your country has long led the field when it comes to the design and deployment of rocketry. Before the war I corresponded with Werner Von Braun and many others now high up in the V2 rocket programme. My Soviet taskmasters were concerned that I had let slip state secrets. Even more ridiculously they considered that I, a Jew, might be a Nazi sympathiser."

"I still don't understand why you want my help?"

"My girls were taken under the orders of Comrade Ilyich Velikovsky. He heads up the NKVD operations here in Berlin. He is also responsible for recruiting agents to work for the Soviet state. When I was shipped out to Berlin as part of the Spear of Destiny project, Velikovsky brought my daughters along with him. In Russia he would allow me to see them for half an hour every other month. He claimed he was doing me a favour bringing them along, so my visiting privileges could be extended while out of the country. However I have not seen them since we came to Germany and I have word he means to use them in some hideous scheme he has cooked up with senior SS members he means to recruit."

"Use them how?"

"There are things that a father does not want to contemplate. I need someone in the SS to help me locate them and get them back. I am desperate, you are my only chance. Will you help me? As I said I can tell you many things."

Karl was not unmoved by Isaac's plight. Nor was he blind to how useful Isaac might be to the operations of the OSS. He handed the photograph back to Isaac. "I can't promise you anything, but I'll see what I can do," he said. Tears clouded Isaac's eyes, he clasped Karl's hand and looked for a moment like he was going to kiss it but then thought better of it and regained his composure.

"Thank you," he said. "You can't know what this means to me."

Karl wasn't certain how useful he could really be to Isaac, but he resolved to do as much as he could to rescue Isaac's children if his information proved to be of use to the OSS. Karl fired a few more shots into the street for the sake of the other NKVD men, who were beginning to come out from their cover. Then Karl fixed a stray alley cat in his sights. It was walking along the top of the building which Karl had claimed was inhabited by a sniper. He clipped the cat's ear with a bullet and the animal yowled in painful protest.

Hoping this would be enough to fool the Russian soldiers, Karl slung his rifle over his shoulder and strode out into the street. "Tell them its all clear," Karl said to Isaac. Isaac shouted to the other men who came out from their hiding places. They seemed a little suspicious of Karl's antics and they spoke with Isaac in a sceptical tone of voice. Isaac appeared to be assuring them of the veracity of Karl's claims as they climbed back into the jeep and went on their way.

CHAPTER TWELVE

The jeep took them back into the central district of Berlin known as Mitte. The roads became less easy to traverse and the going got rougher. On a couple of occasions the roads were so blocked that they had to back track and find another route altogether.

There was a lot of heated debate and much gesticulation between the driver and the NKVD soldier on these occasions. The soldier seemed to be accusing the driver of not knowing the way and the driver was obviously blaming the poor road conditions because he kept pointing at them and throwing his hands up.

Eventually they came to a residential square, surrounded and sheltered on all sides by tall tenement houses. They had to pass through two provisional checkpoints before they entered.

The first was Russian. Three soldiers halted them and made them climb out of the jeep at rifle point. They spoke with the NKVD agent who showed them identification then pointed to Isaac. The Russian soldiers wanted to know about Karl. The NKVD explained something to them and they nodded. They signalled to Karl that he should hand over his rifle and any other weapons before proceeding.

Karl refused point blank. The three soldiers all trained their weapons on him and Karl raised his hands. Isaac began to speak on his behalf and he heard the name Kammler and Helmstadt mentioned. The Russians relented after a short negotiation and let them climb back in the jeep and continue.

As they pulled up to a side street entrance into the square they were pulled over by an officer in the Wehrmacht.

The street was heavily guarded by Wehrmacht soldiers. "State your business here and your level of clearance," said the officer to Karl.

"I am escorting these operatives of the NKVD into the square so that they might report to their superiors," said Karl. "My clearance is standard endorsed by SS Gruppenführer Kammler." He did not want to make too great a claim for his level of clearance, lest he find himself reporting to a chief of staff regarding an operation about which he knew nothing and on which he was simply gathering intelligence.

"What is the nature of the report your charges are making?" asked the officer.

"I am here to report my findings on the viability of the Spear of Destiny project," Isaac said butting in. The officer's face twisted into a contemptuous sneer.

"I do not speak with filthy Yiddisher communists! Kindly tell the animal not to address me again."

"I think you are best to keep your hands in your lap and look at the floor," Karl said to Isaac. Isaac did as Karl told him but was patently seething. Karl then turned back to the officer. "I apologise for his impertinence. The Jew is here to testify to the supremacy of Nazi technology."

"That cannot be denied," said the officer, approving of Karl's sentiment. "You are to proceed down to the end of the street. There you will all disembark. The Russians will report to their command on the left side of the square and you will liaise with your commanding officer amongst the German enclosure on the right. Heil Hitler!"

"Heil Hitler!" said Karl, who then addressed Isaac. "Tell the driver to start the engine then explain the officer's orders."

"We do not take orders from fascists," said Isaac as the jeep started off down the road.

"No," said Karl. "But we have reached a stage in the war where we are not certain who we are taking orders from anymore."

As the jeep trundled down the cramped side street Isaac turned hastily to Karl. "We do not have long. If I am to meet with you without arousing suspicion you must arrange to capture me. I am making one last visit to the silo tomorrow at four in the afternoon. I will not have a guard of more than three men. The route we take will be the same. In the meantime I would be very obliged to you if you would make inquiries regarding the pressing matter we discussed."

"I'll speak to my superiors and see what I can arrange."

The Jeep reached the end of the street and they all got out without acknowledging one another. Karl had no idea where any commanding officer was stationed so he had no idea where to head. He didn't want to draw any attention to himself by trying to bluff his way through a report anyway. Instead he tried to blend inconspicuously into the general comings and goings of the square while making a comprehensive survey of activities and the security of the operation.

There were probably about two platoons of German soldiers and just as many Russians, mostly NKVD troops by the looks of things. Both were keeping very much apart from one another. The seething resentment between the two groups was palpable and it felt as though in-fighting could kick off at any minute. NCOs were strictly controlling all traffic between the two positions, so Karl stayed close to the German side.

The Russians were stationed on the left of the square and the Germans on the right. Karl thought this rather fitting considering their political positions. If the moderate USA were here they would most probably take up the centre ground, he mused, although in actuality that would not be possible. The centre of the square, a large rectangular space of what had once been grass, or perhaps flagstones, had been dug up. Fresh quick drying concrete was being poured in. The Germans were overseeing this operation.

As they were coming into the square, Karl had seen two perimeters. The outer one – made up of a further platoon of forty men – was controlled by the Russians. The inner one was German, and though Karl didn't get enough of a chance to scope it out, it was most probably made up of a platoon the same size.

The purpose of the perimeters, Karl guessed, was to defend the operation from both German and Russian troops. The Russians manned the outer perimeter as there was most danger of an attack from Marshall Zhukov's advancing troops. If they saw that the area was secured by their own men, they would not attack or overrun it. If on the other hand it was caught by a German counter offensive – Hitler had ordered the twelfth and ninth German armies to relieve the siege from the south and was still awaiting them – then the Russian's could fall back and the German's would not attack their own troops on the inner perimeter.

In addition to all this Karl counted at least two snipers on the roofs of all the tenement houses. There were probably more who were better hidden. The fortification of such a small area of an urban battleground was remarkable. Something highly unique and important was being planned here, but Karl did not yet have the information to say what.

He now needed to get back and report his findings to his superiors at the OSS. Whatever was being planned was on a strict timetable and the sooner Karl could make his report to Max the sooner his side could respond to the information. Leaving the area did not appear to be as easy as infiltrating it however.

Any passage in and out of the square was tightly controlled by the Russian and German NCOs, and the various provisional checkpoints. Even if Karl was to break through any of them and attempt to shoot his way out, there was no cover for a hundred metres around the square, making him an easy target for any of the snipers.

He was walking past the southern side street that led out of the square when there was the sudden sound of gunfire. Everyone in the square turned to see what was happening. With his keen sniper's eyesight Karl was able to see that someone had shot dead several men on the Russian and German south perimeters, leaving them open.

A German sergeant began shouting orders and a troop of Wehrmacht soldiers roused themselves. Karl fell in with the men, following them out of the square in the confusion. They raced across the open ground towards a ruined building on the outskirts of the Russian perimeter. Someone inside the building was firing a machine gun at the Russian and German troops.

The approaching Germans scattered as soon as they came within range and Karl dived behind a pile of rubble. He pulled out his binoculars and focused them on the first floor window from which the firing was coming. He could make out four men in the room but wasn't certain whose side they were on. From their dress it was safe to say they definitely weren't Russian or German.

A German NCO crawled up beside him. "Sharfenshützer," he said, "just what we need. Do you think you can pick them off for us?"

"How do we know they're not ours?" said Karl. "They may just think we're communist scum."

The NCO shook his head. "The Russians spotted them and informed my men. They weren't any of theirs. We called out to them and a fight broke out, then they opened fire."

"I can't get a proper shot at this angle. You'll have to give me covering fire till I can get in a better position."

"I'll see what I can do."

Karl left his position and moved cautiously around to another while the NCO fired over his head at the building. In truth he could easily have picked off the men from his last position. He suspected however, that they were friendly agents on the side of the Allies as neither Russians nor Germans could lay claim to them.

Karl let off some shots which went wide for show. He saw two Russians coming in from an angle where they were just out of range of the machine gun. He took out both of them with body shots so as not to draw suspicion.

He hadn't noticed that, in between blasts of firing, a German soldier had gotten close enough to throw a stick grenade through the first floor window of the room next to the one where the machine gunners were. The grenade contained a large charge and the resulting explosion was powerful enough to take out the front of the building and the wall between the rooms.

Karl looked through his binoculars and saw that two of the machine gunners had been killed either by the blast or the collapse of the wall. The other two were heading for the back entrance. Karl got to his feet and started running ahead of the German and Russian troops.

One of the men leaving the building was cut down by sniper fire. His comrade in arms checked to see if he could aid him and upon seeing the man was beyond help left him where he fell. The surviving man darted into a maze of ruined streets a good few minutes ahead of Karl and the pursuing soldiers.

Karl was the first one after the fugitive and he hoped he could reach the man before any of the Russians and Germans. Using simple deduction he followed a route through the streets, catching sight of the man doubling back on himself once through the window of a half demolished building. Karl ran parallel to the fleeing man then turned down a side street to try and head him off. As he got to the top of the street Karl saw the man was caught between him and a Russian soldier at the other end.

Before Karl could say anything the man raced for an alley nearby. The Russian raised his rifle to fire at a range in which it would be hard to miss. Karl whipped his pistol out and shot the Russian through the left eye. The soldier jerked backwards and his rifle fired wildly into the air. The fugitive did not see Karl come to his aid though, and the sound of gunfire only made him run faster.

Karl chased after the man but lost him at the bottom of the alley. He ran out into the street beyond and came to a crossroads. There was no sign of the man anywhere. Then he heard a cry in German one street down; "Over here, quick he's here." Karl raced to the top of the street and nearly ran smack dab into the man, who stopped at the last minute. The street was a short one and a dead end, there was nowhere for the man to run. He was trapped between Karl and the German soldier.

Karl still had his pistol drawn. He raised it. The man flinched. Karl aimed it and shot. The German soldier fell dead. "No wonder you're losing this war if that's the best you can do in the way of shooting," said the man in an

English accent. He was full of the bravado that comes just before death.

"I wasn't aiming at you," Karl said.

The man looked surprised. "A Yankee," he said. "Working deep cover, well I'll be!" He scratched his head and grinned, relieved at the last minute reprieve.

"We don't have much time before the others get here."

"In that case come and give me a hand with this grate," said the man. "I nearly had it off then Fritz here caught me napping."

"Where does this lead?" asked Karl.

"It's a service entrance to the U-Bahn, the German underground, wait you'd call it a subway wouldn't you?" Karl and the man climbed inside and just as they were replacing the grate two Russian soldiers turned down the street. Karl grabbed his pistol and shot twice. The grate fell a little and knocked him. "Hold it," he told the Englishman.

"This is bloody heavy," the Englishman said. One soldier fell but the other was still standing and began to run, shouting. Karl fired again and got him in the back, silencing him.

Karl and the Englishman climbed the long metal ladder down to the disused underground railway tracks. "Do you know where this leads?" asked Karl.

"There's a station in safer territory about a mile and a half from here," said the man as he pulled a flashlight out of his knapsack. "I committed the whole system to memory about a year ago. Most of it's out of use now, but this tunnel is safe. It runs right under the square back there. Three of them do in fact, each one on top of the other. It's a sort of terminus under there. That's why they put this service entrance here. There's one for each of the tunnels. This one's the lowest. The top tunnel is really close to the surface. The service entrance for that is just to the north of the square. That was our planned escape route before things went pear shaped."

The Englishman fell silent for a while. Karl imagined he was dwelling on what went wrong. Then his mood lightened, he pulled himself together and turned to Karl. "I'm Captain Daniel Brown by the way," he said and offered his hand.

"Karl Fairburne. Good to know you Dan."

"That's Daniel old boy, and it's a pleasure to meet you too. A bloody miracle in fact, I thought my goose was definitely cooked back there. You're OSS right?"

"That's right, and you must be SOE, Special Operations Executive?"

"For my sins."

"I thought you guys were staying out of Germany."

"By and large we were. We were having more success with Operation Sussex." Karl looked non-plussed. "Sorry, that's the code word we used for infiltrating British agents into France to aid with the resistance. That's all over now; the whole operation was a great success. Berlin is the last great arena where the future of Europe will be decided, so we've got men on the ground here. Not having much success though."

"So what happened back there?"

"Routine surveillance job gone awry. Some damn Russian spotted us, must have got sloppy I guess. So what do you know about this operation the Germans have got going with the Russians?"

"About as much as you do."

"Ah, playing it cagey are we? We're supposed to be on the same side you know. It won't hurt to trade a little intelligence."

"There's honestly not a lot I can tell you. The area is well fortified, which you probably know, and well manned. I don't know what either side is planning yet, or how it fits into the Russian plans to take Berlin, nor the German plans to stop them. I can't tell which side, if any, are the traitors."

"Well you're about as well informed as I am," said Daniel. "And I lost three good men today. You can imagine how much I'm looking forward to my next briefing."

"What do you know about the Spear of Destiny?" asked Karl as they came to a fork in the tunnel.

"This way," said Daniel pointing out the right hand tunnel with his flashlight. "The Spear of Destiny, it's an ancient relic that's rumoured to have occult powers. Legend has it that it was once owned by a Centurion called Longinus who used it to pierce Christ's side while he was on the cross. Whoever possesses the lance will rule the world. It's been owned by 45 different emperors over the last thousand years and until a few years ago it was on display in the Hapsburg Treasure House in Austria."

"You seem to know a lot about this. You're not a believer are you?"

"Me? Good heavens no, but it's important to understand how your enemy thinks. The philosophies he lives by, the icons that he values. Have you ever read *Mein Kampf*?"

"No," Karl confessed.

"Not exactly a scintillating read, but an important one for gauging and appreciating the Nazi mind set. Hitler writes of his fascination for the artefact as a young man of 21. For three years, while he lived in Vienna, he visited the artefact on display in the treasure house countless times, simply to gaze at it. He even recounts how he went into a trance once and got a vision of the future just looking at it. Supposedly had a vision of how he would come to power and everything. As soon as he invaded Austria in 1938, he had the Spear taken back to Nuremberg, the Nazi's so called 'spiritual home'. That's about all I can tell you. Why do you ask old boy?"

"Several of the people I met while in deep cover referred to the Spear of Destiny project. Have you heard anything about it?"

"Can't say that I have. That's what they're undertaking with the Russians is it? You don't think they actually plan to use the Spear of Destiny do you?"

"It doesn't really have any special powers does it?"

"Oh heavens no. The whole artefact comprises nothing more than three bits of blade and a shaft from the top of an old bronze age spear. It couldn't possibly have any power. But the Nazi's are desperate, they're going to be beaten any day now. Maybe they've become so unhinged they'll try anything."

"Not with this much security," said Karl. "And not with the Russians involved. They don't hold with any of the Nazi's occult philosophy. They're materialists. It's antithetical to their beliefs, or lack of them. There's no way the Soviets would get involved with a plan to use a magical artefact. There's got to be something really big in it for them."

"That'll be where the codename comes from then," said Daniel. "Whatever it is they're planning to do, it involves a power so great whoever possesses it will run the world. A weapon that can change the fate of nations."

"I don't know," said Karl, "if I can imagine a weapon with that capability."

"Modern warfare is going to be an awful lot different from now on. Science is seeing to that. We get closer to the weapon that will end all wars everyday. Maybe the Russians and Germans have hit on something."

"If they have, it'll be our job to find out and stop them,"

said Karl without hiding the irony in his voice.

"Someone has to clean up the mess I suppose," Daniel said, cracking a smile.

They came to a disused stop on the line and hopped up on to the platform. "The stairs are just over here," said Daniel, pointing with his flashlight. They climbed the staircase and came to a metal gate at the top. It was closed and the lock had rusted shut. Karl gave it a few hard shoves, then shot the lock off with his pistol and kicked the gate open.

"Listen old man," said Daniel offering Karl his hand. "You really saved my bacon back there. There's a lot of operatives who would have happily seen me killed rather than break their cover. It could have taken you months to infiltrate that place and you threw it all away to help save me. I owe you my life and that's a favour I mean to repay one day."

"Don't hold yourself in too much esteem," said Karl taking Daniel's hand and shaking it. "My work there had finished and I was looking for a way to sneak out without attracting attention. You created the perfect diversion. You don't owe me anything."

"Yes I do," said Daniel. "And I'll be seeing you about that repayment soon."

"I look forward to that," said Karl as they parted ways.

CHAPTER THIRTEEN

Karl checked the road through his binoculars. He was on the second floor of what had once been a department store but was now a mere shell without a roof. He looked at his watch again. It was 5:15pm, the jeep carrying Isaac was twenty minutes late by his calculation and the light was beginning to die. If they didn't turn up soon it would be too dark and they would have to abandon the plan in favour of something else.

Max had been quick to see the opportunity that Isaac offered them. The OSS had learned a great deal about the joint Russian/German operation. They knew who the key players were on both sides, but they didn't yet have a full picture of what they intended to do and how they hoped to accomplish it. Isaac was the key to putting all the pieces together and he had practically fallen into their lap.

Karl had outlined his plan for kidnapping Isaac from the NKVD and drawn a map of the route they would take, detailing all the men and equipment he would need. Max had cleared his strategy and found him the agents within three hours of their meeting.

Karl had hoped to enlist Chuck's help on the mission but he wasn't available. He would, however, be helping with Isaac's cross-examination later, which pleased Karl no end. He was also pleased that Max had been able to rope his old buddy Tex Jones into the operation.

Tex's pappy, and his grand-pappy before him, ran a huge cattle ranch back in Texas. Tex had been handling rifles out on the range since he was tall enough to sit in a saddle without falling off. He graduated from Westpoint in the same year as Karl. He was the highest ranked graduate sniper ever to leave the institute, knocking Karl into second place. Karl had been leagues ahead of all his fellow trainees, but leagues behind Tex.

Tex had been recruited to work for Allen Dulles at the OSS HQ in Bern, Switzerland when the US entered the war. He ran commando operations as a sniper over the border in Germany and occupied France. Then one night, just over a year ago, full of liquor and fighting drunk, the US sniper with the most number of confirmed kills to his name got into a brawl with a bunch of marines and took a bottle to the face. He lost the use of his right eye and his ability to snipe. Now he sported an eye patch and a fetching scar.

Tex was still an exceptionally skilled and highly trained field operative though. Max took him on and employed his talents in the one arena where the OSS still needed effective men of action, Berlin. Karl felt safer for having Tex on board. He was a friend in a foreign and hostile land and just the kind of man you wanted by your side in a fight.

Backing Tex up were two guys Karl hadn't worked with before, James and Warren. James he knew by reputation, an agent renowned for getting the goods no matter what it took. Warren wasn't Max's choice. Command had insisted on his placement when Max had reported the mission to them. This meant quite simply that he was X-2.

Karl wasn't blind to how things worked in the OSS. They would keep him in the field as long as he kept getting them the results they wanted, but with a large question mark hanging over the loyalty of Karl and his family, they would want to keep him under constant scrutiny. On a personal level, Karl hoped to learn something from Isaac that would help him understand the relationship between Kammler and his father.

Finally the jeep pulled into view, nearly forty minutes

late. Only a Russian would have such blatant disregard of a schedule. Say what you like about Germans but they would rather face death than the dishonour of missing a deadline. The plan Karl had proposed was simple. He would shoot out the front wheel of the jeep and bring it to a halt. On the stretch of road he had chosen there was only one place to shelter from sniper fire. Already wary of sniper attack the Russians would be driven to take cover in that one pre-arranged spot. Tex, James and Warren would be waiting, carefully camouflaged, right next to them.

While Karl pinned the Russians down with sniper fire, the three OSS agents would catch them off guard and quickly dispatch the driver and the two guards. Karl would then meet up with Tex, James, Warren and Isaac at a prearranged spot nearby, where transport was waiting to take them to safety.

Karl drew a bead on the right hand front tire of the jeep, adjusting his aim a notch and a half down on the crossbar of his sights to accommodate for gravity over the distance. The jeep pulled perfectly into range. Karl squeezed the trigger and the tire exploded.

The driver did not handle the jeep as everyone expected though. Karl let off a few close shots over the Russians' heads to spook them and instead of slamming on the brakes the driver accelerated causing the jeep to skid, spin and then turn over.

Karl watched through his binoculars as Isaac climbed out of the up-turned vehicle and ran for cover with his hands up shouting, "Don't shoot, don't shoot, I am an informant," in German.

The two NKVD soldiers pulled themselves free of the jeep, got to their feet and started after Isaac. Karl couldn't tell whether they understood what he was saying but they were obviously intent on capturing and possibly killing him.

Before Karl could get the men in his sights Tex and Warren broke cover. As experienced agents they were used to adapting to changing situations. Isaac was running towards a half demolished wall. This was the cover towards which Karl had hoped to drive the men.

Tex was coming up behind the wall so Isaac and the men on the road couldn't see him yet. Tex could see that Isaac was running wildly, swerving from side to side. This made it difficult for Karl to shoot his pursuers. There was no guarantee that Isaac wouldn't run into the trajectory of a bullet meant for one of the soldiers at the last second. Even though Isaac was in front of the men the bullet could still pass through one of them and hit him.

Tex drew a knife from a sheath on his belt, came out from behind the wall and threw it at the soldier closest to Isaac. The knife whistled past Isaac's ear and caught the Russian in the throat. He had been seconds from grabbing hold of Isaac. Now he stopped and his hands jerked to his throat, surprised to find a knife there. Blood spilled out over his collarbone and soaked his chest, running down in a thick constant stream. The soldier's eyes glazed over, he took two more steps and then his knees gave out and he pitched forward in the dirt and rubble.

James had been hiding on the other side of the wall to Tex and Warren, closer to the road in a dug out of rubble. Isaac was nearly upon him when he leaped from his hole and brought Isaac to the ground. From the flying tackle that he used on Isaac it was obvious that James had played college football.

As soon as Isaac was on the ground, Karl had a free shot at the last NKVD soldier. He fixed the man in his sights, aimed for the position he was just about to run into and fired. It was a clear and precise shot. The top of the soldier's head cracked open, blood and brains burst out in a torrent and his whole body went limp.

Karl drew in his breath and saw that he was shaking. He realised this wasn't from fatigue, it was nerves. Tex, who was still the best marksman Karl had ever known, was watching all his shots. Karl had never gotten anywhere near him. Maybe part of Karl felt guilty that he still had the use of his talents while Tex was denied his, as though Tex were more worthy. At the very least Karl felt he better be at the top of his game in front of the best of his peers.

He watched as James stood up and helped Isaac to his feet. Tex and Warren joined them. Their job from this point was to get Isaac safely to the armoured SS car, parked halfway between their current location and Karl's position 350 metres away.

A bullet ricocheted over their heads. All four men instinctively ducked. James threw himself on Isaac to protect him. The shot came from the up turned jeep. The driver was alive and had crawled out from the wreckage. He was firing his rifle from behind the vehicle. He was either dazed or inexperienced though, because he wasn't using it properly as cover and was still exposed.

Karl reached for his rifle but Warren got there first, firing off a couple of shots from a Colt 45 that he pulled from a shoulder holster. The force of the shots knocked the driver on his back as they thudded into his face and shoulder. Karl was impressed. A Colt wasn't standard US Army issue and couldn't be purchased anywhere in Europe. Warren would have to have brought it all the way from home. When a man goes to that much trouble he has to have a special fondness, and a certain skill with a weapon. The sort of skill Warren had just displayed.

Karl put his rifle away and left his vantage point. The armoured car was parked four streets away. He clambered over the rubble surrounding the former department store until he got onto the flat surface of a road then jogged to the meeting point.

"Thank the Lord it is you," said Isaac as soon as he saw Karl jog up to the armoured car. "I was beginning to worry. I did not know who these men were, and I am a Jew alone in Nazi Germany."

"These men are working with me," said Karl. "They will not harm you."

"Why did you not snatch me earlier? I was terrified you weren't going to come."

"You were late getting to the spot we had designated for your capture," said Karl.

"The driver was an idiot. He kept losing his way. Then he nearly killed us. Did you have to shoot at us like that?"

"You didn't help matters with your actions either," said Karl. "Luckily these men were able to swiftly rectify matters. Now there isn't time for any more talk. We have to get you away from here before we're seen."

James climbed into the driver's seat of the armoured car. Karl and Tex bundled Isaac into the back. Warren rode shotgun as the car pulled out and drove off to a safe house.

Max had found an ideal lock up to hold the meeting. Ten minutes before they arrived Karl blindfolded Isaac, telling him it was for security purposes. It mainly helped reinforce the illusion they were creating.

They walked Isaac around for a few minutes. Led him through the same door, opening and closing it every time, steering him as though he was going around sharp corners in a corridor, everything to disorient him and give him the illusion of being in a large building. Then they sat him down in a chair and Karl took the blindfold off.

There was a desk in the middle of the room with a single angle poise lamp on it. The lamp cast a small pool of light around the three men sitting behind the desk. The men were Karl, Max and Chuck. Max and Chuck were dressed as high-ranking SS officers. Isaac was sitting on a small stool in front of them. This meant he had to constantly look up to the men at the desk in front of him.

These were standard SS interrogation methods. Max had gone to great lengths to get all the details exactly right. There could be nothing to make Isaac suspect that he wasn't in SS custody.

"My lieutenant tells me you have information concerning the activities of the SS that most of us in command don't know about," said Max in German. "Is that true?"

"It is," said Isaac. "But I won't tell you anything until you promise to locate my daughters."

"We've located your daughters," Max bluffed. "I want to know if you have anything worth my time before I do anything more though."

"You've located them? God be praised! Where are they? Can I see them?"

"Not until you've convinced me it's worth my while to help you."

Isaac was not convinced. "I need some proof that you have them, that they're unharmed. I also need to know when you're going to give them back to me."

"We can't give your children back to you," said Max.

"What would you do with them in the middle of Berlin? If we don't return them to your superiors with an explanation that they'll accept, neither you nor they will be safe in Russia."

"Very well," said Isaac.

"Now what do you have that will tempt me to help you?"

"I have vital information about General Helmstadt, SS Gruppenführer Kammler, Comrade Velikovsky and the Spear of Destiny project."

"You also have my interest," said Max. He motioned to Tex, now dressed in full SS regalia and standing in the shadows. Tex stepped up to the desk. Max said a few quiet words in his ear. Tex nodded and left the room. Max turned back to Isaac.

"Perhaps we can start with General Helmstadt. What is he doing here in Berlin?"

"Helmstadt is one of the principle architects of the Spear of Destiny project. He has come to Berlin ostensibly to see it to fruition. He has other motives however. Motives, which concern my superior Comrade Ilyich Velikovsky."

"Go on."

"Comrade Velikovsky has greatly increased his standing in the Bolshevik party of late. He works for the NKVD and is both a zealot to the Soviet cause and exceptionally self-serving. When he found out that Helmstadt's position within the SS was under threat he made great efforts to win him to the Russian side. Helmstadt had already opened negotiations with the United States, but Comrade Velikovsky convinced him to defect to Russia instead. This has brought Velikovsky much prestige within the NKVD and he knows that he can use Helmstadt to greatly increase his power. It is ironic though to think that had Velikovsky failed, the United States would now be engaged in the Spear of Destiny Project with Helmstadt and your Gruppenführer Kammler."

"Tell us something about Gruppenführer Kammler's involvement in this project," said Chuck, speaking for the first time.

"Kammler, as you must know, wants to control your nuclear secrets. He is using the rocket programme that he already controls to do so. He has developed a missile of much greater speed and strength than the V2. The V2 has proved effective in its deployment but it does not have enough range or destructive capacity to strike a deadly blow against the enemies of the Third Reich. Because it only has a maximum range of 234 miles, it is only really possible to use it to attack neighbouring countries on your borders, such as Britain, which is only the other side of the channel. While Britain has proved a thorn in your side, your biggest threats now come from Russia and the United States, who are both continents away. Kammler's new rocket the V10, has a range that is ten times greater so that it is possible to launch a pre-emptive strike against countries a continent away."

"And Kammler has perfected this has he?" said Max. "There are working prototypes that he has tested?"

"I have seen them myself," said Isaac. "Right here in Berlin. I was on my way to do some further tests on them when you took me. I arranged the tests on purpose so you could intercept me."

"We admire your courage and ingenuity," said Chuck half mockingly. "But tell us more about Kammler, how does the V10 help him get control of our nuclear secrets?"

"Now, Germany has the capacity to use an Atom bomb on one of her two main enemies. Kammler insisted that Helmstadt furnish the V10 with a nuclear warhead.

Helmstadt couldn't refuse without appearing to sabotage your war effort. Kammler will finally get his hands on an Atom bomb here in Berlin where he has stationed his rocket."

"What do you think he is going to do with it?" asked Max. "Assuming that General Helmstadt has brought a nuclear warhead into Berlin."

"Helmstadt has definitely brought a nuclear warhead into Berlin," said Isaac. "And Gruppenführer Kammler means to use it. Once he has control of your nuclear secrets I don't think Kammler is much bothered who he will take them to. I imagine he will settle for whoever makes the highest bid. He wants to demonstrate the power he controls though, so a decisive nuclear strike is a necessity for him. I would also imagine it is an act of revenge. America has severely hampered the objectives of the Third Reich, so Kammler must naturally want them to pay."

Karl imagined that Max and Chuck were as astounded and alarmed as he was by Isaac's revelations. None of them could allow it to show through their impassive exteriors though, for fear of blowing the whole masquerade.

"Has General Helmstadt handed the warhead over to Gruppenführer Kammler yet?" asked Max.

"No. Although it has been constructed General Helmstadt still needs to arm the warhead. He intends to do that at the Kaiser Willhelm Institute which, as you must know, is one of the two main centres for Nazi nuclear research. They have three tons of refined uranium oxide that Helmstadt intends to use."

"How loyal is Helmstadt to the Soviets?" asked Chuck, probing Isaac's story. "Could he still be turned by the United States at the last minute?"

"I do not think so. Comrade Velikovsky compiled a comprehensive file on Helmstadt before he approached him and it seems he uncovered something that has given him great leverage with the General. I do not know what this is, but it has ensured Helmstadt's full compliance."

"Can you tell us what target has been selected for the nuclear missile?" Max said.

"The Whitehouse in Washington DC has been chosen as the target that will do the single most damage to the United States. A nuclear strike will wipe out a quarter of the population in the blast alone. The resulting fall out and radiation will severely deplete the surviving populace. The area will not be habitable for the next twenty years at least. Without any central administration the United States will be in chaos. It will take many years to recover from the blow. By that time my country will have marched unchecked through Europe, just as you National Socialists once hoped to."

"America is your ally though," said Chuck. "Why do you turn against it now, just at the moment when your coalition is about to be victorious, especially as you are poised to take Berlin. Why not just seize all the nuclear secrets once you have captured the city?"

"Because Stalin has promised to share Berlin with the Allies and could easily let the secrets slip out of his grasp. Our treaty with you has taught us that today's allies can be tomorrow's foes and our next big enemy will undoubtedly by the United States, who are just as ideologically opposed to us as you were. If Russia can aid in a nuclear strike on the USA, mounted by leading members of the Third Reich, without being directly involved, it will have complete deniability. We are already behind both you and the United States in the race to develop nuclear capabilities. This will put us back in the lead, without having to face the United States in openly declared war."

"What you say is of great interest to us," said Max. "And explains a great many things. How can we count on the validity of your intelligence though? How have you come by so much sensitive information, considering your position in the Soviet hierarchy?"

"I am ideally placed to learn such things. I am the leading Soviet expert on rocket science here in Berlin. I consult with and brief many people. I hear many things. People do not worry about your security clearance when they hold the lives of everyone you hold dear in their hands. They supposed the continued threat to the lives of my family to be security enough to buy my continued devotion and silence. When you hold that over a man you presume him perfectly safe to discuss anything in front of."

"And yet you turned on them," said Max. "Their hold over you couldn't have been that effective."

"I no longer believe that the survival of my family depends on keeping my Soviet paymasters happy. In fact I now believe the opposite, which is why I'm making, what my faith tells me is, an unholy pact with you."

Max was impressed by the validity of Isaac's intelligence and the urgency of responding to it. He did not let the latter show in his voice or manner though. "I accept what you say to be true then."

"I have made good on my side of the deal. Now I want some assurance that you will make good on yours."

"What's to stop us from simply taking you outside and having you shot?" Chuck asked, staying in character as an SS officer and also fishing to see if Isaac had any more intelligence with which to bargain.

"There is much I can still tell you. I can be very useful to you as an informant if you put me back without arousing suspicion. But I need assurances that you can guarantee the safety of my two daughters and me."

"You will be released back into Soviet custody," said Max. "So as to arouse no suspicions among your superiors, we will hand you over to the United States, who will in turn hand you back to the NKVD. You will say that the Wehrmacht attacked your jeep. You were captured but subsequently freed by the intercession of the United States forces who killed your Nazi captors and rescued you. You will say you told the US nothing other than your connection with the NKVD, do you understand?"

"How will you hand me over to United State's custody when you're still at war with them?" Isaac wanted to know.

"We have many secrets the United States want," said Max. "They know we will not fight on much longer and already there are many on their side who want to make deals with us, just as there are on your side. We know of several US operatives who are happy to trade a favour for a favour and hand you back to the Soviets for us."

Isaac nodded, satisfied with Max's answer. Karl was impressed with the ingenuity of Max's planning, forethought and cover story. They had pulled it off. Isaac had, at no time, suspected that he wasn't meeting the SS. "When will you return my daughters?" He asked, and Karl saw the stumbling block to the whole operation.

"As soon as you are safely back with the Soviets and we can guarantee your security, your daughters will be returned unharmed to NKVD command, with instructions that you are to be informed of their safe return," Max lied. They had no idea where Isaac's daughters were. Max knew he couldn't possibly substantiate that promise. Even though he was undercover in another identity, Karl had given Isaac his word to try and help. Isaac had staked a lot on getting this information to them and Karl believed he was owed a little co-operation.

"I'll personally make sure your daughters are returned," Karl said as he walked around the desk and helped Isaac to his feet. Karl caught Max's eye as he said it and caught a hint of disapproval. For the first time there was an air of distrust between them. Max was uncertain of Karl's motives for making that promise, and Karl wasn't sure how sincere Max was about finding Isaac's missing daughters.

Karl put the blindfold back on Isaac and escorted him through the door. Tex and Warren walked Isaac around a bit more to keep up the front and took him away to another part of the city to hand over to two other OSS operatives.

Karl felt very uneasy about his distrust of Max. There were few men he could trust in Berlin and he didn't want to lose one of the only one's who had any pull with the OSS. The secret accusations against Karl and his father had made him even more paranoid. As an undercover agent, in a complicated political situation, Karl didn't think he could get any more paranoid, but here he was, doubting everything.

One of the problems he'd been trained to expect was a growing sympathy for his undercover identity. The longer you played a persona, the more it became a part of you. The dangers involved with this are that you become confused as to who you're really fighting for, the goals you are trying to achieve and the people you are looking after. Your personal and professional agendas become hard to define.

Karl also knew he was fixating on this small point because the enormity of what Isaac had told them was too much to take in. Karl had left his home to fight on foreign soil, safe in the knowledge that the war was overseas.

When he arrived he saw a city he grew up in reduced to smouldering rubble. Now the country for which he fought was threatened with worse. The horror of the war was about to come home to the United States unless Karl, and the handful of men he was working with, could stop it.

CHAPTER FOURTEEN

"What do we make of this?" said Max as soon Karl was back in the room.

"It explains most of the activities we've been monitoring," said Chuck. "But it's more serious than anything we expected."

"Karl you've witnessed these activities in the field," said Max. "What's your take? Does all this seem possible to you?"

"It would make a lot of sense," Karl said. "I've seen the rockets he mentioned. They have the capability to transport them too. The square I infiltrated, full of NKVD and Nazi troops, must be where they plan to launch the missile. Why else would an empty square in the middle of a bombed out city have so many troops guarding it?"

"What do we do now?" Chuck said, framing the one question they'd all been avoiding.

"As soon as this meeting is ended I will report immediately to Major Harwood, head of the OSS German department, and Deputy head Allen Dulles. They in turn will contact General Donovan who is responsible for briefing the President. I will impress upon them the extreme urgency of the situation and the dire need for quick and decisive action. We will then await our orders." Max said.

"It could take days for Washington to formulate a response," said Chuck. "By that time..."

"...by that time there might not be a Washington left to deliberate, I know," said Max. "If we start acting without orders, we stop acting together though. We are a disciplined international organisation and we adhere to a central policy. That doesn't mean however, that we can't act on our own initiative until we know the full strategy. We need to focus on any missions we already have that affect this nuclear missile and continue our guerrilla tactics of sabotage and de-stabilisation."

"We could attack the silos for a start," said Karl. "There's enough explosive material in there to blow the whole port apart. If we can get a few men in there with some form of detonator and get them out safely we could destroy the rockets."

"Good thinking," said Max. "It's unlikely that they have only one silo, but we can look into the possibility of what you're suggesting."

"Launching a rocket is a big operation," said Chuck. "It involves a lot of man power and a lot of equipment has to be mobilised. There have to be fuel convoys coming into Berlin, not to mention other mobile operations that we can attack as they move things into place."

"That's true," said Max, "and I like your thinking. I'll have agents in the field prepared for just those possibilities. There is one mission that's come down the wire that is extremely relevant to our current situation. I'd like you to handle it Karl."

"Okay. I'm happy to do my bit."

"Chuck," said Max. "You'll understand if I ask you to step outside while I brief Karl."

Chuck looked surprised, but he wasn't going to argue. "Sure," he said. "I'll make a sweep of the perimeter and make certain we haven't been compromised."

Chuck left and Max fixed Karl with an inquiring look, the type of look that weighs up all a person's reactions - verbal and physical. "What do you know about Hans Kammler?" Max said. Karl nearly started, but caught himself at the last minute. He couldn't afford to let anything slip with Max scrutinising him. Was it possible that Max knew about what he had learned? Of course not, he told himself and pulled himself together.

"Erm," said Karl after a pause. "Only what you told me in the last briefing and what I learned just now from Isaac."

"We want you to take him out," said Max. "It's not just a straight forward assassination though, in fact that's a secondary feature of the mission. In the main it's a retrieval mission. We need you to infiltrate the Reichstag, where Kammler is currently holed up, and find a certain bit of information for us. We cannot afford a failure in this part of the mission. Your life will be in great danger and you cannot come back empty handed. Do you think you're up to it?"

"Of course. What am I going to be looking for?"

"We have it on good authority that Kammler has gotten hold of the secret access code to disable the nuclear device in Helmstadt's briefcase."

"How has he managed that? I thought that was something only Helmstadt himself knew."

"So did we. It appears that he left some loose ends. He naturally ordered the men who constructed the case and set the combination for him to be killed, but one of them got away and has been on the run for quite some time. The SS were informed that this man was a wanted criminal and should be tracked down. They weren't told why though, and being SS men they simply followed orders. Eventually the man was caught and was due to be sent off to a concentration camp. However, when he revealed who he was and why he was sentenced to death, he was able to strike a bargain."

"With the SS?"

"Naturally," said Max. "As you know they are ripe with in-fighting and are constantly jockeying each other for position. Word got back to Kammler that the man was in custody and Kammler ordered an immediate stay of execution. He had the man moved to Berlin and interrogated him personally, taking down everything the man told him in code."

"What happened to the man?"

"Oh, Kammler had him shot soon afterwards. It's an unfortunate liability of knowing too much when you deal with the SS."

"So you want me to steal the code from Kammler for you."

"It won't be easy. But we have someone inside the Reichstag who can help you."

"Another agent. A man we already put in there? I didn't know we'd been that successful."

"We haven't. It's a double agent close to Kammler that contacted us. She's the source of our information. A Russian agent, working within the Nazis who wants to defect to the West."

"She?"

"Her name is Yelena Petronova. She is Kammler's mistress. He is the fifth high ranking Nazi that she has taken as a lover."

"So she likes a man in Jackboots does she?"

"No, she doesn't have any choice in the matter. She was forced into working for the Soviets, so she claims, by our Comrade Velikovsky."

"That name again," said Karl. "The same ones just keep popping up don't they."

"Indeed, although she is a Russian national her mother was a German communist who left Germany in 1920 after the failure of the Spartacist uprising in Berlin lead by Karl Liebknecht and Rosa Luxembourg. She defected to Russia and married an officer in the Red Guard who was subsequently killed battling the White Guard in the civil war. Yelena and her brother were raised bilingual. This fact and her obvious beauty made her an ideal siren."

"Siren? I don't think I follow."

"It's a Russian term, for a type of agent we don't employ. The NKVD quickly realised that a man will say many things to a trusted mistress during pillow talk that he would not confide to anyone else. A siren is an agent that seduces high ranking enemies of the Soviet state in order to either pump them for information that they will then pass on to the Russians, or in some cases, trap the man into becoming an informant on his own side. They're not the only ones to use this tactic, the Germans have sirens as well."

"Well I'm glad we don't use such tactics."

"No. It's mean, dirty and despicable, and it's ruined the lives of many good men..." Max stopped and bit his lip. In all the time Karl had known him, Max had just come the closest he had seen to losing control. He seemed really perturbed by what he was saying and for a second he shook with anger. Max took a deep breath and composed himself. Karl knew better than to ask him if anything was the matter.

"Nevertheless," Max continued. "In this instance it works to our benefit. Miss Petronova has proven to be a very useful double agent. These are desperate times and I'm not going to turn down help from any quarter."

"Kammler intends to use this code to steal the nuclear secrets from Helmstadt, right?"

"That's correct, yes."

"So, if the code is so top secret, why hasn't he just committed it to memory and destroyed it? Why leave it lying around in the Reichstag? How do we know we're not being set up here? What if I'm walking into a trap?"

"If I thought you were walking into a trap, I wouldn't send you. Kammler hasn't committed the code to memory because he doesn't intend to use it himself, that would be much too dangerous. We don't know when he intends to make the grab, but he will employ a trusted member of the SS and he will make certain that he is outside of Berlin, just in case anything goes wrong. For this reason he has to keep a single copy of the code in the safe in his private chambers at the Reichstag."

"All I have to do is liberate it."

"It won't be easy. It's the most dangerous mission I've sent you on. To be frank, there's no-one else I could entrust this to. The results you've been getting in the field have defied everyone's expectations."

I'll bet they have, thought Karl without saying anything.

"Everyone is seriously impressed with your record so far. You're bound to receive a decoration for this." Max put a hand on Karl's shoulder and smiled. "I'm proud that I brought you into the field Karl, and I'm even prouder to fight your corner."

Karl imagined Max would have had to do a lot of fighting in his corner, if what he had been told was true. He could not remain sceptical in the face of Max's praise though. He knew it was standard practise to give agents a pep talk to prepare them for a particularly hazardous mission. This didn't mean he was unaffected by Max's display of avuncular affection.

Max was the most recent in a long line of father figures that Karl had always sought out. His own father had been distant and disapproving throughout most of Karl's life. He had never received the approval or affection from him that he so desperately craved. So he had looked for it in others. This made him a real sucker for the line Max was feeding him.

"Do we have a plan as to how I get inside the Reichstag?" asked Karl. "I mean I can't just stroll up and knock on the door."

"No. That wouldn't be a good idea. We intercepted news that a special courier is making his way into Berlin by motorbike. He is carrying vital documents for Kammler's eyes only. We have his route. We want you to stop him when he gets into Berlin, kill him and take his place. We've arranged substitute documents that you can trade with one of our operatives before you enter the Reichstag. Once in you should be able to get straight to Kammler. Kill him then contact Miss Petronova, she can get you into the safe where the code is kept. Is that all clear?"

"Perfectly. Do you have the courier's route to hand?"

Max produced his familiar attaché case, pulled out a file and handed it to Karl. "It's all in here, along with a plan of the Reichstag showing Kammler's office and private quarters, plus a photograph of our Russian siren. Commit it all to memory then burn it."

Karl flicked through the contents of the brown cardboard folder and nodded. He took it with him as he got up to leave. Max took his hand at the door. "You make sure and come back now son."

"Oh I will," said Karl.

"You better. 'Cos if you don't, I don't care what filthy pit of hell you find yourself in, I'm gonna come find you and kick your ass, you hear?"

"I hear," said Karl. Max slapped him on the shoulder and he left.

Karl regretted not bringing a tarpaulin with him as he lay behind a pile of rubble next to the Autobahn turn off, just outside of the Mitte district. The ground was damp and sodden, and the moisture had leaked into his clothes making it very uncomfortable to lie still for as long as he needed to.

He listened carefully for the sound of a motorcycle. His interception would have to be done at close quarters. This was not a part of his mission in which his long range sniping skills could be used. He couldn't shoot out the tires on the bike because he would need to drive it himself. Also he couldn't risk getting blood or bullet holes in the courier's uniform because that would draw suspicion towards him at the Reichstag.

The kill would have to be clean, quiet and up close. Tex had suggested the best way to stop the motorcycle without causing too much damage. He lent Karl a crossbow he had looted from a hunting shop in Munich. Tex told him to shoot the bolt between the spokes of the front wheel, just behind the prongs that connect the handlebars with the axle.

It was a tricky shot and Karl had only one chance to make it work, but Tex thought he was up to it. He had shown Karl how to use the bow and Karl had taken a few practice shots, so he knew his way around the weapon.

Just as the water from the damp ground had seeped into every part of his woollen vest, Karl finally heard the 'put-put-put' of a motorcycle engine. The courier pulled off the Autobahn and reduced his speed as he came down the turn off ramp. Karl emptied his lungs and blanked out everything except the shot he was going to take.

The courier drove up to Karl. His front wheel came into range. Karl squeezed the trigger. The bolt shot right between the spokes and the front prong. Had Karl mistimed, the bolt would have passed straight through, but it stuck.

The bike's front wheel came to a dead stop. The back

wheel, powered by the engine, kept going and flew up into the air throwing the courier over the handlebars. The bike flipped over and landed on its side, engine still running.

Karl leaped from his position and charged at the courier while he was still winded. The courier heard him coming though. He had not landed badly and was not injured. As Karl came upon him, he drew a pistol from a side holster and fired.

Karl caught the bullet in his left shoulder. He lost his footing on a piece of rubble and fell on his back.

The courier got to his feet and came at Karl with his pistol drawn. Karl scrabbled about with his right hand and found a rock. He sat up and hurled the rock at the courier's forehead. His head snapped backwards. Blood spurted from his face and he staggered.

Karl stood and threw himself at the man. He grabbed the courier's right forearm with both hands and brought his knee up under it. He pushed down with both hands at the same time and the bone fractured. It made a crackling sound as it broke. The pistol dropped from the courier's hand and let off a shot as it hit the ground.

The courier screamed with pain. To Karl's great luck, the bullet had lodged in the courier's ankle. Karl pushed the man onto his back and put his hand over the courier's mouth, pinching his nose shut at the same time.

The courier kicked and punched Karl ineffectually for a minute, then stopped struggling and gave up. Karl held him down until all the fight ebbed from his body and he died.

Karl got up, turned off the bike's engine and dragged the body to an abandoned checkpoint sentry box. He cursed under his breath at the pain he felt in his shoulder. The wound throbbed and bled as he dropped the courier's corpse on the floor of the sentry box.

He stripped off the top half of his uniform to look at the wound. It was clean and it wasn't too deep, but the bullet was of too small a calibre to get out. He began tearing his wet shirt into strips with his teeth and fingers. Karl wadded up a piece of torn shirt. He found a hip flask of schnapps on the courier. He took a slug from the bottle to help with the pain then doused the wad in the rest of the schnapps as a makeshift disinfectant. He pressed the wad to the wound in his shoulder and tied it in place with strips of shirt, making certain that the blood would not leak through. Moving his left arm was now extremely painful.

He stripped the courier's uniform and put it on. Unfortunately it was very tight as the courier was a size smaller than Karl. This did not help his shoulder.

Karl left the sentry box and went to inspect the motorcycle. The paint on the right hand fender was scratched, but aside from that it was undamaged. He pulled the bolt out of the front wheel, set it straight and climbed on. The engine started on the second kick and he was away.

Fifteen minutes later he pulled up at the corner where he was due to exchange the documents. He made a quick scan of the area and couldn't see anyone. Then Tex stepped out of the shadows not ten feet away.

Karl smiled. It was good to see Tex's skills were just as sharp as ever. "Got something for me there pardner?" Tex said.

"Depends," said Karl. "If you've got something to trade."

"I got just what you need right here," said Tex producing

a set of false documents from under his windcheater.

Karl swapped the fake documents for the ones in the courier's attaché case. Tex put the real documents safely away. "Good luck pardner. You make sure you come back now."

"I will." Tex punched him affectionately on the shoulder for good luck. It was Karl's left shoulder and he couldn't help wincing.

"Whoa, hold on there cowboy. Ol' Tex has a pretty mean right hook, but I barely tapped you there. What's up?"

"I caught a bullet in this shoulder. Back when I took out the courier."

"Now wait a minute, back up there pardner. I don't mean to question your judgement, but are you fit enough to carry on? Cos you don't wanna be riding into that Reichstag unless you're completely able to fight your way out."

"I'm fine. There's too much at stake for me to quit now."

"There's too much at stake for you to fail."

"I won't fail. It'll take a lot more than a flesh wound for that."

"Make sure you don't," said Tex. "Or you'll have me to answer to."

"Everyone's on my back all of a sudden," said Karl laughing off Tex's concern and revving the bike up.

"That's 'cos a lot rests on your shoulders," said Tex. Karl pulled away. "Don't you forget that," Tex shouted after him.

CHAPTER FIFTEEN

Karl drove past the old Reichstag building. Burned in 1933, it was still a hugely impressive structure with its four monumental facades. The large flight of steps and the high portico of the main entrance, with its four Corinthian columns, dwarfed the current seat of government, a building that had been taken over by the SS in the final stages of the war, when Berlin became all but uninhabitable.

Karl pulled up to the new Reichstag. The guard checked his papers then directed him to a courtyard entrance at the rear. Another guard checked his papers there and told him where to park. He entered through a goods entrance.

The new Reichstag was in a building that had been a luxurious hotel before the Nazis came to power. A consortium of Jewish businessmen had owned it, but Hitler's administration soon seized control. Under the SS, Karl noted, the building was a strange mixture of army barracks, officious bureaucracy and luxury boarding house.

He strode into the main foyer. A man at a desk told him the lift was out. Since the last round of Allied bombings there was only enough auxiliary power for a few electric lights and the refrigerators in the kitchen. Karl would have to take the central staircase.

The men Karl passed on his way up to the top floor looked bored, tense and weary. Membership of the SS encouraged a particular breed of fanaticism. Karl suspected that was all that was keeping the men in their posts. More Russian troops were pouring into Berlin every day. With British and Americans soon to back them up, there was little the men could look forward to except one heroic last-stand. Karl imagined that would probably come as a welcome relief to the tension and tedium they were currently displaying.

He reached the top of the stairs and turned left down a corridor to General Kammler's offices. One of two guards stopped him at the second set of doors. "Heil Hitler!"

"Heil Hitler," Karl returned.

"What is your business with Gruppenführer Kammler?"

"I have important documents for the Gruppenführer," said Karl.

"Let me see them."

"They are for Gruppenführer Kammler's eyes only."

"Give them to me then and I will see he gets them." The guard held out his hand but Karl kept hold of his attaché case.

"My orders are to hand these personally to Gruppenführer Kammler and no-one else."

The guard eyed Karl for a moment, weighing up whether he was a security risk and if he should be personally affronted by his refusal. "Show me your papers," he said eventually. Karl handed him the courier's ID and clearances. "Wait here a minute," said the guard, and walked to an office at the other end of the corridor.

Karl looked around the building under the none-too watchful eye of the other guard. Karl had been checking out the layout of the place since he arrived. Making certain that it was still the same as the plans he had memorised, that there were no alterations or amendments to any of the floors due to bombing raids or other business.

All of this was essential to the escape routes he had planned. There were three, one direct route and two contingencies. The last thing he wanted was to get halfway out of the building and find someone had built a wall where they shouldn't have or that a staircase was missing due to bomb damage.

He heard raised voices in the office. It sounded as though the guard was being scolded. The door opened. The guard stepped out, still facing the room, clicked his heels and bowed. He had been chastened but did not want to show it. Karl received the guard in a supercilious manner, which made the man seethe inwardly.

"Gruppenführer Kammler will see you now. Go to the last door on your left and knock. You are expected." Karl walked straight past the guard, without paying him any more attention and knocked on the door.

"Come," said a voice within. Karl opened the door and stepped into the office. Kammler was sitting behind his desk, poring over some papers. He did not look up. Like most high ranking Nazis, he looked nothing like the ideal of the master race he espoused.

Karl felt strangely let down now that he was finally face to face with Kammler. He wasn't sure what he had been expecting, but Kammler was a short stocky man with absolutely no hair and half moon spectacles perched on the end of his nose.

Karl hadn't realised till now how much he had invested in this meeting. He needed Kammler to tell him the truth about his father. Kammler held the key to clearing his name and the honour of his family.

"Well?" said Kammler impatiently. He was patently not a man who was used to being kept waiting.

"I have important documents for your attention mein Gruppenführer."

"I know that, that fool of a guard told me as much and I ordered the documents to be sent to me personally. You're already fifteen minutes late. Do you intend to make me wait even longer to see them?"

"No mein Gruppenführer. My apologies, here they are."

Karl put the false documents on Kammler's desk and reached into his pocket for the cord he had there. "I will need you to sign my remittance form mein Gruppenführer. To prove I have carried out my orders to the letter."

"Yes, yes, I know that man," said Kammler, flicking through the documents with a puzzled expression. "Wait a minute, these aren't in order."

Before Kammler could say anymore, Karl kicked the back of his revolving chair so that he spun round. He removed the cord from his pocket, took it in both hands and slipped it around Kammler's throat, twisting the ends to form a tourniquet. Kammler gasped for breath as the chord tightened. His whole head went bright red and the veins at the side of his forehead throbbed. Karl took hold of the tourniquet in his left hand, wrapping the ends of the cord around his fist and pulled out his pistol with his right hand. He placed the pistol at the base of Kammler's skull.

"This is a P-38 with a silencer attached. If I pull the trigger you'll be dead and I'll be out of the building before anyone will realise. Alternatively if I don't let go of this cord you'll choke to death in less than two minutes. I'm going to ask you a series of questions before I release this cord and you're going to tell me exactly what I want to know. Nod if you understand." Kammler nodded.

"If you cry out or attempt to escape you will be dead before you can draw your next breath. Is that clear?" Kammler nodded again. "I'm going to release the cord a little, just enough so you can breath," said Karl. "Now, before the war you met with a man called Frederick Fairburne, an American diplomat. What was the nature of the meeting?"

Kammler's tongue flicked out and moistened his dry lips. "Before the war I met with many people. I do not recall the man you mentioned."

Karl twisted the cord. "Try harder. He was stationed at the American Embassy here in Berlin throughout most of the Weimar Republic and the beginning of the Nazi regime. What was your connection to him?" Karl loosened the cord again.

Kammler coughed and wheezed. "I had no connection to him. If I ever met him the matter was not of enough consequence for me to remember." Karl tightened the cord, choking Kammler once more.

"It is now a matter of such consequence, that your life hangs in the balance if you don't remember."

He loosened his hold a little and Kammler sounded like he had a hacking cough. Then Karl realised that he was laughing. "Do you think I am that afraid of death that I will play your little games? Do you think if I cared about dying I would be sitting in an office in the middle of Berlin with half of the Red Army about to descend on me? Oh no, I have something you want and if you were going to kill me you would have done it properly by now."

This was not going the way Karl had planned. He was not in control of the situation. He did not have enough time to get Kammler to give him what he wanted. Mainly because he was not sure what he needed to know. "You are American aren't you? I can tell by your accent. It's not immediately apparent, your German is excellent, but there's a certain accent that you only get from attending a German American academy as a child, which you obviously did. I have something your pay masters want, no? Are you here to do the hard bargaining?"

"Was Frederick Fairburne a traitor?" Karl said, trying

to force the conversation back to where he wanted it. He shook Kammler as he did so. This was a mistake.

Kammler rocked forward then threw himself backwards. He pushed up with his legs and straightened his body smacking right into Karl's wounded shoulder. Karl toppled backwards and Kammler landed on top of him. Kammler thrust his elbow into Karl's stomach and knocked the breath out of him. Kammler broke free and ran for the door shouting for help as loudly as his hoarse voice would allow.

Karl grabbed his ankles and brought him to the ground. The door to the office burst open and the officious guard rushed in. Karl shot him twice in the face with his silenced P-38. The guard flew backwards into his counterpart who was bringing up the rear.

On seeing Karl the other guard dashed back down the corridor to get help. Karl got to his feet and sprinted across the office and out of the door. He shot the guard twice in the back and the man fell without ever reaching the first set of doors.

Karl heard Kammler get to his feet and run. He dashed back into the office in time to see him leave by another door. He raced after Kammler, chasing him through a suite of rooms without catching him.

Karl reached a huge bedroom with expensive decor and realised Kammler was nowhere in sight.

"He left through a servant's exit," said a female voice. Karl turned and saw Yelena Petronova for the first time. The photo he had been given did not do her justice. She was stunning. Karl almost forgot himself and his situation just looking at her auburn hair, her blue eyes and her curvaceous figure.

"You will not catch him," Yelena said. "And we do not have much time to get to the safe before he returns with many armed men."

"I'll catch him. Which way did he go?"

"You will not have time to get back here afterwards and get to the safe if you pursue him. Which is more important to you, Kammler's death or the combination to Helmstadt's case? What is going to help your cause more?"

Yelena's argument made sense and it brought Karl back to his senses. He had been sloppy with Kammler. Too eager to find answers to questions he didn't know how to frame. He had to let that go now and focus on the bigger issues. "Where is this safe?"

She led him into a small adjoining room and walked up to a picture of a rural setting within an ornate, gold frame. She took hold of the frame and pushed the picture to one side. It was on runners. Behind it was the safe. "Do you wish me to open it?" Yelena asked. Karl nodded and she turned the dial on the front several times, released a lever and pulled the safe open.

Inside were substantial sums of money in at least five different currencies and a small envelope. Yelena took the envelope and handed it to Karl. It read 'Codename - Sesame', in German, on the front. "This is the combination?"

"It's the only copy. Kammler will be back any minute. Come we must go. I know which route to take to avoid any soldiers. I have spent many bored, desperate hours exploring this place."

Yelena took him back to the bedroom and out into a corridor, then into another suite of rooms that were not being used. The curtains were drawn and dust cloths were thrown over all the furniture. The rooms smelt of damp and neglect.

She guided Karl right to the other end of the building

through a series of vacant and untouched rooms. In other rooms and corridors they heard distant footsteps racing up and down looking for them. At the end of the last room she took Karl back into a corridor and through another door onto a flight of rough concrete stairs that would only have been used by the hotel staff.

"This leads down into the basement," she said. They followed the stairs all the way down and went through a set of large doors into a basement with a low ceiling where the boiler was kept. "There are stairs leading up to the rear courtyard on the other side."

They made their way through the labyrinthine rooms of the basement to the other side. It was dark and the air was hot and oppressive. Yelena took Karl's hand to lead him. They turned a corner and, in the gloom, Karl crashed into a doorjamb with his left shoulder.

It was the second blow he had received to the wound and the pain was unbearable. It swept through his left side and his legs went from under him. He pulled Yelena down with him. "What is the matter?" she asked. "Are you hurt? I didn't see you get shot in the fight back there."

"I was hit by a bullet before I arrived," Karl told her, trying hard not to show any pain in his voice. His mind was fighting to regain control and to block out the pain so he could get up, get out of the building and finish his mission.

Yelena helped him to his feet. He was sweating and unsteady. His mind was screaming at him to get a grip. The whole building was crawling with SS soldiers all of whom wanted to find and kill him. In his pocket was a sheet of paper containing information that was essential to the survival of hundred's of thousands of his countrymen. He had to get out of this alive and get that information into the right hands.

"The steps to the courtyard are up here," Yelena said leading him. Karl started to use the pain so it worked for and not against him. They climbed the steps and peered out of the door at the top. The courtyard was clear, but the motorcycle Karl came in on was way over the other side and there was no cover to use to stop from being spotted.

"Thank you for your help," he said. "But I will have to go it alone from here. It is too dangerous for you to get involved any more."

"I am coming with you."

"No. It is too dangerous. I can't guarantee I can keep you alive."

"So far it is I who have been keeping you alive. You would have been dead without me. I will not survive either, if I do not leave with you. They will know that I helped you escape and kill me. Even if they didn't, I am a prisoner in this place. I sit around all day waiting to die when the Russians come to take the building and the SS makes its last stand." There wasn't time to argue. Karl realised he wasn't going to shake Yelena and he probably did owe her his life.

A single guard sat smoking a cigarette in an armoured car not twelve feet from them. He was probably the driver. Karl walked silently up beside the vehicle, then barked. "What's this man, loafing around when there's a crisis on? There's an assassin loose in the building who's just tried to kill Gruppenführer Kammler and you've got time to smoke a cigarette!"

The guard jumped to attention at the sound of Karl's voice. "Give me the keys," Karl demanded in a tone of voice that would brook no contradiction. Without thinking the guard responded. He was so used to following orders that he opened the door and reached for the keys.

It was only when the guard had the keys in his hand that he stopped to question what he was doing. Karl was right up next to him by that point. The guard could see that Karl was not dressed as an officer and should not be giving him orders. He put his hand on his pistol.

Karl brought his foot up and smashed the door into the guard's face as he was coming out of the car. The man was stunned and Karl kicked the door a further two times. He heard a rib snap on his third kick. Before the guard could respond Karl drove his fist into the man's gut.

The guard doubled over and slid to the ground. Karl reached down and took his keys and pistol. He left the man gasping for breath and spitting blood and teeth onto the cold cobblestone floor.

Karl signalled for Yelena to join him. They climbed into the armoured car and he started up the engine. As they approached the road they came upon a cordon of twenty men. "Get down," said Karl and put his foot to the floor.

The soldiers opened fire. Four were using sub-machine guns. The bullets thudded into the car. Yelena curled up under the seat as shards of glass rained down.

One of the SS men threw a grenade. Karl swerved at the last moment to avoid it. It exploded mere feet away from them. There was a wave of fierce heat and flames that engulfed the car. The force of the explosion lifted it onto two wheels.

Karl fought for control, wincing at the pain in his shoulder. He righted the car and headed out onto the road and away. There was sporadic firing as the men chased after them but Karl soon left them behind.

As soon as he was properly clear, Karl let out a deep breath. He had just survived the most dangerous mission of his career. It was far from a complete success. He had let his personal agenda get in the way of killing Kammler and that had nearly ruined everything.

Nevertheless, he had in his possession one of the single most important pieces of intelligence his country had ever gathered. All he needed to do now was make certain it got into the right hands.

CHAPTER SIXTEEN

Once Karl had put enough distance between himself and the Reichstag, he drove the armoured car into a side street and torched it. The street was near an abandoned bunker where Karl had hidden provisions and a change of clothes.

Yelena followed him down the steps into the bunker. She pulled a face the minute she stepped inside. The room stank of urine, fear and neglect. Yelena knew better than to complain though. Karl moved aside a pile of firewood and pulled out the backpack he had left there. He removed the Russian uniform he had taken from the dead soldier on the train and threw the rations to Yelena.

"What am I supposed to do with these?"

"Fix us something to eat."

"Sorry darling, I don't do domestic. You'll have to fix your own dinner." Karl rolled his eyes and took off his top. "Now this is more my line," said Yelena playfully.

The wound in Karl's shoulder was still bleeding heavily, in spite of the makeshift bandage. The blood had matted and stuck to the inside of the courier's jacket. Karl drew a deep breath as he pulled it off. Yelena moved in close to inspect the wound and frowned.

"This does not look good," she said and placed a hand on his chest. "You are shaking. I think you ought to let me take a look at that. Come, sit." She pointed to an old packing crate. Karl sat down, glad to take the weight off his legs.

Yelena knelt next to him and removed the knife from his boot. Karl's hand instinctively caught her wrist and she raised an eyebrow. "You don't like me handling your weapon. It's not the first one I've had in my hand."

"I'll bet."

"No, and most men don't tend to object." She cut the strips of shirt holding the bandage in place. "Not when you know what you're doing."

"And you know what you're doing, do you?"

"I've never had any complaints."

Yelena peeled the blood soaked wad of fabric away from the wound. Karl swore in English. "Such language," said Yelena in English. "What would your mother say?"

"You speak English," said Karl in surprise.

"Fluently," said Yelena. "I have been a hostess to many visiting American and British dignitaries in my time."

"I'll bet you have."

"Not in that way." She spoke English with a soft, east European drawl. The accent suited her a lot better than her perfect German.

"I'm going to have to get the bullet out. It will poison your blood otherwise and your wound will not heal."

"It won't come out. It's lodged in there."

"Nonsense. All I need is the right tools."

She reached into the bag of provisions and pulled out a metal spoon. "Perfect," she said and placed a thick strip of beef jerky in Karl's mouth. "Bite down hard on this, there will be a lot of pain."

Using the tip of the knife, Yelena located the bullet then pulled it out carefully between the blade and the handle of the spoon. She slipped twice and almost lost the bullet at one stage. She was perfectly right there was a lot of pain. Karl bit the jerky in half and ground his teeth. Finally the bullet dropped to the floor.

"You are bleeding heavily. We must cauterise the wound. I need a bullet and a match." Karl reached for his backpack and his head spun. There were flashes in front of his eyes and he lost all vision for a minute. He was faint from loss of blood, hunger and fatigue.

"This is going to hurt even more," said Yelena when he regained his focus. She had taken a bullet from a clip in his pack and dismantled it. She emptied the powder from the cartridge into the gaping bullet hole. Then she set a match to it.

The pain was beyond excruciating. Karl could not keep from screaming every obscenity he knew. The smell of cordite and his own burning flesh filled his nostrils. He bent forward, put his head between his knees and threw up.

Yelena found a flask of water in Karl's pack and handed it to him. He rinsed out his mouth and spat. He started to shiver violently and Yelena put the Russian great coat around his shoulders. "Better now?" She asked.

Karl nodded. "I better get dressed."

"Rest a moment," Yelena told him, putting her hands on his shoulders to stop him from standing. "I'll break a lifetime rule and prepare us something to eat." Karl did as he was told. After years in the field, it occurred to him that this was the first time he'd been looked after by anyone in a long time. Ironically the last time it happened he would have been as a child in this very city.

His nanny had been not been as disarmingly beautiful as Yelena though, or as bad a cook. Karl didn't think you could make army rations taste any worse, but somehow Yelena managed. "You know," he said between mouthfuls. "I forgot there's often a reason why people have lifetime rules."

"And you can taste the reason for mine," said Yelena with a smile.

She rummaged about in his pack some more. "What are you looking for?"

"Your cigarettes."

"I don't smoke. I'm a sniper. It draws enemy attention."

"Just my luck. How is your shoulder?"

"It's sore. But it's going to heal now so I guess I should thank you."

"Don't trouble yourself."

"Okay, I'm not big on gratitude. I don't spend time with many people and those that I do spend time with don't expect many 'pleases' or 'thank yous'."

"You could have fooled me," Yelena said, then sighed. "God I could use a drink right now."

"I doused that bandage in schnapps pretty good. Maybe you could still squeeze a few drops out of it."

"Great. Sucking alcohol out of a blood stained dressing. This war has not yet reduced me to those depths."

Karl stood and rolled his shoulder. "Careful," warned Yelena. "You'll tear the burnt tissue. Give it time to heal." Karl heeded her words. He bent down slowly and began to put on the NKVD uniform. "Hold on a minute," said Yelena. "I thought you worked for the USA. What are you doing with an NKVD uniform?"

"Relax, I liberated it, shall we say, from one of your countrymen. I thought it might come in handy, and it just has."

"Why, I thought your orders were to go undercover as a member of the SS."

"They are. Or rather they were. The thing about my mission here in Berlin is that I'm constantly changing my allegiance and uniform. This is just the most recent change. See, what's left of the whole SS here in Berlin is going to be looking for an American disguised as a German courier. So I've got to change my appearance in order to get this code to my superiors."

"And what about me?"

"They're going to be looking for you too. We need to

disguise your appearance. You better wear the courier's clothes."

"I thought you said they would be looking for a courier," said Yelena. "And I'm not wearing any clothes soaked with your blood."

"The jacket and pants are fine. We'll adapt your appearance so you don't look entirely like a courier. Besides you won't be on a motorbike and you're entirely the wrong build."

"I'm a woman. Of course I'm the wrong build, but don't you think they'll notice?"

"Not if we disguise you properly. At this point in the war, practically every able bodied man has been enlisted, even if they're as small and slight as a woman."

"So I've got to wear this stinking, bug infested uniform?"

"It's not bug infested, and yes you have to wear it. You might look a little out of place, but nowhere near as conspicuous as you do dressed like a woman. Especially a woman that's wanted by the entire SS."

"Okay, okay," said Yelena. "I'll wear your wretched pants and jacket, even if they don't fit." She stripped down to her underwear and began putting on the uniform. Karl turned his back and averted his eyes. "It's alright," said Yelena. "You're quite welcome to look. I made sure I got a good eye-full while you were changing."

"Are all Russian girls like you? 'Cos the girls I know back home certainly aren't."

Yelena laughed. "No. All Russian girls are not like me. I have simply seen too much to cling to hypocritical old values."

"You mean like modesty," said Karl, "and shame."

"Hah! Shame is an invention of your Capitalist state, backed up by a corrupt clergy. It is meant only to suppress

149

your women, to keep them in your kitchens, working as your unpaid drudges. Russian women certainly don't suffer from that."

"So they're free to seduce enemy Generals, is that it? I'm glad our women aren't so liberated, if that's the case."

"I never said I was liberated. In my own way I was as captive as any prisoner of war. I have simply stopped pretending to hold a lot of pointless double standards. All men chase women for the same thing. When we give it to them, they condemn us as whores. So we play along, pretending that we don't want it as much as you. This is what you call modesty. It has no part in the world where I have to survive."

Karl shrugged. He had nothing to say in return. Partly because he had to admit she had a point and partly because he was completely distracted by her nearly naked body. It had been a long time since he'd seen a woman wearing so few clothes. Even then it would probably have been on a pin-up in some soldier's locker.

"You see," said Yelena, who was purposefully taking a long time to dress. "You like looking at my body, no? Why should I pretend that you don't? Or begrudge you that pleasure. Your girls back home would be just the same if you let them."

Karl shook his head to clear it. "We're wasting time. We have to be away from here as quickly as we can. We have a distance to walk and you can't wear your old shoes. You'll have to pad out those spare boots with some rags."

"You certainly know how to make a girl feel glamorous don't you?"

"Nothing is going to be easy with you, is it?"

"And a second ago I thought you were accusing me of being too easy." Karl rolled his eyes. He knew he wasn't going to win any argument with her.

They gathered their possessions and left the bunker. Their eventual destination was a safe house in Charlottenburg but they would have to go through the Tiergarten district to get there. The Tiergarten district was not held by either the Russians or the Germans. This did not make it any less hazardous to cross. In their present situation they were open to attack from either side.

Karl chose a route that would keep them as far from any line of fire as he could. It meant a lot of stopping and starting, and a lot of doubling back on themselves, which did not please Yelena. "Why are we taking such a convoluted route? We could have been there by now if we hadn't gone so far out of our way."

"You don't even know where we're going," Karl replied. "How can you know whether we'd be there or not?"

"I've spent enough time in Berlin to know it shouldn't take this long."

"We have to stay off the main roads and away from the main thoroughfares. It's the only way to avoid detection."

"That's easy for you to say. At least your boots fit you properly."

"You always have to have the last word, don't you?"

"Yes."

"And there's nothing..."

"...you could say to stop me in my tracks."

"Or..."

"...shut me up, no."

Karl exhaled loudly in exasperation. If he ever had doubts about working alone in the field, they were now proving groundless.

"What are you thinking?" asked Yelena, after a period of welcome silence.

"How good it was to be left alone with my thoughts."

"I'm surprised you have them."

"What?"

"Thoughts."

"You just asked me what I was thinking," said Karl. "Of course I have thoughts."

"No," said Yelena. "You have reactions, not thoughts. Such as: 'how can I kill this man?' 'Where can I leave this weapon so I can use it later?' 'How much water will I need for this journey?' Those are not thoughts. Thoughts are deeper and more involved. Such as 'have I done enough things in my life to counteract all the pain I have caused?' Or 'why does man invest so much time and energy into futile pursuits like war?' Do you ever think about such things?"

"No."

"So you don't have thoughts."

"Why did you ask me what I was thinking then?"

"I wanted you to surprise me."

"Alright," said Karl, stopping at the entrance to an underpass. "You want to know what I'm thinking right now?"

"Surprise me."

"I'm wondering how in hell you managed to seduce so many men when you ask so many damn questions?"

"I might as well ask you how you managed to kill so many men when you get so riled by a few simple questions. I seduced those men because it was my job to do so, just like it is your job to kill. Like you I was good at my job, but unlike you I didn't have a choice about doing it."

"What makes you think I have a choice?"

"No-one is threatening the lives of those you love back home."

"I wouldn't be so sure of that," said Karl. "But I know the way your country works."

"Do not suppose that just because you put on a Russian uniform you know anything about my country."

"To ensure your loyalty, your superiors took a member of your family into custody and shipped them off to a labour camp, your mother perhaps or your brother."

"Congratulations."

"What?"

"You surprised me. Perhaps you are more perceptive than I realised. They took my brother. He was a medical student and an idealist. He really believed in the revolution and the destiny of the proletariat. Like so many others they broke his heart."

"Aren't you afraid that what you're doing now is going to endanger the lives of your family?"

"I no longer have one. My mother died of grief. She believed in communism her whole life. She fought for it in Munich then fled to Russia. The Soviets slowly murdered all her belief in a socialist state. When that was dead they took away her children and she had nothing left to live for."

"And your brother?"

"He died in the camp. There was a plague of influenza, none of the inmates survived."

"I heard about that," said Karl. "I'm sorry."

"So now my country no longer has any hold on me and I no longer have to seduce men. I am free to ask as many questions as I like."

"And soon you'll be free to start a new life in the free world," Karl added. Yelena laughed. "What's so funny?"

"I am always astonished by how you people in the West refer to yourselves as the 'free world', as though you enjoyed any more freedom than we do."

"No-one forced me to seduce the enemy by kidnapping my family."

"No," said Yelena. "But you told me they were in danger and that you didn't have a choice about fighting."

"That's because of your country, not mine. Besides, I don't see anyone from my country defecting to yours."

"That is because your so called 'free press' never tells you about them, anymore than our state press reports such matters."

"Why do you want to come over to our side then, if your own country is so free?"

"That is a stupid question. My country murdered my family and forced me to become a whore. Your country does not offer me freedom. It offers the opportunity to revenge myself on the people who destroyed everything I hold dear."

"Well you'll get your chance at all the revenge you want as soon as I hand you over to command."

"What?" said Yelena, the calm disappearing from her demeanour. "No you can't."

"What do you, mean? I thought that was what you wanted."

"You can't just hand me over to men I don't know. I have no idea what they would do to me."

"It's alright," said Karl. "These are good men. You have nothing to fear from them."

"I have everything to fear from secret service agents from another country," said Yelena. "I have seen what the men from my own country do to enemy agents, even those that wanted to co-operate."

"But I've told you, our side aren't like that."

"And I've told you I don't believe that. Your country is fighting Germany and soon it will be fighting my country, we both know that. I have seen what the Germans and the Soviets are like. You don't have any more men or any better technology. You think you will win this war by being more honourable? No, you will win it by being more ruthless and more dangerous than your enemies. That is how all wars are won. You think I will receive any better treatment at the hands of your commanders than I could expect at the hands of my own? Of course not."

"That's ridiculous."

"You think so?" said Yelena. "You put a lot of trust in your OSS. Do you think it puts as much trust in you?"

This last question stung Karl more deeply than Yelena could realise. His own side apparently didn't trust him. That was his personal reason for fighting – it's why he had messed up the hit on Kammler – he wanted to regain his country's trust, to exonerate his family name, to remove any doubts they might have had about him. He had to believe that he could do that, that his country was different, or else why was he killing so many people in its name?

"You don't have any choice," said Karl. "You can't go back to the Nazis, or your own side. You said so yourself, remember?"

"But you're from the free world, remember? Of course I have a choice. I can stay with you."

"What!" said Karl forgetting himself and raising his voice. "You have got to be joking. I work alone in the field. I can't do my job any other way. Why on earth would you want to stay with me?"

"Because I trust you."

Karl shook his head in disbelief. "I'm fighting the Germans, and your country, remember? If I'm going to win I'm going to have to be more ruthless and dangerous. What makes you think you can trust me?"

"Because I know you."

"You only met me a few hours ago."

"I know," said Yelena. "But in that time I have saved your life at least twice. You owe me. I have a hold over you."

"Don't be so sure."

"Oh but I am sure. You might not realise it but I have been testing you. You could very easily have left me at the Reichstag. It might have been in your best interests, but you didn't. You did the honourable thing. I stood nearly naked in front of you back in the bunker. You probably haven't been with a woman in months, yet you never laid a finger on me. You turned your head like a bashful schoolboy. You would be surprised by how few men have ever done that with me."

"No I wouldn't," said Karl.

They were about five minutes from the location of the rendezvous. Without warning Karl felt the muzzle of a Luger at the back of his head. "Hande hoch!" barked a high German voice. Karl and Yelena raised their hands as two more Wehrmacht soldiers stepped into view.

CHAPTER SEVENTEEN

Karl could have kicked himself. His attention had been taken up with Yelena and he had completely lost his focus. He had walked into the ambush like a rookie.

The Wehrmacht soldiers pointed their rifles at Karl and Yelena. They were at a range where it would be hard to miss. The soldier in back of Karl took his rifle. He then made Karl take off his great coat, patted him down and found the P-38.

As he removed the pistol Karl saw from the German's uniform that he was a corporal and was most likely in charge of the other two men. The corporal took a step away from Karl, still covering them with the Luger. He surveyed the weapons he had taken.

"An American pistol and a German rifle. An interesting collection for a Russian soldier, don't you think?" He threw Karl's pistol to one of his men. "Here Dieter. You need a pistol."

"Stealing SS property is considered a serious crime," said Karl. "It could see you shot or sent to the front after my superiors speak to your officer."

"He is German," said Dieter, who now looked decidedly worried. "Perhaps we should just let them go."

The corporal shook his head. "What is he doing dressed as a Russian soldier? The SS do not go undercover and we weren't told of any SS detail in this area. They're all holed up in the Reichstag waiting to die."

"Since when did the SS discuss tactics and details with a common corporal in the Wehrmacht?" said Karl superciliously. "Return the weapons and I will see that you are only disciplined lightly for this infraction."

"And let go of such a fine rifle? I don't think so."

"We don't want him telling his superiors," said Dieter, who was clearly losing his nerve. "We don't want to get in trouble."

"We're already in trouble," said the corporal. "And he won't be able to tell a soul if he's dead."

"Ah, so you men are the deserters who shot their officer," said Karl, trying to bluff his way out with guess work. "I thought it was strange to see a mere corporal carrying a Luger."

"God in heaven he knows," said Dieter. "They're already after us, we'll never get away with it. I told you we wouldn't."

"Shut your mouth," said the corporal. "He doesn't know anything, how could he?"

"We don't take kindly to the murder of German officers in the SS," Karl said, pressing his advantage. "Did you really think we would let it go unpunished? In these dark hours for the Reich discipline is more important than ever. Do you think I am here alone?"

Dieter and the other Wehrmacht soldier began to look nervously around them. "While I distracted you my men have surrounded you. Lay down your weapons this instant." Karl was probing for the weak link in the three soldiers, hoping to get them to falter just enough to give him an opening for attack.

"Ridiculous," sneered the corporal. "If your men are all around us let them show themselves."

"They await my signal. You can still walk away from this with your lives."

"Alright then," said the corporal. "Give them the signal."

"I do not take orders from a corporal! Neither do my men."

"If you know so much about us," said the corporal, "tell

me what company we're from. What was the name of the officer we shot? Which post did we desert? How did you find out about it when it only happened hours ago?"

Karl was waiting for the right moment to make his move. The two soldiers were rattled by what he was saying, but they were too far away to jump and the corporal still had him covered with the Luger. "See?" said the corporal when Karl didn't answer. Then he turned his attention to Yelena. She had her hands up but she was looking at the floor and had not raised her head since the men had ambushed them.

"Who is your companion?" The corporal said and put the barrel of his Luger under Yelena's chin, raising her face. "Ah," he said, sounding pleasantly surprise when he saw Yelena's face under the peaked courier's cap. "Are the SS so desperate that they've started recruiting women to track down deserters?"

"Please do not hurt us," said Yelena. "I am SS Gruppenführer Kammler's mistress, this man is my lover. He is helping me escape. We are fleeing the city just like you. I do not want to die at the hands of the Russians. If you let us continue in peace I can make it worth your while."

"And what do you have that we might want? Money, which we can't spend, or pilfered jewels which we can't pawn?"

"No," said Yelena, tilting her head provocatively and looking straight at all three men. "Something you probably haven't had in a long while."

The men exchanged furtive glances. They were suddenly transformed into excited schoolboys, unable to believe their good luck. Karl was astonished by the power that Yelena was exerting. She had achieved more in one look than all his bluff and bravado had managed. He was in awe of her sexual power. If he was honest, he was also a little afraid of it.

"Come," said the corporal. "There is a place I know, near here." He turned to Dieter and the other soldier. "Keep this man under constant cover. If he even blinks wrong, shoot him."

The corporal took them to a bombed out store. The front window was completely smashed and the store's contents had long since been looted. A door at the back led down a corridor to two backrooms and a lavatory. In the far room was a canvas bed that the owner might have used to take a nap during his lunchtime, or where he might have slept on those nights when he was out of favour with his wife.

The corporal stopped at the door. "We'll take it in turns," he said. "Don't take your eyes off the prisoner for a moment. He went into the backroom with Yelena and the two men kept their rifles trained on Karl. Dieter was more interested in what was taking place in the backroom. "He's left the door open," he said peering through.

"We're going to give your girl the time of her life," said the other soldier. "What do you think about that?"

"Won't be the first time that's happened," said Karl shrugging philosophically.

"That's the price you pay for being with a girl that beautiful."

"We'll show her a trick or two alright," said Dieter.

"She's more likely to show you a trick," said Karl. "You won't believe what she can do with her lips."

"I've seen them," said the other man.

"Not the ones I'm talking about you haven't."

"Oh my God she's taking her top off," said Dieter. "You've got to see this!" The other man's gaze flicked between Karl and the door Dieter was peering through.

He could not resist the temptation to join his comrade there.

"You move and I'll kill you," he said to Karl. "I swear I'll kill you." Karl's attitude to the whole matter had lulled them into a sense of security. The two men jostled for space at the crack in the door, excited by antics going on just beyond it.

When he was sure they were paying him no attention Karl slowly lifted his right foot and pulled out the knife he kept there. Without making a sound he walked up behind the other man and tapped him on the shoulder. The soldier straightened up in surprise, angry that Karl had moved. Before he could say anything Karl brought his arm up and sliced through the man's trachea and the artery in his neck in one single movement.

The man keeled over backwards making a wet gurgling sound as he breathed in and out through the slit in his throat. A fine mist of blood shot from his neck as he fell and Karl stepped aside to avoid it.

Dieter heard the thump as the man hit the ground and looked round for the first time. Karl put his arm round the startled soldier's throat and drove the knife through his left eyeball and into the front cerebellum of his brain. Karl held Dieter as he kicked and jerked, his body went into convulsions. Neither man had cried out or been given any time to realise what was happening to them.

With the two soldiers quietly dispatched, Karl slipped through the door and proceeded silently down the corridor. The door to the far backroom was wide open and both the corporal and Yelena were too distracted to see Karl come in.

The corporal had his trousers round his ankles. Yelena was kneeling in front of him on the bed. His top lip was curled up like a snarl and he was uttering groans and insults in equal measure.

Karl came at him from behind. He grabbed the corporal by the throat with his left and hand and pulled him backwards. Off balance and off his guard he fell against Karl.

Before the corporal could react, Karl brought his right arm around and drove his knife into the corporal's chest. The blade sliced clean through the tissue of his heart. His body went into shock convulsions and Karl threw him to the floor.

"You took your time," said Yelena, dressing hastily. "I thought I was going to have to do all three of them before you roused yourself."

"I came as quickly as I could."

He went and picked up his rifle from where the corporal had left it lying against the wall and took a hunting knife and the Luger from the corpse. He then went and retrieved his pistol from Dieter.

Karl waited for Yelena outside the store, surveying the derelict cityscape. "Which way now?" she said joining him. He walked off without answering and Yelena followed silently. He knew that she wanted him to thank her for her quick thinking. She had proven she was useful in a tight corner, but her constant need for gratitude and acknowledgement was wearing on him. He left her to seethe quietly.

A few streets later they came to a terrace of houses that were uninhabited, but still standing. Karl was due to meet Max and his associates in the central house. There should have been a green scarf hanging in the downstairs window, to show the men were waiting and the coast was clear. There wasn't. This immediately made Karl suspicious.

He motioned for Yelena to step back into the shadows of the alley they were standing in. He pulled out his binoculars and surveyed the surrounding streets. Through a gap in the terrace of houses Karl saw Russian soldiers in the streets beyond.

It looked like the tail end of a whole platoon that must have been advancing on the centre of Berlin. He waited until they had passed out of sight. When he was sure there were no more Russian soldiers in the area, Karl walked up to the front door of the central house. It wasn't locked. He pushed it open and stepped into the hall. The whole house was silent. "I don't think there's anyone here," whispered Yelena. He didn't reply.

He checked both front rooms, which were completely bare. They also smelled differently to the hall. "Is that some sort of polish?" Yelena asked sniffing the air.

"I don't think so," said Karl. His stomach sank as it began to dawn on him what it might be.

He went up the first flight of stairs then stopped. Another flight led to the first floor landing but the closer Karl got the stronger the smell was. It was a sweet smell, a little like almonds. The stronger the smell got, the more it stung Karl's nose and made the back of his throat burn.

He charged back down the stairs and into the small kitchen at the ground floor. There was a large earthenware sink with an old faucet. He tried the faucet and it rattled into life with a groan and a splatter. Karl tore a frayed curtain from the cracked window and doused it in water. Then he wrapped the soaking fabric around the bottom of his face.

Yelena didn't know what to make of his behaviour as he went back up to the first floor landing and told her to stay out of the hall and open every possible window. His eyes began to sting and he took very shallow breaths.

There were four doors, three of which were open. The fourth led to the largest room at the back of the house.

Karl kicked the door open and ducked down low. A cloud of cyanide gas wafted out.

Keeping his face less than an inch from the floor, Karl crept into the room on his stomach. The air nearest the floor was breathable but his eyes stung as he looked around the room and Karl knew that if he lifted his head even a fraction too high he could still be poisoned.

The gas was dispersing out of the door and a smashed window at the end of the room where someone had obviously tried to jump out and escape. Eight bodies, possibly more, lay on the floor. Their skin was waxen and blood red froth was dripping from their mouths and nostrils.

In the centre of the room was Hank's corpse. Karl hadn't seen the man since they'd taken on the Gestapo and he was sorry to see him now. Hank had three bullet holes in his chest. Karl guessed that he had sustained those before breaking the capsule of cyanide gas he kept behind his eye patch.

If he were to reconstruct the events that led up to this, Karl would have said that the meeting was abandoned when the platoon of Russian soldiers overran the area on their way to the centre of Berlin. As Max and the others would have been dressed as German reserves, they wouldn't have been able to explain that they were on the Allied side, even if they had gotten the chance.

Hank would have volunteered to fight a rear guard action to give Max and the others time to get away. After holding out as long as possible and taking three bullets, Hank must have lured the Russians into the room and taken as many of them with him as he could. His face, like all the other corpses, was stretched in a grimace of acute agony. No-one in the room had died a merciful or painless death.

Karl crawled backwards out of the room on his stomach. He slithered down the stairs too to avoid any escaped gas. He didn't take a deep breath until he got out of the back door. When he did, he coughed so hard he threw up and his lungs burned so that it hurt to draw the smallest breath.

There were more corpses at the rear of the house. Several would have died from the gas as they jumped from the first floor window. The others must have been shot by Hank. Karl sat with his back to the outside and tried to regain his breath. Yelena came to sit next to him.

She took Karl's hand in hers. His first instinct was to shake her off, but then he realised how welcome the human contact felt, especially after what he had witnessed in the room upstairs. "We need to decide on a new plan," Yelena said, "and quickly." Karl hadn't given it any thought until that moment but it dawned on him that he was carrying a document that was of tantamount importance to the war effort. He was running out of time to get it into the right hands and he currently had no idea how he was going to do that.

"It seems like we will be spending a little longer in each other's company," said Yelena.

Karl shook his head. "I need to find some way to get you quickly to safety. I work much better alone."

"So you say. But I have yet to see any evidence of that."

"I need to get this code to my superiors then await further orders."

"There may not be time for that. You are trying to stop Kammler from launching his new rocket aren't you? It can go as far as the USA they say. It must have quite a lot of fire power."

"More than you know."

"You would be surprised just how much I do know. Men who keep as many secrets as Hans did, have a need to unburden themselves. A man will say things in the arms of his mistress that he wouldn't even dream of saying to his closest family or friends. Such is the power we hold. It frightens men. This is why my lovers tried to keep me locked up and my NKVD masters held so much over me."

"Perhaps you do frighten them," said Karl. "Perhaps you do know many secrets. You don't know how I can get in touch with my chain of command though."

"Maybe not. But I might know something just as important."

"What's that?"

"I know where the convoy carrying the fuel for the V10 is coming into Berlin. I overheard Hans discussing it with one of his lackeys. The newly built Autobahn had been damaged in crucial places so they had to devise an alternate route."

"Alright, but what good is that to me at the moment?"

"You need to stall for time, don't you? If you deprive the rocket of fuel then you'll force them to reschedule the launch. That will buy you time to get the code into the right hands and to wait for more orders."

"How am I going to do that?"

"You are a sniper, are you not? This fuel is highly combustible. Surely if you shoot it in the right place you can cause enough of an explosion to wipe it out."

Yelena's idea made a lot of sense. "Can you remember the exact route?"

"I sat there and watched them while they drew it up on a map of Berlin. I was feigning indifference of course, but I knew it was important and that it would come in handy later on, so I paid much closer attention than they realised."

"So you can draw me a map?"

"No, I do not want you to leave me somewhere while you go off on a mission. If you tell me exactly the sort of spot you will need to ambush the convoy I will take you there."

"That's ridiculous," said Karl. "I can't possibly take on a task of this nature with a... with someone in tow."

"With a woman in tow, that's what you were going to say isn't it?"

"What if I was? I can't possibly do this job if I'm thinking about your safety the whole while."

"It seems to me," said Yelena. "That you can't possibly do this job unless I'm worrying about *your* safety."

"Oh it's back to this is it? Okay, you're right, you did help me out of a couple of tricky situations and I'm grateful. Are you happy now? Will you finally let the matter drop?"

"Seeing as you've been so gracious about it," said Yelena sarcastically. "How could I possibly refuse?"

"Alright, those matters were one thing, but sniping is an entirely different ball game. I have to put myself in situations and inhabit locations where only one person can go. I have to be able to move incredibly quickly and to travel incredibly light. I can't do that with another person around. It takes inordinate amounts of patience and concentration and I can't afford any distractions."

"Like it or not," said Yelena. "You can't afford to let this opportunity go by. And the only way you're going to be able to take advantage of it is on my terms. As a single woman alone in Berlin I am in constant danger. As a conspirator in an attempted murder on a high ranking Nazi and a traitor to my own people, in a city occupied by their armies I am as good as dead. I need someone I can trust to protect me."

Karl threw up his arms. "You're impossible!"

"Never the less," said Yelena. "I am also intractable. We have wasted too much time on this pointless conversation already. If you have your breath back we must go."

CHAPTER EIGHTEEN

Yelena took Karl east to a flyover on the borders of the Marzahn and Hellersdorf districts. There was a station, S Bahnhof, in Hellersdorf with working rail links to the city of Kleve, near the Dutch/German border.

Kleve was where the Gruppe Nord V2 mobile rocket unit was based. Under the command of Major Schulz it had been doing considerable damage to the Allied strongholds in Europe. Yelena told Karl they had now been mobilised to launch the V10. From what she had learned from Kammler, much of the Abteilung Batterie 485, the motorised artillery group, had already made its way to Berlin. The SS Werfer Abteilung Batterie, the technical battery, was now following. For security purposes they were not coming in full force but a platoon at a time. The first of these was the fuelling platoon.

The S Bahnhof was in a district of Berlin that was occupied by Russian forces. They had strict orders, however, to give the motorised artillery group safe passage. Most of the platoon had come ahead of the fuel by road. Because of its volatile nature, the fuel had to make the majority of the journey by rail. The platoon was due to meet the train at S Bahnhof and transport the fuel from there to its destination in the Mitte district.

Karl had specified to Yelena the type of location that was crucial to the operation they had planned. He needed the target to be in a completely open space with no buildings on either side. His vantage point had to be from a higher position so he could shoot at a downward angle. In spite of his annoyance at being coerced into taking her along with him, Karl had to admit that Yelena had chosen an ideal spot. It met every one of his specifications.

The flyover was a mile and a half from S Bahnhof. It was part of an uncompleted construction programme. The road the convoy was to take had been built in 1943, but another flyover had been planned to run overhead. Work on this flyover had been abandoned in 1944 due to cuts in subsidy arising out of the mounting cost of Germany's war effort. All that remained of the scheme were two large concrete support columns that flanked the existing flyover.

One concrete column still had metal rungs fixed to the side that the labourers had used to scale it during construction. Karl insisted on leaving Yelena in a builder's hut near the base of the column. She had little head for heights and was quite glad not to have to make the climb. She agreed to wait for him out of the firing line.

Karl made his way up the rungs. The closer he got to the top of the column the more aware he became of the crosswinds blowing around it. He fixed his gaze straight ahead and tried not to think of how high up he was, or how precariously he was balanced.

Towards the very top, rungs were missing. Karl had to reach for hand holds in the concrete like a mountaineer. He had no rope to hold him though, and the rungs appeared sporadically, forcing him to improvise. He didn't want to think of how he was going to get down, or if that were even possible.

With a bit of desperate scrambling, and a few unsure footholds, Karl dragged himself to the top of the tall column. His muscles ached with the exertion, but he felt exhilarated to be up so high. He had a perfect downward angle with which to aim at the fuel convoy. There were no buildings in between him and the target either.

The top of the column had not been properly finished and it did not have a flat surface. It was highly uneven and pitted with dips and hollows. Karl clambered over each hollow until he got to the edge. He found a perfect dip in the concrete where he could lie, completely out of sight from anyone on the road below. From then on it was simply a matter of waiting.

Six hours later Karl was going through his twentieth set of stretching exercises, to keep his muscles from seizing up, when he spotted activity on the flyover below him. Two troop carriers, about fifty metres apart, passed beneath him on the road. He checked them both through his binoculars; they were carrying the bulk of the platoon. The fuel would not be far behind.

Sure enough, less than a minute later, travelling at a much slower speed, vehicles pulled into view. There were two armoured cars with machine guns mounted on them at the front and the rear of the convoy to provide protection for the middle three vehicles. These consisted of two tankers either side of a smaller truck towing a very large canister that had a portable pump strapped to its back.

From the time he had spent in the missile silo Karl could tell that the two tankers were carrying alcohol, the principle propellant for the rocket. The canister would contain liquid oxygen, which was more volatile and more difficult to produce than the alcohol. There would also be a store of Hydrogen peroxide somewhere on the convoy.

Karl's target was the canister of liquid oxygen. The main shell of the container was far too thick to pierce with the calibre of the bullets he had to hand. The same was true of the tankers carrying the alcohol. Even if he did pierce the tankers all he would cause would be a leak anyway. He would need an explosion fierce enough and hot enough to ignite the alcohol. This was the principle that the German scientists used to power the rockets.

It was what Karl now intended to use to destroy the convoy.

In order to create this fierce explosion Karl would have to detonate the highly combustible liquid oxygen. The canister had one weak point that would allow him to do this: the nozzle on the top of the canister out of which the compressed liquid oxygen is pumped into the rocket. It could be shot off with a single well aimed bullet. Not only that but the resulting sparks, from the bullet ricocheting off the metal, would ignite the compressed liquid oxygen escaping at a high speed.

The nozzle was not an easy target though. It was not large and there was no margin for error in the shot. What's more it was a moving target and the wind was blowing quite strong around the flyover. He would have at most two shots before he gave away his position. With his position compromised he wouldn't have a particularly quick or easy escape route.

There was no room for error. He had to make the shot. The convoy couldn't be allowed to get to the centre of Berlin.

Karl adjusted his sights for 300 metres and found the nozzle in his cross hairs. He tracked its progress. He made allowances for the wind blowing around the exposed flyover and focused on the spot the nozzle was about to move into. Karl emptied his lungs, steadied his aim and squeezed the trigger.

The shot narrowly missed and pinged off the canister. Karl's heart sank and he swore. He quickly reviewed the shot in his mind, trying to determine what went wrong. It should have been perfect but it wasn't. The only variable for which he hadn't fully accommodated was the wind. Either a freak gust had appeared or it was stronger than he had allowed.

Before he head time to re-aim, the convoy ground to a halt. Only the armoured car at the front kept moving. The driver of the first tanker got out and waved to it to halt its progress. Karl watched through his binoculars as the drivers of the truck and the tanker got out. They were joined by a couple of soldiers from the armoured car in back of the second tanker. The driver of the second tanker pointed to the top of the column where Karl lay.

They had made his position. There was no time to spare. With the convoy stationary he would never have a better opportunity. Once again he emptied his lungs and drew a bead on the nozzle. To allow for the wind he moved across half a notch to the left on his horizontal bar.

The shot was dead on. The result was spectacular.

The canister of liquid oxygen erupted into a white hot ball of flame which spread outwards at a rapid pace. Karl couldn't look directly at it for fear of being blinded. The ball of flaming oxygen tore through the tanker containers, shredding them and igniting the alcohol within. They exploded in two huge columns of fire.

The remains of all the vehicles on the bridge flew up in the air. They were torn apart by the force of the explosion and rained down as flaming debris. The wall of heat that came off the explosions was so intense that Karl had to bury his head and curl up into a ball inside the hollow where he was lying.

Burning body parts flew past him. A dismembered forearm landed right next to him. Karl could smell the flesh burning as the flames licked at it. The watch on the wrist of the arm had melted.

A burning skull landed right on his backside. He yowled with pain and knocked it aside. It rolled a little way off then stopped. The skin had been completely charred away. The bared teeth grinned at him from within the blackened bone, as though the skull were pleased to have committed one last act of posthumous revenge.

The flyover cracked in two places and collapsed onto the road below, taking whatever remained of the convoy with it. Melted tarmac and shattered concrete tumbled down on to the road along with mangled vehicles and machinery; all that efficient German technology ruthlessly lain to waste.

Karl stood up and surveyed the aftermath. The flyover was in ruins and the convoy was destroyed. He was frankly quite astonished by the destruction he had wrought. He had expected a big explosion but nothing quite like this.

As Karl was taking one last look before descending, a bullet bit the concrete close to him. He whirled round and saw that in all the commotion he hadn't seen or heard that one of the troop carriers had doubled back to see what had caused the explosion.

They must have spotted him through their binoculars. When they saw the Russian uniform and the rifle they would have assumed he was a Russian sniper and saboteur. Karl hit the ground and crawled over the dip and hollows until he got near the edge of the column and could see down to the ground.

He could make out around ten men at the base of the column. They could not see him from where he was lying. He had the advantage over them with the elevated angle. One of the German soldiers from the troop carrier had a rifle and was trying to find Karl. Karl fixed his aim and shot the man straight through the heart. He staggered backwards, dropped his rifle and keeled over. A pool of blood spread out underneath him.

This panicked the other nine men and they ran for cover. Karl aimed for the soldier at the head of the other nine. He picked the spot the man was about to reach and took him out with a headshot. The soldier directly behind the headshot victim sprawled over the corpse and the other seven scattered, heading off to their left.

They were running scared now. Karl picked off another on the far left of the group. He caught the man with a shot that shattered his pelvis, crippling but not killing him. The unfortunate individual writhed on the ground in agony and even from his high position Karl could hear his wails of pain.

The remaining six backed up, then turned and ran to the right. They were joined by the soldier who had fallen over the corpse. Karl shot once again and narrowly missed his target. By which time the men had managed to make it back to the troop carrier they had arrived in. They took cover. One idiot was foolish enough to stick his head out to try and locate Karl. He died within seconds from a bullet through his right eye.

The troop carrier was parked near to the builder's hut where Yelena was hidden. He hoped she had the good sense to stay out of sight and let him finish off the group from where he was. Then again, he reminded himself, she had proven she wasn't stupid already and would know not to get involved.

There was no movement for a while. Karl imagined that they would try to board the troop carrier and drive off. He checked out the vehicle with his binoculars, taking careful note of every place that they might board so he could pick them off when they tried. After a thorough survey of the vehicle he felt sure he could anticipate their movements.

However there was no way he could have anticipated their next move.

Karl watched as one of the men placed a weapon on the bonnet of the troop carrier and began to aim.

The weapon was a Panzerschreck. An anti-tank rocket launcher, similar to a bazooka. It fired a 3.2kg rocket powered grenade.

Karl grabbed his rifle. Before he could aim it, the German soldier fired. The rocket struck the concrete column Karl was lying on. The force of the impact was so great he was thrown up in the air. He flipped over and landed on his back.

He couldn't breath for a minute and his ears were ringing from the explosion. He was disoriented, and he may even have blacked out for a second for his mind raced to work out what had happened to him.

Then it came back to him. He felt as though the column was moving under him. He heard a rumbling sound and realised it was. Karl jumped to his feet and saw a giant crack had appeared in the concrete ahead of him. It was widening into a large gulf. He picked up his rifle, sprinted towards the crack and then leaped as the section of column he was standing on fell out from under him.

Karl grabbed hold of the section that was still standing as a huge, wedge shaped chunk came away and tumbled to the ground below with a resounding crash, throwing up a giant cloud of dust that covered everything for a wide radius. The chunk of falling concrete comprised approximately a third of the column and over three quarters of the top section on which Karl had been standing.

He was left dangling from a thin ledge of flat concrete. He swung himself up on to the ledge and his rifle fell from his shoulder. It clattered down the steep concrete slope behind him and, luckily, caught on the broken steel support roughly 15 metres below.

Karl could not afford to be unarmed. Reluctantly he lowered himself off the ledge on to the steep slope and began to clamber down, finding hand and foot holds in the powdery, jagged concrete.

Several times he put his weight on a piece of concrete that broke away and fell to the ground. The third time this happened Karl slid several metres on his stomach until his feet found the steel support where the strap of his rifle had caught.

His heart was pounding so hard it felt like it could stand no more and wanted to burst out of his chest. From where he was currently perched he was vulnerable to attack from the ground. To guarantee his safety he really should try and get off the column, but his only route down was by the steel rungs on the other side. If he used those he was a sitting duck to any half decent marksman.

Karl retrieved his rifle but before he could climb back up to the ledge he heard the roar of another rocket being launched from the Panzershcreck. Karl clung tightly to the steel support and braced himself for the impact. The whole column shook as the rocket tore into it and a giant crack appeared right up the centre of the remaining column, effectively cleaving it in two. The only things keeping it standing were the steel supports it was built around.

The column started to sway and twisted dangerously to one side as the supports began to buckle. Karl's stomach turned over. He broke out in a sweat and a deathly cold fear crept through him.

He fought to keep down the hysteria that was rising in him. For the first time he started to think he wasn't going to make it. This was the end.

He would never get the documents into the right hands to save his country. He would never clear his family name. He would be crushed hundreds of feet below in a matter of moments. His corpse would never be recovered and his name would be forgotten for all time.

His natural survival mechanisms tried to kick in. To drown out the terror that was screaming inside his head, but they just weren't loud enough.

He didn't know what to do next. He had minutes to act and he couldn't think of any action that would save him from dying.

There was another explosion and Karl almost lost it altogether. He heard a tiny voice muttering something over and over. It was his voice. Karl was saying a prayer. The only one he knew. One he had learned years ago in Kindergarten.

"Gentle Jesus meek and mild, smile upon this humble child."

The prayer had a calming influence. He was going to see God. Karl didn't think the big guy would be too pleased to see him though.

He waited for the column to topple. Nothing happened. It rocked and swayed a little but didn't fall.

Had the soldiers missed? Why didn't they fire again? What was happening?

After an interminable wait, Karl started to climb up the slope to the top of the column. He reached the ledge and pulled himself up. He couldn't see anything on the ground below. He inched himself over to the side of the column where the steel rungs were. Luckily it was the one side that was the least damaged, even if it did lean dangerously to one side.

Karl swung himself over and began to climb down. With every rung that his feet or hands found he expected a bullet to find him. But none did.

A lifetime later his feet touched the ground. He stepped back from the column. He wanted to run as far away from it as he could but the ground was shaking so much that he could hardly stand. Except it wasn't the ground shaking, it was his legs.

Every muscle in his body was going into violent spasm. He toppled to the ground and lay there shaking. When the spasms died down he saw a pair of boots right in front of his face. He looked up and was relieved to see they were worn by Yelena.

She offered him a hand. He took it and got slowly to his feet. "You're alive," she said.

"Much to my surprise. What happened to the soldiers?"

"I killed them."

"You killed them," said Karl unable to hide his surprise. "How?"

"It was easier than I imagined. I came up behind them and threw a grenade. They were too busy trying to kill you to notice me."

"A grenade; where the hell did you get a grenade?"

"You are not the only one who scavenges from dead soldiers."

"How did you take out seven men with one grenade?"

"I missed actually. The grenade rolled under their truck and blew up the gas tank. Only two men survived the explosion. They were both wounded. I picked up a pistol that was lying on the ground, and shot them both. I have watched you kill many times now, so it did not seem so impossible to me."

"And how do you feel?"

Yelena paused and gazed off into the distance before she spoke. "I have seen a lot during this war. I did not think there was anything left inside me that could die while I still remained alive. I was wrong."

Karl nodded with complete understanding. They walked past the wreck of the troop carrier and the dead soldiers in silence.

He knew he ought to say some words of consolation. If Yelena had been a man he would have known exactly what to say. Because she was a woman he was unsure. So he said the one sincere thing he could think of. "Listen, I didn't think I was going to make it back there. You saved my life and you haven't rubbed my nose in it. I don't make a habit of saying this, but thank you."

"You're very welcome," said Yelena. "And I don't make a habit of saying that either."

CHAPTER NINETEEN

"Aha," said Yelena in triumph, holding up half a loaf and some opened tins of rations. "Food at last."

"You just fished those out of the trash and that bread is mouldy."

"Only on one corner," said Yelena. "The rest is perfectly edible."

Karl pulled a face. Yelena dismissed his squeamishness. "You Americans are spoilt by the surplus of your capitalist system. You throw away food while the rest of the world starves. There is a meal for two here. We have no food and I haven't eaten in ages. No Russian soldier would have let this go to waste."

Yelena threw away the mouldy corner of the loaf and used the rest to mop out the discarded cans of rations. Karl turned away in disgust and ignored the growl of hunger in his stomach. They were standing in a former accountant's office in the Lichtenberg district. There was no hint of it in the abandoned office, but at one point it had been the OSS nerve centre in Berlin.

It was the second OSS hideout that Karl and Yelena had visited since blowing up the fuel convoy. They had walked miles. Both of them were tired and dusk was falling. There was one more place Karl wanted to visit before they called it a day though.

"Are you sure you won't have anything to eat?" asked Yelena, offering him a chunk of stale bread dipped in congealed gravy. In spite of himself Karl accepted the food. It tasted as bad as he had expected, but he tried to forget the flavour and swallowed it as quickly as he could without gagging.

While Yelena had searched first the cupboards and

then the bins for food, Karl had searched the building for any clues as to where the operation might have moved. There was none. They'd done a very professional job of stripping the place of any record of OSS presence. Karl felt that sudden fear that grips everyone who works deep cover at one time or another, the fear that he had lost contact with his own side's support network. He was out of the loop and out on a limb with no-one to help him.

There was nothing worse than being alone in the field. Not when you had vital information that you had to pass on as quickly as possible. With every hour that he failed to hand it over, his country came closer to destruction.

"Come on," Karl said slinging his pack over his shoulder. "We've got to move on."

"What?" said Yelena. "It's getting dark and I have walked miles today. You don't know who or what is out on those streets tonight. We are safe here for the time being. Why do you want to leave?"

"I don't know how much time I've got left to get this access code into the right hands. There's one more place I can make tonight, but we have to leave now."

"No-one is going to be there at this time of night," said Yelena. "I understand how urgently you need to get the codes to your superiors. I realise that something has caused the OSS operation to move and you need to find where its new base is. But even if they're still working out of this location that you want to check out, it's not likely they'll be there by the time we get to it. They'll have gone to ground, like we should. We can leave by first light tomorrow."

Karl could see the sense in what Yelena was saying. In his single mindedness he had not been thinking properly. He needed to get the codes to Max as soon as possible, but he shouldn't lose sight of the need to be cautious or patient. Those were two traits he didn't lack as a sniper. Now he needed to employ them as an agent.

"Alright," he said. He was suddenly very tired. An imminent need to lie down and rest overcame his whole body. "We can bed down in one of the top rooms. I've got one blanket. We'll sleep in shifts and keep look out for one another."

Karl had been asleep two hours when Yelena shook him awake.

His sleep had been deep but he sat straight up. Years of combat had conditioned him to be alert in an instant. In the dim light of the room Yelena cautioned him to be silent and signalled that he should listen. There were footsteps in the office below.

Karl un-holstered his pistol and went out on to the stairs without making a sound. He listened to the noises coming from below. Whoever was in there thought that the building was empty. Otherwise they wouldn't be making so much noise and drawing attention to themselves.

Karl descended the old staircase making certain he didn't make a sound. He walked over to the office door, which was half open, and peered inside. A man dressed all in black was pulling up the floorboards in the far corner of the room. He had his back to Karl.

Karl came up quietly behind him. The man was making so much noise he didn't hear. Karl put his pistol away. He didn't want to kill the intruder. He wanted to find out what he was doing. He caught the man in a headlock. The minute Karl had him the man began to struggle.

Before Karl could properly subdue him, the man brought his elbow up hard. He struck Karl just below his rib cage. The pain caused Karl to loosen his grip and the intruder wriggled free.

The man bolted for the exit, where Karl noticed Yelena was now standing. Karl dived for his legs and tackled him. The intruder came crashing to the ground. Karl drew his pistol once again and smashed the butt of it into the bridge of the man's nose. The man cried out in pain and held his hand up to ward off another blow, shouting something in Russian.

"What did he say?" Karl asked Yelena.

"He said don't kill him he is a friend," she said.

"Wait," said the man, in an American accent. "You speak English. I'm sorry I thought you were Russians."

"You're American?" Karl said in surprise.

"Born and bred in LA."

"How come you speak Russian?" Karl wanted to know.

"I work under cover. I speak German and French as well."

"Who do you work for?"

"I'm not sure I can tell you."

Karl raised his gun to strike again. "You better."

"Wait!" said Yelena. "I think he's on our side."

"Is he?" said Karl. He addressed the man. "Why are you tearing up floorboards?"

"While we're asking questions, why is an American dressed as a Russian with a Russian dressed as a German?"

"How," said Karl, "do you know our nationalities?"

"Your accents make it pretty obvious."

Karl put his pistol away and got off the man. "You must know this place was used by the OSS. Do you know where they're now operating?"

"If you know this was OSS HQ," said the man "Then you must be working for the secret service too. Who's your contact?"

"Max Avery."

The man whistled to show he was impressed. "The main man himself! I just run errands. We had to leave here fast and I came back to clear up some loose ends."

"I need very badly to get in touch with Max," said Karl. "I have information that could affect the security of the United States. I was supposed to pass it on at our last meeting, but something happened and they had to leave before I got there."

"Our whole operation has been compromised. We've lost a few good people and had to destroy a lot of records. The Russians are working with the German's on something and they don't want us to know about it, allies or no allies."

"Can you take me to where they are?"

"I can take you to my contact, Chuck Fleischer"

"I know him well. We worked together recently."

"My name's Hanna," said the man, offering his hand. "Joe Hanna."

"Karl Fairburne. And this here's Yelena Petronova."

"Pleased to know you ma'am," Joe nodded deferentially to Yelena and cleaned the blood off his nose with a handkerchief.

"We should leave straight away," said Karl. "I'll grab our things."

"I've got a job to do first," said Joe. "Maybe you can lend a hand."

"Okay. So long as it's quick."

"Quicker we get to it, the quicker it'll be done."

Joe went back to the far corner and tore up a few more floorboards. Below them were a stack of folders and documents. "They had to move out of here too quickly to burn everything. So they hid these and sent me back to burn them now. We should stick them in the fireplace and set a match to them."

"The smoke from the chimney would draw attention," said Karl. "Someone could even get here and fish something out before it was all burned. Our best bet is to set light to them right there. No-one's going to think there's anything unusual about a burning building in Berlin. That way you guarantee they'll be destroyed along with every other trace of OSS presence."

Karl and Joe arranged the documents so they would burn better and piled the loose floorboards over them. Karl went and grabbed their things. Joe set light to the documents. Then they all left the building.

Chuck could not hide his surprise at seeing Karl.

"We thought you were dead," he said with a start. Then he collected himself. "When you didn't come back from your mission I mean. When we found out Kammler was still alive. We naturally assumed you hadn't made it."

"It didn't all go according to plan," said Karl. "But I got the goods. That's why I've got to see Max right away."

"He'll be pretty keen to see you I expect," said Chuck. He turned to Yelena. "So this is Miss Petronova then. You've been a great help to us. We'll be sorry not to have such a reliable source so close to Kammler anymore."

"I can still be quite a lot of use to you," said Yelena.

They were standing on the platform of a disused U-Bahn station in the Mitte district. "You wouldn't know anything about a fuel convoy that blew up, would you?" said Chuck.

Karl smiled "I'm not sure I can say."

Chuck laughed and punched his shoulder. "You wily old dog, we were wondering who was responsible. We heard the British were in town. We thought maybe they were up to their old tricks. I did think it strange that it was a strategy we'd discussed though."

Karl could see that Yelena wasn't pleased about him getting all the credit. "I couldn't have done it without the information Yelena gave me. She proved herself very handy in the field as well."

Chuck smiled and bowed like a perfect gentleman. "Good to have you on board."

Karl admired Chuck's professionalism. Even though he could handle himself in most situations, his charm was his most deadly weapon. He put people at ease and that made their guard drop. Though Chuck himself would never let his own guard down.

Chuck switched on a flashlight and hopped down on to the tracks. "This way folks," he said pointing with his flashlight beam.

"Where are we going?" said Yelena, she looked less than certain about entering the tunnel up ahead.

"To our new HQ," said Chuck. "It's in the station office at the next stop on this line. You can't get to it from the sidewalk because the entrance is covered with rubble, so we have to use this route in. It's kinda handy because it doesn't leave us prone to detection."

"It's okay," said Karl sensing the reason for Yelena's caution. "I trust Chuck."

Karl helped Yelena down and they walked through the tunnel to the next station. "Course, this was electrified before the war," said Chuck. "We wouldn't have been able to walk along here at all, for fear of stepping on the electric rail. All the same, you wouldn't believe some of the things we've found down here. Even in the short time we've been here." Chuck listed a few of the improbable things, including a giant tin bath, a stuffed moose head and an old chest full of erotic publications from the last century.

Karl knew Chuck was trying to put them at their ease and distract them from the eerie nature of their surroundings. Karl wondered if he had ever ridden the U-Bahn between the two stations when he was a young boy living in the city.

Finally they came to the office. Behind the heavy wooden door on sprung hinges were two large rooms with low ceilings. The thick white paint on the walls was peeling and coming off in flakes. There were boxes of files piled up in the corners and two desks in the main room. Two agents sat behind the desks engrossed in paperwork. They looked up only briefly to scrutinise Karl and Yelena. The place had been swept and dusted in a perfunctory fashion, but still bore the musty weight of antiquity.

Chuck told them Max was in the room beyond the door to their left. He went in first and announced Karl and Yelena. Karl followed him in with Yelena in tow. Max stood up behind the small desk fighting even harder than Chuck had to hide his surprise. "Karl... I... I had no idea," he said. He walked round the desk and grasped Karl's hand, slapping him on the shoulder. "We had no word. You were late to the meeting and, as you probably know, we had to leave quickly. With the communication silence surrounding the relocation of the operation, we all just assumed that you'd been killed. Now you've come in from the cold."

"And I have some incredibly hot Intel," said Karl.

"We'll get to that in a minute, if you don't mind," said Max. "First you must introduce me. I imagine that this is Miss Petronova, about whom I've heard so much."

"It's a pleasure," said Yelena offering her hand and smiling for the first time. She was still dressed in the oversized courier's uniform. Her face was streaked with dirt and her hair was unkempt. This did nothing to diminish her charm as soon as she turned it on. Max and Chuck were instantly in her thrall. Karl was astounded yet again.

"I ran into a spot of bother in the Reichstag," Karl explained. "Things didn't go quite as planned and Yelena here pulled my ass out of the fire. Unfortunately that blew her cover with the Nazis so she had to leave the Reichstag with me."

"I completely understand," said Max. "We'll look after you for a couple of days Miss Petronova and then arrange your safe passage out of Berlin."

"I appreciate your kindness and concern," said Yelena. "But my preference is to stay under Karl's protection."

"I'm afraid," explained Karl, "that Yelena's formed a sort of, err... attachment to me."

"And I'm afraid," said Yelena, in a withering tone. "That Karl seems to think I've developed a crush on him." Max and Chuck laughed at this. They were rather smitten by Yelena and they found it amusing that she should find Karl attractive. This wounded his pride, as Yelena knew it would.

"I'm sure you have many capable agents," Yelena continued. "But I have not worked with them and in a desperate situation like this, in a dangerous place like Berlin, it is not wise to put your safety in the hands of people you do not know."

"I've tried talking to her," said Karl. "But she won't listen."

"Yelena," said Max. "I quite appreciate your concerns and I wouldn't want you to feel that your safety wasn't of tantamount importance to us. I'll discuss this matter, and everything else that pertains to your future, in great detail, if you'll allow me, in just a little while. In the meantime there are a few pressing matters I need to talk with Karl about. If you accompany Chuck next door he'll see that you're well looked after."

Chuck held open the door for Yelena in an exaggeratedly chivalrous fashion. She walked provocatively past him to show her appreciation. Max whistled as soon as the door closed. "She's something ain't she?"

"I thought you didn't like her type," said Karl.

Max's expression changed to one of displeasure at being reminded. Karl felt as though he had said something inappropriate. He knew he shouldn't have brought up Max's uncharacteristic outburst. He should have forgotten it for the sake of politeness.

Max regained his demeanour, Karl's comment was forgotten and his smile returned, although Karl thought it a little forced. "So, you came back after all," said Max. "Just like I told you to. Glad to see that you still follow orders. Take a seat Karl."

Karl sat on a wooden chair and Max returned to the leather chair behind the desk. "I'm sorry that I didn't succeed in killing Kammler," Karl said.

"I take it that you did succeed in the other part of your mission though. Do you have the code with you?"

"It's right here." Karl removed the crumpled sheet of paper from his pocket. He handed it to Max who looked at it thoughtfully for a moment.

"I'll see that this is passed on to the relevant people. I understand you've been busying yourself with fuel convoys as well."

"Err, yes I have."

"You know that was an unauthorised mission," said Max. "While I applaud agents working under their own initiative in the field, that was a major act of sabotage you undertook without the consultation of your superiors."

"I was cut off from any contact. I attempted to consult

you but you weren't available. The information I received came with a specific window of opportunity. If I hadn't acted the moment would have passed. As it was a strategy we had previously discussed I didn't think you'd mind."

"Which is probably the only reason I won't be disciplining you. That, and the fact that I want you to blow something else up for me."

"Is that my remit now?" said Karl. "I thought I was still to be deployed as a sniper."

"You are," said Max. "This mission will involve all your abilities both as a marksman and an undercover operative. In your last report you told us about a missile silo you infiltrated."

"That's right."

"We've been instructed by Washington to initiate a policy of sabotage on the Spear of Destiny project while they reach a final decision about the intelligence we sent them. The silo is a prime target. I doubt it's the only one they have in operation but it would do severe damage to their plans if we were to put it out of action."

"Okay," said Karl. "I take it you have a plan."

"I do. It's thanks to the informant you handed us as well."

"Isaac," said Karl. "I thought we gave him back to the Soviets."

"That was the plan. It seems he cut another deal with the agents who were supposed to arrange his return. I used two guys from Bern so we wouldn't blow our cover here. This meant they reported directly to Deputy Head Dulles, who's heading up the Swiss operation. Isaac evidently had a change of heart about working with the Nazis. He told the two agents handling his return that he wanted to come over to our side. They weren't working under my chain of command so they weren't obliged to consult me. Dulles didn't care what operations we had planned, it looked good for him to snatch a top Russian rocket scientist."

"What about his children?"

"That was his main condition for defecting," said Max. "That we did everything in our power to find them. He thought we would be his best bet. That means our operation is charged with finding Isaac's girls, while Dulles gets all the credit for his defection."

"That's hardly fair."

"That's OSS politics for you. We do get to use Isaac's specialist knowledge in all our operations though."

"Which brings us back to the silo. What's the plan?"

"You'll be working with Tex Jones again, which I know will please you. Tex is going to pose as an SS lieutenant and engineer from Von Braun and General Dornberger's research compound in Peenemünde where they developed both the V2 and the V10. You've visited the silo once as an SS member, so you already have an established cover. You're to accompany Tex to the silo as his guard. You're a face they know so they'll be less wary. We've contacted the silo, using what the Nazi's thought was a secret channel, to let them know you're coming. Your cover story is that he has come to fit a prototype device intended to fix a potential problem with the rocket. We've rigged up an incendiary device, disguised to look like the radio control component. It'll be activated by the same radio signal that the rocket uses. It will have enough power to ignite all the fuel in the silo. Isaac has drawn us up some schematics and Tex has been briefed in how to fit the thing without drawing any suspicion. Once you're out of the silo and far enough away you can detonate the device by radio control. Do you have any questions?"

"Yes. What are we going to do about Yelena? She could

also be of use to us, but she refuses to be handled by anyone else. I can't undertake this mission if I have to baby-sit her."

"Don't worry about that. Chuck and I will take care of her, you worry about completing this mission." Max handed him an envelope. "This contains a map and the co-ordinates of where you're due to meet Tex. He has a new SS uniform for you so you can ditch those Russian duds once and for all." Karl opened the envelope and had a quick look inside. "Memorise it and burn it as ever," said Max. "Oh, and you might want to go out of this door." He pointed to a small metal door behind him. "It leads into a side tunnel that ends in steps to the street above. That way you won't have to see Yelena before you leave. It'll make it easier for us to deal with her for you."

"Okay," said Karl.

Max stopped him just as he was about to leave. "If I hear any reports about your death on this mission, I'll consider them exaggerations shall I?"

Karl smiled. "I've got a good man watching my back. I don't think I'll have much to worry about." Max nodded and Karl slipped through the back door, groped his way down the pitch-black tunnel beyond it until he found the steps to the street above.

He felt a little guilty about abandoning Yelena when she had been counting on him. He couldn't help thinking he still owed her for coming to his rescue on several occasions. He didn't envy Max and Chuck the task of trying to talk her round. It dawned on him that he would rather take on a life-threatening mission than attempt that himself. Such was the place the woman held in his estimation.

CHAPTER TWENTY

"Freeze!" said a thick German voice. Karl felt a cold gun barrel pressed against the base of his skull and stopped moving instantly.

Then he heard a familiar chuckle. "Got you that time pardner," said a voice with a broad Texas accent. Karl recognised it instantly as Tex's. He turned to confront the old reprobate.

"You're lucky I didn't snatch that gun off you and shove it where the sun don't shine."

"No," said Tex, "*You're* lucky you didn't *try* and snatch this gun offa me. Cos it wouldn't have ended up in my rear, that's fer sure."

They were standing outside an old tram terminus in the Neukölln district, roughly twenty minutes from the port of Hafen Neukölln where the silo was. "Come on," said Tex beckoning to Karl as he walked off. "I've got a few things for you."

They walked around the side of the terminus where a vehicle was sitting under an old tarpaulin. Tex pulled it away to reveal a brand new German jeep. On the backseat were provisions, an SS uniform in Karl's size and a large metal case containing the incendiary device. "How in hell did you get all this?" Karl asked.

"Ah. If I was to tell you that, then I'd have to kill you."

"You'd die trying."

"Die laughing more like."

Karl tapped the metal case. "So this is the little firebug is it?"

"Careful! That thing could take your hand off if you don't watch out, it's very delicate."

"You better watch out for potholes in the road then," Karl said. He took the SS uniform from the back seat. "Time to change. That old Soviet uniform was beginning to stink."

"How d'you think I always get the drop on you? I can practically sniff you out, wherever you are."

"Bloodhound eh?"

"Nope, just an all round hound."

Karl took off his jacket and shirt. Tex pointed to his wounded shoulder. "How's the bullet hole doing?"

Karl shrugged. "The bullet's out and it seems to be healing. It hurts from time to time but not so it slows me down or stops me doing anything."

Tex nodded. "So long as it doesn't get in the way of the mission. You've got my back on this one. I've gotta know you're firing on all cylinders."

"You couldn't be in safer hands."

"So long as you keep them to yourself," said Tex in a camp voice. "I'm not that sort of boy."

"That ain't what your momma says."

"Well she's just taking pity on you," said Tex. "Cos she knows you can't get a gal."

Karl finished changing and climbed in the front seat. "I'm driving," said Tex rattling the keys. "Pop said if I let anything happen to his wheels he's gonna have my hide."

They arrived, just outside of Hafen Neukölln, twenty minutes before they were expected. Tex had made good time. You had to when you were posing as a member of the German military. Punctuality was like an article of faith to them.

They wanted to scout out the area before they

proceeded with the mission. Preparation was key. Too many missions had gone to the wall due to a lack of it. They had to identify the best escape routes and locate the ideal position to set off the incendiary.

Both Tex and Karl had a sniper's eye for the terrain. This meant they were very adept at judging distances. They had a calculated figure of 1,175 metres for the blast radius of the explosion and based on this they were looking for a landmark beyond which it would be safe to activate the device. They were looking for somewhere that was close enough to the target to be able to verify it had worked, but far enough away to be outside the radius of the blast. They chose an old rusty crane that lay idling by the side of the Spree, then carried on to their destination.

They pulled up at the silo dead on time. The guards at the door told them to get out of the jeep and checked their credentials. "A moment Lieutenant Oberman," a guard said to Tex after they stated their business. He went inside and announced their arrival.

A white-coated technician came to the door and greeted them. The man did not look pleased and they received a frosty reception as they were ushered inside. "I have to say," the technician said in a harassed tone. "This is most irregular and highly inconvenient. We've been working around the clock to get the rocket fully operational. Most of us have hardly slept. There's a matter of days till the launch and now you tell us the whole radio piloting is malfunctioning. This is not the conclusion that we arrived at."

"You did not design the system," said Tex in an equally officious tone. "Therefore you cannot be expected to have our knowledge of the finer points of its operational facilities. If such matters were left in your hands then we'd be lucky to hit the United States at all." The technician bristled at Tex's put down, but he didn't continue to argue.

Another senior technician came over to join them. His expression was anxious and he appeared more eager to fix the apparent problem. "We received word that the gyroscope is not functioning properly," he said. "This did not come up in our diagnostic."

"Your diagnostic is flawed by a paucity of information and training," said Tex. He had really done his homework and had the role of an officious rocket scientist down to a tee. Yet again Karl was impressed by his performance in the field. "It is only to be expected," continued Tex. "Your training was on V1 and V2 rockets. The V10 is an entirely different beast and cannot be measured and evaluated by the same standards and procedures."

"Where exactly does the problem lie?" asked the senior technician.

"The problem," said Tex. "Lies in the gyroscope controlling rudders 2 and 4, which, as you know, control the angle of the upward ascent. Over such a long period of time the signal controlling them becomes weaker and their response is less accurate. As the angle of ascent determines the angle at which the rocket eventually approaches the target, we have a major concern. Over such large distances even the smallest error in the initial trajectory can result in the rocket missing its target by as much as 100 kilometres. What is designed to be a master stroke for the Third Reich, could easily end up as an empty gesture when it strikes an uninhabited stretch of land, or worse still, the ocean."

A look of grave concern stole over the faces of the technicians. Karl could tell they were torn between panic at the time they had left and the sinking feeling that always comes when you realise you have to go right back to the drawing board.

"However, all is not lost gentlemen," said Tex, playing them with expert precision. "I do not come empty handed." He clicked his fingers and Karl produced the incendiary device from within the metal case. "We at Peenemünde have been working on this problem for some month's now and have constructed a solution."

"But why were we not told?" said the first technician.

"It is not your place to *be* told," Tex snapped at the technician. "It is your place to simply do as you *are* told." The technician blushed and looked at the floor. He was severely embarrassed to be given such a dressing down in front of his colleagues.

"Now," continued Tex, making certain that he had all the technicians' undivided attention. "You are required to fit this gyroscope to the radio control devices and begin tests immediately." The technicians wasted no time in placing a rocket in harness and readying it for a battery of tests. "Make certain the rocket is fully fuelled and primed as well," Tex ordered.

"Won't that be a little dangerous?" asked the senior technician timidly.

Tex drew himself up to his full height. "Is everyone in this detail so desperate for disciplinary action that you must question everything I tell you?"

The bullying worked and the technicians began fuelling the rocket without any further questions. If the mission were to be a success Tex had to keep a tight grip of the whole proceedings. While the technicians were still Nazis and used to following orders, they were men with inquiring minds who were also used to asking questions. This might prove dangerous if their suspicions were aroused at any time.

"I am not obliged to answer any questions from a subordinate," Tex said. "However, as you are to be trained in the use of this equipment I will explain my orders on this one occasion only. As you know the crucial factor in any equation governing the angle of flight is weight. The gyroscope will function quite differently in an empty rocket than it will in one that has been fuelled. While this increases the dangers to you during installation, it is necessary that you learn to fit the prototype under these conditions as you will need to fit the perfected device to a fuelled rocket when we come to launch it."

This seemed to head off any further questions the technicians had and they busied themselves preparing the rocket to be fuelled. Tex oversaw the operation while Karl hung back. "Your commanding officer," said a voice behind him. "I think he needs to eat more fibre." Karl turned and saw the moustached technician he had spoken to last time he visited the silo. The man had a mischievous half smile.

"I'm sorry?"

"I said he needs to eat more fibre," said the technician. "I do not think he has had a bowel movement in some time."

Karl smiled at the subtle joke. "No he just talks shit instead," he replied and the two shared a quiet laugh.

The rocket was moved around in its harness and suspended over the back of a truck with a large trailer with a huge mechanical arm. "That's a Meillerwagen," said the technician. "It's used by the mobile firing units." The Meillerwagen backed the rocket up to a welded steel platform. "That's the Abschuss platform."

"The what?" asked Karl.

"The launching table. It's 3,600 pounds and quite portable, ingenious really." The mechanical arm lifted the rocket up until it was standing completely vertical. "It has to be upright so they can fuel it."

When the fuelling was complete Tex and another technician climbed a tall stepladder to the top of the rocket. Tex was carefully carrying the incendiary device. "That's where the gyroscopes are fitted," said the technician. "Just below the nose cone, where the warhead will be."

Karl appreciated the man's commentary. He felt a sudden pang of conscience about his mission. He liked the man and enjoyed his company. Yet here he and Tex were, engaged in a plot that would kill him and all his colleagues.

"Your officer, he's from Peenemünde you say?" Karl nodded. "That's funny," said the technician. "I was trained and worked at Peenemünde myself and I don't remember him."

"He either joined after you left or you just never saw him."

"I doubt it," said the technician. "Peenemünde was not a large place and men qualified to work there are not easily come by. Don't you find it strange that one might have joined so late in the war-effort?"

Karl shrugged. "I don't ask questions. I just follow orders."

"You don't ask questions," said the technician, raising an eyebrow. "And I had you pegged for a man of intelligence."

Karl wondered if the technician was hinting at anything with the phrase 'man of intelligence'. It had the same double meaning in both German and English, but Germans were not as given to wordplay. Before Karl could say anything the technician excused himself, commenting that it was good to see Karl again.

Karl heard Tex raising his voice and took a few steps closer to the rocket to hear what was being said. "But lieutenant," the technician was saying. "It may not be my place to question a superior; however you have not connected the wires correctly."

Tex was just about to give the man a dressing down when the senior technician called up to him. "A moment Lieutenant Oberman." Karl sensed a subtle mood change in the silo. There was a sudden air of expectancy and suspicion.

Tex had not picked up on it. He was too distracted by his task. "What do you mean interrupting me at this crucial point in the proceedings?" he snapped at the senior technician.

"I have just been on the radio to General Dornberger, the chief of staff at Peenemünde. He left Peenemünde over a week ago after overseeing its closure. He is now in Thuringia with Project Leader Von Braun. They know nothing of a new gyroscopic device."

"Of course they haven't heard about it," Tex said over his shoulder as he came quickly down the ladder. "They are no longer in charge of this project. Gruppenführer General Kammler is. That's why Peenemünde was closed down. I am General Kammler's representative on the Spear of Destiny project and I answer to him alone. Of course I know more about gyroscopes than Dornberger and Von Braun do, they are no longer involved with the project."

Karl had to admire Tex's nerve. None of the technicians had expected such a brazen rebuttal of their attempt to expose his cover story. This bought them crucial time as the technicians and soldiers decided how to respond.

Karl took stock of all the guards posted around the silo. There were five on the front and back entrances, two a piece on the side entrances, and two more outside the front entrance. It was not likely that Tex and he could shoot their way out.

Tex was to toe to toe with the senior technician. His manner was so overbearing he nearly convinced the other technicians into believing him, even though his cover had been blown. The guards were another matter though. They were definitely getting ready to act. No-one dared fire a shot however, for fear of igniting all the fuel that was stored in the silo.

The senior technician was about to speak when Tex pushed his shoulder and swung him round. As the blind-sided technician spun, Tex pulled out his pistol with his right hand and gripped the technician in a neck lock with his left. Before anyone could react he had a gun at the man's temple.

"Listen all of you," Tex said in a loud voice, addressing the guards. "I want you to put your weapons on the floor and walk away from them. You have twenty seconds before I shoot your project leader through the head. Then I fire another bullet into one of those fuel canisters and we all go up in flames."

The guards exchanged glances and decided to play along. They placed their weapons carefully on the floor. Few walked more than a step away from them though.

"My colleague and I are going to leave now and none of you are going to stop us," Tex said, backing slowly towards the main entrance. Karl drew his pistol and moved in to cover Tex. Back to back they moved towards the door.

Karl was facing the entrance as they reached it. He scanned each of the guards, switching his aim between them to let them know he could put a bullet in any of them. He took his eyes off the man furthest to his left for no more than a second and the man jumped for his rifle.

Karl fired downwards. The bullet went through the top of the man's head and came out of the bottom of his face, blowing his jaw off. It ricocheted off the concrete floor and lodged in his leg. The other four guards went white with the thought of what might have happened if the bullet had not been stopped.

They backed off then. Karl and Tex left the building without any further trouble. One thing Karl had learned from his tour of duty is that most confrontations in a war don't come down to who's better equipped or got more men. They come down to who's got the most front.

Outside Karl came up behind the two sentries. He put his pistol against the back of the left sentry's skull. "Drop your weapon," he ordered. "Tell your friend to do the same." The other sentry spun round, saw what was happening and dropped his weapon out of fright. Karl noted that he was barely into his teens.

Karl blew the left sentry's brains out. Tex took his pistol off the technician for a second and shot the teen sentry through the heart. They could not afford to have either man try and put a bullet in their back as they were leaving. What's more it made the guards inside wary of coming out the main entrance for fear of catching a bullet.

They moved over to the jeep. Karl reached over to open the door when out of nowhere a pistol was pointing at Tex's head. It was the technician with the moustache. Suspicious, he must have sneaked out after talking to Karl and hidden in the backseat. "Drop your weapon and let go of my colleague," he demanded. Karl put his pistol to the technician's temple. They were in a Mexican stand off.

"Put down your pistol and I will let you live," said

Karl. "I don't want to, but I will kill you before you can blink."

"But not before I kill your friend here," said the technician. "How do you fancy your chances of surviving and getting away alone?"

"I've faced worse odds. I like you though. You don't have to die like this. You can still have your chance to visit the stars."

"I like you too," said the technician. "And much as I want to visit the stars I see in the night sky, I love the country from which I look up at them more. You, it grieves me to say, are an enemy of that country."

While the moustached technician was momentarily distracted by Karl, Tex batted his gun to one side. Then he pushed his hostage over, whipped out his knife and buried it in the technician's chest in one single movement. By the time the technician reacted he had a cold steel blade in his heart. He pulled the trigger of his pistol and his colleague on the floor screamed as the stray bullet tore through his shoulder.

The technician fell sideways and Karl caught him. The man's eyes rolled upwards as he took one last look at the stratosphere he would never breach.

Tex made kissing noises to deride Karl. "Mmm, mmm, mmm, I like you too. Do you want to ride my pocket rocket to the stars." Karl ignored him and laid the technician's body on the ground.

He pulled Tex's knife out the man's chest and handed it back to him. "We have to leave. There isn't time to waste."

They climbed into the jeep and started up the engine. It sputtered into life and then died. Karl looked over his shoulder and saw the guards coming out of the side entrance. Tex turned the key again. The engine coughed but refused to start. The guards were almost on them.

A bullet whistled past them and put a hole in the windscreen. Several more shots followed. Karl grabbed his rifle and took out one of the guards. "Come on baby," Tex said to the jeep. "Show me what German engineering can really do."

As though Tex had somehow hit upon the magic words and inspired some latent nationalism in the jeep, it finally sputtered into life. And not a moment too soon. They pulled away at speed as the guards bore rapidly down on them.

Tex accelerated to top speed. Karl watched as many of the guards climbed into two waiting jeeps and began pursuing them. The distance between them and their pursuers began to quickly decrease.

"How long until we get past the crane?" Karl shouted.

"Just a few more minutes," Tex replied. Karl looked at the two jeeps coming up behind them. Guards on both vehicles were firing at them.

"We're not going to make it before they catch us," said Karl.

"I'm flooring the jeep but it doesn't seem to have the power we need."

"We've got to slow them down!"

"Look on the floor behind the seats," said Tex.

There was a large canvas sack on the floor in front of the back seat. Karl picked it up and opened it. Inside was a brand new Panzerfaust. "Nice," said Karl, surveying the disposable launcher with its pre-loaded, rocket propelled grenade. "This is just what we need."

He hunkered down in his seat and aimed the Panzerfaust at the jeep closest to them. Once he had it in his sights he activated the launcher and braced himself. The rocket screamed off and crashed dead into the bonnet of the jeep.

The explosion tore the front of the vehicle apart and the back wheels flew up in the air, with the onward momentum, flipping what was left of the jeep. The guards in the front seat were burnt to a crisp and dismembered. Those in the back were thrown out of the jeep in flames. Charred and severed body parts rained down around them as they smacked into the ground at a bone breaking velocity.

Karl and Tex whooped in delight at the carnage. "Whooooeee," screamed Tex. "Git along little doggie!"

"Where are the other rockets?" Karl asked.

"Other rockets? That was the only one. You were supposed to take out both vehicles with one shot."

"Why didn't you tell me that?"

"Well excuse me for thinking you knew what you were doing!"

The second jeep had to avoid the remains of the first and lost vital time in doing so. This slowed it down enough for Tex to steal more of a lead on it. "Here comes the crane," said Tex. He pulled the detonator out of his pocket. "T- minus one minute and counting," he said. They shot past the crane and Tex pressed the button.

Nothing happened.

Tex and Karl exchanged puzzled glances. Tex pressed the button again. And again. And again. And several times more with increasing annoyance, but all to no avail. "Well how about that," said Tex. "Looks like that German technician was right about that wiring after all."

"Well excuse me for thinking you knew what you were doing," Karl countered. Tex shot him a foul look.

The remaining jeep was beginning to gain on them and they started firing again. One bullet hit their back tire and caused a blow out. Tex fought to keep control of the vehicle and stop it skidding out of control. "There's only one thing for it," he said and pulled into a four-storey storage depot just beyond the crane.

"What are you playing at?" said Karl as Tex brought the jeep to a stop inside the depot. "You've got to shoot the detonator to set off the explosion," said Tex. "It's the only way."

"There's a whole squad of guards on our tail," said Karl. "Are you crazy?"

"No," said Tex. "If we get up to the top floor you'll just about have the angle for the shot. There's only one staircase up. I'll post myself at the top of it and pick off anyone who follows."

"There's no way I can make the shot at this range."

"What are you firing, a Gewehr 43?"

"Yes."

"That's got a 1,200 km range. The blast radius is 1,175km, you can make it."

"But we're outside of the blast radius here."

"Look," said Tex, fixing Karl with his cold blue eyes. "Are you a freakin' marksman or not?" With that he bounded up the staircase without waiting to see if Karl was following.

They got to the biggest window on the top floor. It looked directly out on to the missile silo. They could see the upright rocket still in position. Karl studied it through his binoculars. "The incendiary device is triggered by a radio controlled circuit. When the circuit is broken it sets off the device and ignites the fuel. All you need to do is shoot through the green and red wires to detonate the device."

"Is that all? I can't see any wires at this distance."

"Give me the binoculars," said Tex. He put his one good eye to Karl's binoculars and tried to locate the wires. "Uh huh, there they are, right on the rim of the opening."

Karl took the binoculars and Tex pointed out the wires to him. "I can hardly see them," he said. "And these binoculars are much more powerful than my scope, there's no way I can draw a bead on them."

"Are you gonna beat your gums and moan? Or are you gonna complete this mission?"

"I can't shoot them at this angle," Karl said. "I need to be higher to get a proper shot." Before Tex could reply he knocked out several panes of glass with his rifle butt. "Give me a hand up on to the roof," he said. "And make certain you keep those guards from getting up the stairs."

"You can count on it," said Tex giving him a bunk up.

Karl climbed out of the window. He shimmied along a ledge and then caught hold of the guttering. He began to pull himself up on to the roof when, without any prior warning, a bullet nicked his inside thigh. Two more thudded into the wall next to him. He felt blood trickling down his leg but the pain wasn't great enough for the bullet to have done any real damage.

The guards must have spotted him just before they chased them into the depot. He didn't dare look down to see how many were firing at him. He scrambled up on to the roof and got out of range of their guns. Beneath him he could hear them charging into the depot and up the stairs. The sound of footfall on the stairs was quickly silenced by Tex's gunfire.

The top of the depot consisted of two slanting roofs. Karl lay nestled in the gutter between the two. From there he had the best possible view of the top of the rocket through the window of the silo. He set his sights to the maximum range and picked out the wires where Tex had shown him.

There was a stiff breeze blowing off the river Spree and there was a long shortfall between Karl and the target. There was a lot of gravity and wind speed to account for. This was not going to be easy.

As Karl was making the necessary adjustments he saw one of the technicians in the silo climb up the stepladder next to the upright rocket. He got to the top and bent over the incendiary device. He was obviously intent on disconnecting it.

Karl drew a bead on the man and fired, using the shot as a test. He aimed for the heart, through the back of the rib cage, but hit the man in the base of the spine. This gave Karl the best indication of how to shoot out the wires. The technician fell from the ladder as his legs gave way.

Karl heard gunfire below him. The guards must have rushed the stairs. He had very little time left. He emptied his lungs. Waited for his heart to calm then, before his muscles started to shake, he fired.

Karl could have lived and died twice over in the split second between making the shot and the bullet finding its target. That's how long it felt. There was no way he could have seen the bullet slice through the two wires. There was no way he could have missed the resulting explosion.

He seemed to feel it before he saw it. It rattled through him, shaking his innards. There was an immense roar that increased in volume until it was agonising to hear.

The walls of the silo crumbled and flew apart like they were made of sugar paste. The roof dissolved into tatters and was flung miles up into the air with the force of the blast.

A blinding ball of white heat burst from within the silo and grew exponentially outwards and upwards, eviscerating everything within its path. It had the same intensity as the exhaust from the back of a rocket only so much larger.

Karl looked at it a microsecond too long. The blinding light filled his vision and he felt the back of his eyeballs frazzle and throb with pain. He closed his eyes tight but the blinding light was still there.

He turned away from the blistering heat and the light was all around him, whether his eyes were open or shut. The explosion died away. The heat and noise subsided, but the light that filled his sight didn't. Nor did the pain in his eyes.

He was on a rooftop, four storeys up with no easy way down. A few metres below him was a squad of enemy soldiers intent on killing him and he couldn't see a thing. He was totally blind.

CHAPTER TWENTY-ONE

Karl hugged the roof and made his way carefully along it, trying to find a skylight or some other way down. He reached out to explore the surface he was inching along, but all he could feel beneath his fingers was the cold slate of the roof tiles.

Below him he heard more gunshots. Tex, it appeared, was engaged in a fierce battle. Karl felt angry that he was of no use to his friend just when Tex really needed his help. After a fierce exchange of shots the firing stopped.

There was silence for a long while after that. Karl had no way of knowing how the gunfight had gone. Or whether Tex had survived. He didn't know if his blindness was temporary or permanent. It might clear up in a day, an hour, or never. In which case he would probably never get down and would starve to death if some enemy soldier didn't pick him off. Not a comforting thought.

After what could have been an eternity as far as Karl was concerned, he heard scrabbling on what was probably the edge of the roof. He turned his head to listen better. "Where the hell were you?" said a familiar voice.

"Tex," said Karl, with no little relief.

"Of course it is. Have you gone blind or something?"

"Actually yes," said Karl with an apologetic smile. "The blast was quite intense and I didn't look away in time."

"Aw hell! Right, the first thing we gotta do is get you down from there. That ain't gonna be easy."

"You ain't whistling Dixie."

"No I ain't. How'd you get all the way over there anyway?"

"Guess I must have walked. Am I far from the edge?"

"Twenty or thirty metres," said Tex. "Follow the sound

of my voice. I'll tell you if there's anything to watch out for."

Karl stumbled back along the roof with Tex's assistance until he got to the edge. "Steady pardner," said Tex. "That's the easy bit out of the way. Now, I'll drop back down and climb in the window. When I tell you, lower yourself gently over the edge and I'll reach out and guide your legs into place, so your feet are on the ledge."

Karl listened until Tex was back in the window and gave him the word, and then he lowered himself over the edge. His legs dangled as he inched down and then he felt Tex's hands on the back of his calves. He took hold of the guttering and dropped on to the window ledge.

At that very minute the guttering in his left hand snapped and came away from the wall. He dropped it like hot lead and reached out for a handhold but found none. He careened around to his right and the guttering in his other hand broke too.

For a moment he seemed to hang in mid air as he tried to lean forwards and get hold of the wall. Then he toppled backwards.

Just as he felt his toes start to leave the ledge he stopped falling. The front of his jacket was being held by something. He put his hands to his chest and found Tex gripping him. "This just ain't your day is it pardner?"

"I've had better," Karl admitted.

Tex pulled him forwards towards the open window and guided his hands so he could pull himself inside. Karl collapsed on the floor as soon as he got into the depot. "What happened with the guards who were chasing us?" Karl asked, still lying on his back.

"The blast killed the two that were outside. Another couple were crushed by one of the doors that got blown off. I killed the rest. Wasn't too difficult, they were pretty shell shocked by the explosion."

Karl got to his feet. "Come on. We better get back and report to Max."

Tex took Karl's arm. "The stairs are this way."

Karl did not like having to be so reliant on another person. He was very self-contained. That's what made him such a good sniper. He didn't need other people and he didn't like having to depend on them. Working the field with an old friend like Tex was one thing. But having Tex guide his every action like an invalid did not sit well with him. He tried to hide this so as not to appear ungrateful but he knew Tex could tell. Tex did his best not to wound Karl's pride.

"Jeep's just here," said Tex, after leading Karl down the stairs and across the ground floor of the depot. "What happened to your leg?" Tex asked.

"Bullet nicked it." Karl said.

"I thought you were walking kinda funny. Didn't realise you were hit."

"It doesn't feel like there's any real damage done. Perhaps you ought to take a look at it."

"Whoa there pardner! You're gonna have to take off your pants for me to take a look at it. And I ain't having no man drop their pants for ol' Tex. Way I see it, my job is to get you back safely and put you in the hands of someone who knows about taking other men's pants down."

"Fair enough," said Karl as Tex led him round to the passenger seat of the jeep.

"Hey, I just realised," Tex said. "You know what this is?"

"No."

"It's a case of the one eyed leading the blind."

"In the land of the blind, the one eyed man is king,"

said Karl climbing in to the jeep. "Should I call you 'Your Majesty'?"

"Naw," said Tex getting in the driver's seat. "Let's keep it informal and stick with 'Your Highness'."

Karl heard Tex put the key in the ignition and turn the engine over without any problems. "*Now* she starts first time. Soon as we don't have a squadron of krauts on our tail." He pulled the jeep out of the depot and then stopped, leaving the engine running.

"What's the problem?" asked Karl. "Why aren't we going anywhere?"

"There isn't anywhere to go pardner," said Tex. "Least ways, not as far as I can see."

"Why not?"

"Well you can't see it at the moment but you made an awfully big mess with that explosion of yours. The whole port is covered with rubble and smoking bits of metal. It's like Armageddon just hit. I can't see any clear route outta here."

Finally Tex turned the jeep right round. "I'm gonna drive back through this depot and out the other side. I'll try and weave my way through the buildings that would've shielded the blast." Karl felt the jeep twist and turn often stopping and going back on itself. He remained silent as he couldn't think of a single useful thing to say to Tex. Tex for his part simply swore a lot and uttered phrases like: "What! I don't believe it," or, "This is too much", over and over again.

Eventually they must have hit a proper road as the jeep seemed to follow a straight line and Tex stopped cussing. They carried on without exchanging any more words for a while. Karl tried to fight back the anger and frustration he was feeling at his sudden visual impairment.

He tried focusing and un-focusing his eyes but nothing improved his vision. His sight was still filled with the white-hot glare of the explosion. Occasional swirls and blotches of red and orange drifted across his field of vision, but that was the only variation in what he saw. He cursed himself silently for not looking away soon enough and promised himself that if he were ever in that situation again he would not make the same mistake.

They had been travelling for about twenty minutes when Tex said: "'Course you know this is going to get you loads more pussy."

"How'd you reckon that?"

"Chicks dig a disability. You wouldn't believe how often this ol' eye patch has got me laid. If I'd known just how much, I woulda plucked my eye out myself years ago."

"Yeah right."

"Honestly. Why would I lie? There was this one French girl in Bern, she had the finest pair of..."

There was the sudden deafening roar of an explosion. Karl felt the jeep rise suddenly in the air. He was thrown backwards, unable to determine if he was falling or rising until his shoulder connected with a hard paving stone. Then he heard a buckling of metal and shattering of glass that must have been the jeep landing either on its side or its head.

He sat up and felt the sharp stab of a dislocated shoulder. He put his hand on the ground, rested most of his weight on it and twisted, popping his shoulder back in to its socket with no little amount of pain. Just as his did so he heard the 'schvvip - ping' and smelled the cordite of a bullet striking the ground less than a metre to his right. Another followed it even closer to his left.

Karl began to piece together what had just happened. The jeep must have hit a stray mine buried in the road. A trap laid by a sniper who was now trying to pick them off. Karl knew he had to get under cover, but without his sight he had no way of telling where there was any cover.

He called out to Tex and listened. He heard a faint groan about six metres ahead of him. Another bullet struck the ground just in front of him. The shots were getting closer, the sniper was honing in. Karl stood in a crouch and made his way over to where he had heard Tex's voice, weaving side to side to make himself a more difficult target.

Karl bashed his head as he ran into the jeep. Feeling his way along it he surmised that it was upside down at an angle with the passenger seat in the air and the driver's seat closer to the ground.

Karl located Tex. He wasn't moving and there was fresh blood on his face and hair. Karl felt for a pulse and found that it was quite strong. Tex was alive but out cold.

A bullet struck the upturned jeep. By Karl's reckoning the sniper would be trying to hit the gas tank so he could take them both out. He would be adjusting his sights and firing test shots until he found it. This meant Karl had a limited amount of time to get Tex and himself under cover.

The one thing he had going for him was that the sniper wasn't very good. As Karl and Tex were dressed as SS officers, it was a safe bet that the sniper was Russian, which might account for his inaccuracy.

The Russians had led the field in sniping at the beginning of the war, particularly on the Eastern Front. In 1941, with the Russian army in retreat and the Germans advancing on Stalingrad, the majority of casualties scored against the German lines were by snipers. Four years later however they were thrusting rifles with sights into the hands of anyone who could shoot straight, and even a few who couldn't.

Even still Karl couldn't count on the sniper continuing to miss indefinitely. He had to find somewhere nearby that was out of the sniper's line of fire. Without his vision he would have to find other ways of assessing his environment.

He picked up a handful of rocks and began tossing them straight ahead of him. The first two didn't yield anything but the third hit a pane of glass and Karl heard it shatter. He threw another one at roughly the same point but a little to the right. This time he heard it strike a wall. From the sound it made, and the speed at which he threw it, the wall was only about seven or eight metres away.

Karl threw three more stones, each at the same wall but a little to the right of the last. The first two hit the wall, the third carried on going and struck the ground beyond. This meant there was probably a door in the wall. Karl threw more stones each in a slightly different place as he measured the dimensions of the doorway based on the noises made by the stones as they struck it.

From this crude form of sonar – 'stonar' he mentally dubbed it – he was able to determine the size of the door, it's relative position and distance from him, all within minutes. The shooting stopped for a moment. Karl had not been counting the shots but at a rough guess he imagined the sniper was reloading. This was his one window of opportunity.

He tugged Tex out of the driver's seat and dragged him across the street towards the door. Halfway there his heel caught on a length of pipe, or it might have been a post, and he tumbled, dropping Tex. He jumped to his feet picked up his friend and started again.

A bullet hit the ground inches from his foot. He picked up speed and practically sprinted for the last two metres. He came to the point at which he was sure there was a doorway. The sound of his footsteps, and of Tex's body dragging along the floor, altered. It echoed slightly off walls and a ceiling. Karl was fairly certain he had made it through the door and into a room.

He put Tex down and began to explore the space he was in. He walked forward with his arms outstretched until he came to a wall. Then he felt his way along that wall until he came to a corner and explored the joining wall. Halfway along he barked his shins on a chair and nearly fell. When he was done he had a fairly good idea of the dimensions of the space he was in.

He needed to find a different route out of the building though. One that, if possible, would afford cover from the sniper. Although he was out of the sniper's line of fire he was still pinned down in the building until he could find another way to leave. All the sniper had to do was simply wait until Karl tried to escape with Tex and then pick them off. Sniping was a waiting game and patience was always the best weapon in the sniper's arsenal. He couldn't drag Tex along the whole way however, he needed to revive him.

Before he could do that, Karl heard an explosion outside in the street. He thought at first that it might be the fuel tank of the jeep but it was too far away and sounded more like a grenade. Then he made out footsteps coming towards the room. He pulled the knife from his boot and crouched in a defensive position, waiting to spring if he was attacked.

"Karl Fairburne, as I live and breathe," said a voice with an English accent.

"Daniel, is that you?"

"In the flesh old man," Daniel replied. Then a tone of concern crept into his voice. "Is there something the matter with your eyes?"

"I can't see. An explosion took my sight."

"I thought something was up, when I saw you," said Daniel. "I must confess I nearly took a shot at you. I thought you were a Hun. There was something about the way you moved though. It looked familiar. So I checked you out through the old binoculars and lo and behold there you are."

"What was the explosion that I heard?" said Karl.

"Grenade. I saw you were under fire from a sniper. He hadn't spotted me but I made his position. So I snuck up and had the blighter. I probably shouldn't have, he was a Russkie and they are supposed to be our allies. But then again, plenty have taken pot shots at me and I do owe you my life."

"Consider the debt paid in full," said Karl, relaxing and returning his knife to his boot.

"Who's your companion?" said Daniel. "I take it he's out cold and not dead."

"This is Tex. He's another OSS operative. He was knocked unconscious when our jeep hit a mine."

"I'm afraid that was one of mine old man. You rather blundered into a bit of sabotage I had set up. I'd laid the mines to take out a wagon carrying some of these new rockets to a makeshift silo nearby."

"We've just taken out a missile silo housing those very rockets," said Karl. "But that was miles away to the south."

"Must be more than one of them then," said Daniel.

"So it would seem."

"Anyway. I was just about to come and help you when that sniper appeared out of nowhere."

"That's how a sniper strikes," said Karl. "Out of nowhere."

"Quite. And that's how the grenade that killed him

219

appeared, out of nowhere. He never saw it coming."

"I have to revive Tex," said Karl. "Can you help me? Has he sustained any other injuries? I can't see him so I can't tell."

"Here take my arm. We'll go and take a look at him." They walked over to where Tex lay unconscious and knelt beside him. "He's had a nasty bump on the noggin," said Daniel. "He's going to have an awful bruise and a scar when he wakes up, but aside from that he seems fine. I can't tell you anymore until he wakes up, maybe he'll have a slight touch of concussion, and perhaps it will be worse. Maybe I'm worrying unnecessarily, he looks like he has a hard enough head."

"Oh it's solid through and through."

Karl heard the sloshing of a canteen. "I've got some water here," said Daniel. "I'll wash his head wound and try and get some liquid into him. See if it doesn't revive him." After a minute or so Karl heard Tex groan. "That's better old chap. You gave your partner here quite a scare for a minute. How are you feeling now?"

"Like someone took a jackhammer to my skull. Who in hell are you?"

"This is Captain Daniel Brown of the SOE," said Karl. "He blew up our jeep and saved our lives."

"That's what you get when you have the English for your Allies," said Tex. "Couldn't you have just saved our lives and left it at that?"

"You were the ones who drove over my mines and wrecked my operation," said Daniel. "Still that's what you get when you work with a Yank."

"Steady there Limey," said Tex. "You might have sucker punched me with your landmine, but Ol' Tex has still got a few more rounds in him."

"And they'd be rounds of ammunition if it wasn't for

the sniper I killed," said Daniel.

Karl heard Tex laugh. "You're alright Danny boy, even for a Brit."

"Charmed I'm sure. Now you boys will probably want a lift out of here. I've got transport parked nearby. I can give you a lift back to a location that's safe for you. And I know where the mines are buried on the roads."

"That'd be real good of you. We need a lift and I've got to keep this lunkhead from getting himself into any more trouble."

"You know I'd say that bump on the head caused some brain damage," said Karl. "If I thought you had any brain left to damage."

"Good thing my balls are still intact then," said Tex.

Karl heard Tex get to his feet. Daniel took Karl's arm and led the pair of them to his vehicle.

CHAPTER TWENTY-TWO

Tex directed Daniel to drop them off close enough to the OSS HQ for Karl to walk there, without giving the exact location away. Daniel wished them well and let them out.

Karl thanked him for his intervention and he shrugged it off. "Told you I always make good on my debts," Daniel said. "You make sure you find your eyesight and don't go losing it again."

"I won't," said Karl and listened to Daniel's vehicle drive off. He tried to hold on to the belief that his eyesight would come back. He couldn't allow himself to fear that it was gone forever, and with it his military career and his chance to clear his family name.

Tex helped Karl down to the U-Bahn platform and they climbed on to the tracks. Neither had a torch and the tunnel was pitch black, so their positions were reversed. Karl, who by now was used to operating without being able to see, had to help Tex find his way to the OSS hideout.

When they arrived the men in the front office sat them both down and reported their arrival to Max. Karl heard Max send one of the men for a military doctor then he came out of his office to hear their report.

Once the debriefing was over they drank hot tea and waited for the arrival of the doctor. The doctor checked them both over then stitched up Tex's head wound. He shone a bright light into Karl's eyes to test for dilatory response. It was the first thing that Karl had seen since the explosion.

The doctor couldn't detect any long-term damage to Karl's retinal tissue and assured him that his eyesight would return, although he couldn't tell how long that would take.

Karl was sent to a safe house to recover. It was a poky little garret, in a terrace of abandoned houses, with a single mattress on the floor, bare walls and floorboards. He could console himself that at least the place had been swept before he arrived.

Twice a day an operative called to check up on him, and to bring food with a fresh canteen of water. Usually it was Joe Hanna, the agent who had led Karl and Yelena to Chuck when they had been out in the cold. He didn't speak much, which suited Karl as there was little he wanted to say.

The forced inactivity gave him time to dwell on his situation. He knew he was being looked after because he had valuable information about the Spear of Destiny project. Without it he would not be afforded quite so much concern and attention. It also allowed them to keep him under observation. They were assessing his loyalty to his country and his continued usefulness in the field. If they had any doubts about either they would soon cut him loose.

Karl also assessed his search for information about his father's loyalty to his country. So far he had turned up nothing to either support or disprove the charge. His encounter with Kammler had been frustrating. He had hoped it would clear everything up but it had simply left him more confused.

He did start to wonder if Gary's deathbed confession was really true. Maybe it was all an elaborate psychological test that command was putting him through. To see how he would react if his loyalty was questioned and whether such suspicions could become self-fulfilling prophecies. If it was a test he was determined to come out of it untarnished.

Karl's sight came back by slow increments. The blinding light began to recede and he started to see things at the borders of his vision. Slowly the blind spot got smaller until it was really only a blotch in his left eye. Three days after he lost his eyesight he was back in Max's office reporting for duty.

Max was concerned that having been blinded temporarily, Karl would have lost his ability to snipe for good. Karl assured him that this wasn't the case.

"If I keep you in the field as part of the elite sniper unit," said Max, "I have to assure Washington that you can still do the job to the same high standard. It's not just your job and reputation that's on the line here."

"With Tex out of commission I'm the highest ranking marksman in the US army," snapped Karl, getting to his feet. "Even with one eye closed and the other hanging out of its socket I can still outshoot any man you have in the field."

"Okay Karl," said Max, in a tone that was intended to calm him down. "I have to ask these questions. I wouldn't be a good officer if I didn't. I don't mean it as a personal attack."

Karl realised his outburst was bordering on insubordination. He sat down. The last three days of inaction had left him wound up tight with frustration and just about anybody could set him off. Max had unwittingly hit a sore spot when he mentioned reputations. Or maybe it wasn't unwitting. Maybe he was probing Karl to see how he would respond.

Karl shrugged off those thoughts. A healthy dose of suspicion might keep you alive as a double agent, but you couldn't let it get out of hand. Not where your senior officer is concerned. Especially as Max was still the best ally Karl had in Berlin.

"Your main mission won't start for a few days yet anyway," said Max. "So you'll have enough time to recover from any temporary damage your eyes might have sustained. Your suspicions about there being another missile silo in Berlin have been confirmed. We exchanged a bit of information with SOE and found out they've located one not far from the launch site you uncovered. This is all to the good though, as it fits in rather nicely with our new game plan. Washington has had time to go over everything we've told them and they want us to hamper the Spear of Destiny Project with acts of sabotage, not derail it entirely."

"They've got other plans," said Karl.

"They've got other plans. I know what you're thinking, the dangers of not doing everything in our power to stop this look a lot different when you view them from behind a desk in the Pentagon, than down here on the ground. However, you've got to remember that for once they are in the hot seat too. The missile is going to be pointed at them. If anything goes wrong they stand to lose everything."

"Never mind what they have to lose, we've already given everything to get them that information," said Karl with impatience. "What do they want us to do now?"

"The strategic and military importance of capturing an intercontinental nuclear missile is too important not to act on. We have the perfect opportunity to catch the Russians and Germans off guard and to take the missile fully assembled and ready to fire. All we have to do then, is ship it safely back to the States and get our boys to backwards engineer it. It could put us leagues ahead of our nearest competitors in the nuclear stakes and guarantee a lasting peace through superior fire power."

"There's only one problem," said Karl. "They have over five platoons guarding the launch site and we are seriously under manned here in Berlin. How are we going to capture a missile with only a handful of agents?"

"We won't have only a handful of agents. Donovan has petitioned Roosevelt for as many troops as he can spare. Eisenhower is sending us a whole contingent under the command of Major Leon Kowalski."

"Kowalski? Not Kangaroo Kowalski?"

Max chuckled. "The very same." Major Kowalski had earned a reputation as a formidable commander and tactician. The nickname 'Kangaroo Kowalski' came from his ability to move troops at a swift pace through territory held by the enemy, as though he were hopping over their lines. This was probably why he had been chosen for the job, because he could mobilise a lot of men in a very short space of time.

"To be honest with you," said Max. "I think Eisenhower is rather glad of the excuse to get troops into Berlin ahead of schedule. None of us really trust either Marshall Zhukov or Marshall Konev. All this business with the rocket only goes to confirm those suspicions."

"I take it that you're briefing me on this," said Karl. "Because I'm to be involved in the operation."

"You are. Initially your role will be to brief Major Kowalski while he plans the offensive. He's an experienced tactician who has made good use of sniper cover in the past, so I imagine he'll want to make use of your talents during the combat as well. That's not for me to presuppose though, so for the duration of the offensive, Kowalski will effectively act as your commanding officer. However, as soon as the site has been secured and the missile has been captured without any incident, there is an exceptionally important mission I want you to undertake. The lives of every person in the city, civilian, soldier, German or ally depend on its successful completion."

"Alright," said Karl. "What is it and will I be working alone?"

"It's a three-hander. I need people who can get the job done so your principal support will be Tex Jones."

"That's good to know. Who else am I working with?"

"I'll get to that in a minute. First let me outline the mission. As you're probably aware one of the most dangerous features of this whole operation is the fact that we'll be dealing with the capture of an armed atom bomb. This isn't the only nuclear device to take into consideration though."

"We've still got General Helmstadt and his case," said Karl, as the real danger of everything that was being planned suddenly dawned on him.

"Exactly. This matter is a crucial part of securing both the site and the missile, but it needs to be handled ever so carefully."

"We have the codes now though," said Karl. "Can't we just mount a separate operation to capture him and neutralise the device in his case? I don't understand why we haven't tried that already."

"Because it would jeopardise the whole operation," said Max. "Helmstadt has a tight control on the Nazi nuclear programme. He controls the warhead and its entire construction. Without him they won't be able to assemble it and the Spear of Destiny project would have to be abandoned. We'd miss this whole opportunity."

"So what do we do?" said Karl.

"Once we have full control of the missile Helmstadt will not want to surrender," said Max. "He will use the nuclear device within the case to hold us all hostage and to negotiate a way out of the secured area. From there it is most likely that he will make his way into Russian territory where the Soviets will look after him. Kammler was able to discover his pre-arranged escape route. Yelena knows exactly where he'll be going so we'll be able to get to the rendezvous point where Helmstadt is due to meet up with the NKVD and cross over to the Soviet side, before he does. This will give us enough time to plan an ambush. As luck would have it, Helmstadt will be crossing over far enough away from the centre of Berlin so that if the worst happens, and the device does go off, it won't endanger the warhead."

"Where's the rendezvous point?"

"That's where we have a slight problem."

"We don't know where it is?"

"We do and we don't. We know for certain that it's in the Russian controlled district of Hellersdorf. We just don't know the exact location."

"But I thought you said thanks to Yelena we'll be able to get to the rendezvous point where Helmstadt is going to meet the Russians. What's the problem?"

"Do you remember I said this was going to be a three-hander?"

"Yes."

"Well the third person is going to be Yelena. She refuses point blank to tell us the exact location. She insists on accompanying you in person and showing you where it is. Command in Bern have complied with her demands and ordered you to take her along. Between you and me I think she wants to get even with you for dumping her on Chuck and me earlier."

Karl sighed. "Couldn't we just torture her?" he said hopefully.

Max shook his head. "We're Americans," he said. "We don't do that sort of thing, at least not officially.

Besides even if we did, it takes time to get that sort of information out of a person and we don't have the time. I'm afraid you're the one who's going to have to suffer in this instance. And anyway she's not exactly hard on the old eye. It might not be that much of a hardship after all." Karl grunted and looked down at his boots, preferring not to discuss the matter further.

"What's the plan once we get to the rendezvous point?"

"That's where your sharp shooting comes in. You'll arrive ahead of time and position yourself so you've got a clear shot at the whole area. When Helmstadt arrives he plans to leave his vehicle and travel with the NKVD. Ilyich Velikovsky, NKVD chief of operations over here, who incidentally is the same man who recruited both Yelena and Isaac, will meet him. Wait until everyone is out in the open then disable both vehicles and take out everyone from the NKVD. It's essential that you don't kill Helmstadt, just disable him. When you've accomplished this, Tex will move in and defuse the case using the code you obtained for us. In the case of anything happening to Tex, you will have to leave your position, defuse the case and retrieve it."

"How does the combination on the case work?"

"You'll be given some training on that. We came across one of the technicians who constructed it for Helmstadt recently and he'll brief you in what you need to do."

"I thought Helmstadt had everyone who worked on the case killed."

"That's what we were led to believe," said Max. "However, our boys liberated a concentration camp at Buchenwald recently, and in amongst the surviving inmates was one of the technicians who constructed the case. He came forward and let the officers in charge know of his connection to Helmstadt. They got in touch with Washington who arranged for the man to come into Berlin with Kowalski. You'll meet the man tomorrow at 09:00 hours, prior to your briefing with Major Kowalski. Now, do you have any more questions?"

"Is there any way I can get out of bringing Yelena along on the mission?"

"No," said Max quite conclusively.

"In that case, I have just one question."

"What's that?"

"Where can I go to get steaming drunk?"

CHAPTER TWENTY-THREE

The next morning Joe Hanna drove Karl to the Kreuzberg district. He was nestling a particularly bad hangover and Joe took great delight in hitting every pothole along the way. Karl began to wish he'd killed the man back when he had the chance the first time they met. At least that way he could have blamed it on mistaken identity.

Kowalski and his men had set up camp around what had been a large municipal park. Endless Allied bombing raids had done little for the meticulous German landscaping that had once made it one of the jewels of the district. Kreuzberg was in the west of the city and was part of the sector that the Allies had agreed would come under American control once the city fell. This made it an ideal outpost for Kowalski and his men, as there was no Russian presence in this part of Berlin.

Karl's head was throbbing violently as they drove up to the camp. Out of the blue, a burst of machine gun fire shattered the windscreen of their vehicle and punched holes in the bonnet. Joe slammed on the breaks and they both rolled out of the vehicle and took cover behind it.

"Wait, we're on your side," Karl called out. "We're expected by Major Kowalski." Karl's attempt to talk to the soldiers firing on them was met with another burst of fire that tore into the vehicle and the ground next to them, throwing up clumps of earth.

"What the hell are they playing at?" Karl said to Joe. "They should know that we're coming."

"Beats me," said Joe and shrugged.

"We're not German," shouted Karl. "We're OSS, ask your commanding officer." Karl pulled out his binoculars and focused on the machine gun nest. It was right on the border of the camp. There two men manning a DP28 MP model 1910 heavy machine gun, capable of firing 500 to 600 rounds a minute. Karl could tell that the men were not very experienced, as they had left themselves wide open to enemy fire. For the first time in the war he had a clear shot at two people who were firing on him, yet he was unable to take it.

"Should we wave a white flag or something," said Joe. "Pretend to surrender, then explain ourselves later?"

"Over my dead body," said Karl.

"If you catch a stray bullet, it might have to be." Just at that moment Karl saw a young lieutenant charge over to the nest waving his arms. A few feet behind him was Tex. The two machine gunners stood down and the lieutenant called out to them. "It's okay, we know who you are, you can come out now."

Karl put away his binoculars and came out from behind their vehicle. Joe followed him uncertainly. "What the hell were you guys playing at?" Karl demanded as the lieutenant came to greet him.

"I'm sorry about that," the lieutenant said. "But you were supposed to come in to the camp by a different route. No-one told the sentries on this side of the perimeter to expect you. They thought you were Nazis."

Karl turned to Joe. "Did you know about this route?"

"I might have done," Joe smirked. "But there were more bumps along this road and you've still got a hangover."

"Ol' Karl's been blowing the froth off too many sarsaparillas has he?" laughed Tex.

Karl massaged his temple and nodded. "Okay Joe," he said offering his hand. "I guess you got me there." Joe's smirk turned into a broad grin and he reached for Karl's hand. Before he could take it Karl sucker punched him with a powerful right hook. Joe fell on his backside and spat out a tooth.

"Hey," he whined. "That's assault, I could report you for that!"

"Steady on ol' buddy," said Tex helping Joe to his feet. "Let's not go jumping any guns. He got you good alright. You lost a tooth huh? Let's have a look at that." Tex lifted Joe's chin and Joe tilted his head back and grinned to let Tex get a better look at his tooth. Tex smashed his forehead into the bridge of Joe's nose. There was an audible crack as Joe's nose broke in several places and blood gushed out. Joe's legs gave out from under him and he slumped to the floor again. "Looks like you took one too many bumps on that road," said Tex. "Guess you should have taken a different route after all."

Karl and Tex left Joe to lick his wounds. The lieutenant took them to the largest tent in the camp to meet Major Kowalski. The Major was a short man of no more than five foot six. He was in his late thirties and his iron grey hair was clipped into a buzz cut. He had very Polish features and an aggressive, phlegmatic manner. Karl didn't imagine he suffered fools very gladly.

"So you're the OSS boys causing all the ruckus in my camp, are you?" he barked at them when they entered his tent with the lieutenant. "You better have something worth dragging me and my men all the way into Berlin."

"Don't you worry about that Major," said Tex.

The Major fixed Tex with an intimidating glare. "I'll tell you what I do worry about soldier. Military protocol. I don't know what kind of rogue operation you're running out here in Berlin, but in the US army we don't address a commanding officer like that. Do I make myself clear?"

"Perfectly sir!" said Tex snapping to attention. Karl followed suit.

"Dismissed," Kowalski said to the lieutenant, who

seemed relieved and left as quickly as he could. "At ease," Kowalski said to Karl and Tex. Then he lit a foul smelling cigar and walked over to a folding table where a map of the centre of Berlin was spread out. He looked down at the map and blew a cloud of blue smoke at it. "What we have here gentlemen," he said, in a portentous voice, "is a siege situation."

After a pause he looked up. "I don't like siege situations." Tex shot Karl a glance that said 'we've got a tough one here'. Karl rolled his eyes in reply, saying 'tell me about it'.

"Say what you like about the German army," said Kowalski chewing on his cigar. "They know how to run a military operation. They've got this area fortified well. They've found the only tenement square still standing in the centre of Berlin and they've turned it into a fortress. They could defend this ground for days against an army twice the size of the one I've brought and we've got a matter of hours to take it. I'm going to lose a lot of men to no good purpose unless you can give me something to work with." Kowalski emphasized this last point by waving his cigar under Karl's nose and poking him in the chest. "I understand you're the only agent we've got who has had a good look at the defences of this launch site,"

"That's right," said Karl.

"So what can you tell me?"

Karl picked up a piece of paper and a pencil from the side of the table. He began to sketch out the tenement square. "There are two perimeters, the Russians control the outer perimeter, the Germans have charge of the inner. There are four roads into the square, each of them has sentries and a checkpoint. The Germans control the two entrances on their side of the square, the Russians man the entrances on theirs. There's a lot of hostility between the two nationalities and the rank and file troops are kept as far from each other as possible. We could use this to our advantage."

"They could just as easily band together against a common foe," said Kowalski. "Namely us. The Russians aren't going to be our allies for very much longer. There's a whole different war coming and this little plot is just the start of it. Carry on."

"By my estimation, there are two platoons of Nazis posted in the square. The majority of these are involved in some way with the launch of the rocket. There are another two NKVD platoons, they're providing security for the operation and making sure the Nazis do as they're told. I estimate that there are also about four snipers positioned on the roofs of the buildings. I can't tell you if they are Russian or German."

"It doesn't matter what side they're on," said Kowalski. "They'll be firing on my men. Now, I make that around 240 men in total. That puts the odds in our favour as long as we can find a way of getting a lot of men into that square in a short space of time. Otherwise they'll be able to hold us off with more than enough time to fire that damn rocket of theirs on Washington."

"Sir," said Tex. "Couldn't we take out one row of buildings with mortar fire and blow a path directly into the square?"

"Do you have any idea how many mortars we'd need to do that boy? We might blow a hole in their fortifications large enough to get our men through. But what if just one stray mortar hit the rocket? From what I've been told about the A bomb, it could send us all up and wipe out the centre of Berlin."

"Sir, the idea does have some merit though," said Karl, coming to Tex's defence. "You just admitted that if we could blow a hole large enough in one of the rows of buildings then we could get our men quickly into the square. Probably quickly enough to over run the Nazis and the NKVD and capture the missile to boot."

"Yes," said Kowalski. "But it would be suicidally irresponsible to use mortar fire to do so."

"What if there was another way of taking out a row of buildings, even more effectively and without endangering the rocket or the warhead?"

"I'm listening."

"When I left the square after infiltrating it, I met a British agent working for the SOE. He was running a surveillance operation on the square that went wrong. I helped him escape and we got away down a service hatch that led to the U-Bahn system. The agent, Captain Daniel Brown is his name, is well trained in sabotage and explosives, and has committed the whole system of underground tunnels to memory. There's a disused tunnel that runs right under the square. It isn't very far from the surface. If we laid enough explosives, with his help, we could collapse the tunnel under the southern row of buildings and they would just fall into the crater left behind."

Major Kowalski didn't reply. He turned his back on Tex and Karl and walked away from them. Then he turned on his heel as if he had made a decision and fixed them with another question. "This British agent. You can vouch for him?"

"Me and Tex both sir."

"Sir I met Captain Brown when I got this," Tex pointed to a freshly stitched wound on his forehead. "If he hadn't have come to help us it could have been a hell of a lot worse."

Kowalski nodded. "It's not a standard siege strategy,

but it has some tactical advantage. If we attack from one side of the square only, we cut the platoons on the perimeter in half. By the time the soldiers on the opposite side of the square realise they're under attack and retreat into the centre we'll already be waiting for them. The collapse of the buildings will not only cause casualties to the NKVD troops posted on the south side, it will throw them all into disarray making it easier for us to secure the whole area quickly and cleanly."

Kowalski strode out of the entrance of his tent and barked at the guard. "Get me Lieutenant Binkley right now! I've got lists to make. I've got to get in touch with the Major-General Gubbins, head of SOE, and get this Captain assigned to my command. I've got to get my hands on enough explosive to demolish a street." The Major stopped talking to himself and fired a question a Karl. "I need to take out the snipers on the roofs and replace them with men of my own. I've got to do it before the main offensive, so I can't call any attention to the manoeuvre. How am I going to do that?"

"Sir," said Karl. "We could use a crossbow. Tex liberated one back in Munich and with his help I've become proficient with it. It doesn't have the range of a rifle but get close enough and it's just at deadly, and completely silent."

"How do you plan to get close enough?"

"There's a service entrance in the tunnel that comes out near the opposite wall," Karl suddenly remembered. "It's inside the perimeter so I shouldn't be seen. I could join the tunnel party along with the other members of the sniper corps. Once the other side's snipers are taken care of we can take our positions on the roof with little likelihood of being detected."

Karl and Tex saw Kowalski do something for the very

first time. He smiled. Even though it lit his face up, it was apparent that he didn't do it very often. They could tell that those facial muscles were not well used. "Gentlemen," he said. "You've definitely earned your pay today. And I'm gonna make damn certain that you earn it come zero hour, so you better be prepared."

"Yes sir," said Tex, he and Karl saluted and held it until the Major returned the gesture. As he did Lieutenant Binkley returned.

"Binkley, get me a working telephone and a radio operator," Kowalski ordered. "These men are due to see that wretch from the liberated camp as well. See that they're escorted will you?"

"Yes Major," said Binkley and showed Karl and Tex out of the tent.

He instructed one of his men to take them to see Herr Mann. The private took them to a small wooden building at edge of the park that had probably once belonged to the park keeper. The two guards on the door waved them through and the private left them to it.

Herr Mann stood up nervously the minute they walked in. Then sat down again straight afterwards otherwise his impossibly frail legs would have collapsed under him. He was skeletally thin and emaciated. His head had been shaved and the hair was just beginning to grow back. His cheeks were sunken, as were his eyes. The skin hung loose all over his body.

"Excuse me," he said timidly. "I do not seem to have enough strength to stand to attention."

"That's alright pardner," said Tex. "You sit tight where you are."

"You speak very good English," said Karl. "I can hardly

determine an accent."

"I studied for my doctorate in Physics at Cambridge University. It was my second. I wrote my first thesis in mathematics at Heidelberg."

"So you're a double doctor," said Tex, impressed. "We should call you Herr Docktor not Herr Mann."

"My name is not Mann," he said. "It is a joke of the guards. One of them said I looked like his Uncle Herman so they started calling me Herr Mann."

"What's your real name?" asked Karl.

"For the past two years it has been simply inmate 21792/45."

"We'll stick with Herr Docktor," said Karl. "If you don't mind."

"I am told that you gentlemen wish to know about the nuclear charge on mein General's case. Am I to assume that you will be attempting to relieve him of it? It will be a dangerous enterprise and you risk many lives in the taking."

"Just how powerful is the charge?" asked Karl.

"It can do two megatons worth of damage," said Herr Docktor. "The blast will kill everyone within a radius of miles. The fall out will kill many more. There is unlikely to be a safe place to be in the whole of Berlin if the case is detonated. Please take great care with what you are doing gentlemen."

"We intend to," said Tex. "Now, I've been told that opening the case, or taking it more than ten feet away from General Helmstadt will detonate the charge. Is that right?"

"That is correct. If the case is opened, or if mein General's heart stops, the devices planted in his body and the case will break the circuit that is keeping the bomb disarmed, thereby arming it and causing its detonation.

In this way he can guarantee both his life and complete control of our country's nuclear secrets."

"You can open the case if you use the right code though," said Karl. "That also disarms it right?"

"It is unlikely that you will ever get hold of this code. Everyone who ever knew it apart from General Helmstadt has been executed. Although I worked on arming and constructing the case, I was merely sent to a camp because I didn't know the code. My ignorance is the only reason I am still alive, albeit barely."

"All the same," said Tex. "If we did have the code, how would we use it?"

"I wonder if you have a pencil and paper about you?" said Herr Docktor. "I will have to draw you a diagram to show you properly."

"Right here," said Tex, producing a note pad and pencil from his top pocket.

Herr Docktor took the pencil and pad and started to sketch the top of the case, showing the handle and the clasps. His pencil strokes were precise and clear but his hand shook and it seemed a gargantuan effort for him just to hold the pencil. "You must forgive the time it takes for me to draw. I am weak from lack of food."

"Why?" said Karl, "aren't they feeding you?"

"I have not eaten proper food for some years. Your American rations are too rich for me. They feed me three times a day but I can keep very little of it down. Hence my condition."

"I'm sorry," said Karl. "Would you please continue with what you were saying?"

"Certainly," said Herr Docktor. He pointed at the diagram with his pencil. "This is the top of the case, either side of the ivory handle are three sets of tumblers. The code tells you what successive combinations of numbers to turn the tumblers to. There are twelve numbers in the code, broken into four sets of three. You put the first and fourth sets of three into the left tumbler, and the second and third sets of three into the right tumbler. Are you following me?"

"So far," said Tex.

"There are six tiny glass bulbs just above the handle, split into two groups. After you have put the code in, they will flash in a sequence of green, red, red, green. When they have, you will hear a hiss from inside the case and then a low hum. On the left side of the case there are three more tiny bulbs. If they flash green then red then green, then the case is disarmed and you can move it away from mein General and open it. If they flash red one more time after that it is an indication that something has not worked with the code and that you should enter it again. Please take note of this, otherwise the case might not be disarmed and cannot be moved away from General Helmstadt."

"I will," said Tex. "You've been a great help to the United States, thanks."

"Is there anything we can get you?" asked Karl.

"I am content merely to be of service in the downfall of my former masters. There is nothing that I need, except to assuage my conscience while I wait quietly to die."

"Hey there doc," said Tex. "I know you've been through an ordeal, but you're safe in US custody now. They've got people here who can help you. You don't have to throw in the towel yet."

"But I want to, as you put it, throw in the towel. I have seen too many atrocities to want to go on living and, God help me, I have committed some myself. This is my judgement on myself. I have been to hell gentlemen. Your soldiers may have liberated our bodies from the camp in

Buchenwald but they have not liberated our hearts or our minds. There they will always remain. Perhaps in death I may be allowed to finally escape, although I doubt it."

"I've heard rumours about what goes on in these camps," said Karl. "But you know, there's a lot of propaganda cooked up by all sides about the enemies we're facing. I never knew how much of it was true."

"More than you have been told. It seems too impossible. That's why it is so easy to dismiss the camps and to deny they ever existed. They did though, and the truth of their existence must be faced not just by the German people, but by humanity as a whole. The simple fact that they could be allowed to exist here in the twentieth century condemns us all. That is why I am content to spend my last hours betraying my country to enemies of the Fatherland like you."

"Hey now buddy," said Tex. "You're doing a good thing here, you should know that after what you've seen. I mean we all love our country..."

"Yes we do," said Herr Docktor. "And perhaps men like us are guilty of loving it too much, maybe that is why we can do the things we do in its name. But I wonder how much the blood on our hands actually helps our fellow countrymen. I was a bitter man before the war. In spite of my academic achievements I could not find a suitable post in my own country. I was full of anger and I needed someone to blame for my situation. Like many young men of that time I blamed the Jews. They were very prominent in my country and very successful. They seemed to hold all the best jobs, to control all the universities, the banks and the economy. They were running them all for the benefit of themselves and their quislings.

"The Fatherland was on its knees after the last war. We did not lose because of the superiority of the enemy forces. We lost because we were stabbed in the back by the enemies within our own country. The socialists, the liberals, the Jews and homosexuals, all of whom were now profiting from the sorry state they had put us in. I thought this to be most unjust. I wanted something to be done about it. I wanted the prestige and recognition that I felt I deserved.

"When the Nazis seized power I was sure all of this would change, and it did. I joined the SS and rose to prominence. My achievements were properly recognised at last and I came to the attention of General Helmstadt, the man who was to prove my undoing."

"Because he sent you to the camp?" said Karl. "For knowing too much about the case."

"No. If the truth be told I chose to go to the camp. I had a warning you see. I could have escaped before they came for me, but I decided not to. I decided that I should be punished for what I had done. I caused the death of many brilliant minds, captured scientists, Polish, Jewish and Czechoslovakian, leading thinkers in their field. Men whose papers I had read before the war. I watched them die of radiation poisoning, their bodies swelling out all proportion, their skin blistering and their teeth and hair falling out, all in the name of Nazi science.

"I could have lived with that though. The amount that we were able to learn, the scientific progress we achieved in such a short space of time seemed to almost justify it. They were still vermin I told myself, little better than lab rats with freakishly developed intellect. What I couldn't live with was what happened to other members of their family and my part in that.

"General Helmstadt has certain tastes, certain predispositions that, out of personal shame for my part in assisting with them, I daren't tell you about. In a way they are the final condemnation of the third Reich, in that they allowed a man of General Helmstadt's character to rise to such prominence. Someone should have put a stop to him a long time ago. With the information I have given you I hope you will now be able to."

"We'll put a stop to him," said Karl.

"Don't you worry about that," added Tex. "And we'll make certain the information he's carrying gets into safe hands."

"Ah yes," said Herr Docktor. "By that you mean American hands of course. It is dangerous information gentlemen. It contains secrets that will change the face of the world forever. I wonder if it will be any safer in American hands than it is in German."

One of the guards entered the room and told Karl and Tex that Major Kowalski required them to return to the main tent and review street maps. They excused themselves from Herr Docktor's company and left with the most perfunctory of farewells. Herr Docktor had as little strength for goodbyes as he had for anything else.

"What do you make of the ghoul?" asked the guard who showed them out. Tex shook his head and Karl said nothing. It was as hard to shake off Herr Docktor's cynicism and resignation as it was to shake off the air of death that hung all around him.

After all the things that the man had seen and done, Karl could not help wonder what he considered so shameful about his relationship with General Helmstadt that he still didn't dare reveal it. What had he helped Helmstadt do that was so unspeakable he had condemned himself to a lingering death in a concentration camp?

CHAPTER TWENTY-FOUR

"Fancy a fag old man?" said a British SOE agent, slapping Tex playfully on the back. Tex swung round and glared angrily.

"Steady on cowboy," said Daniel stepping in to the breach. "He means a smoke, not what you're thinking."

"Why, what was he thinking?" asked the British agent, whose name was Roger Landes

Daniel smiled. "He thinks you meant a poof."

"Heaven's no! A puff of smoke more like."

"That would send the whole tunnel sky high though," said Karl a little non-plussed.

"That's why it was a joke old man," said Roger teasingly. "Still, in the dark, all this way under ground would you really mind who had their hands on you?"

"Just try putting them on my fanny," snarled Tex. "Then you'll find out."

"You Americans have fannies do you?" said Roger, now sounding non-plussed himself.

"Yeah," said Karl. "Don't you British?"

"Well the British army does," said Daniel. "In the form of the FANYs; the First Aid Nursing Yeomanry. They provided a good front for us to bring women agents into the field in France, helped us get around a few tricky clauses in the Geneva Convention saying women can't participate in active warfare. In Britain however only ladies have fannies, around the front that is. Gentlemen have, err... other appendages."

"You know," said Roger. "I speak five languages fluently, but I don't think I'll ever properly understand American."

"Thank God we're allies then," said Daniel.

"Amen to that," said Tex, and finished connecting the charges to the load of explosive over their heads. They were standing in the uppermost of the three U-Bahn tunnels that ran beneath the south street of tenement buildings in the launch site square.

Karl's hunch about Daniel's invaluable knowledge of explosives and the U-Bahn tunnels had really paid off. Daniel had co-opted his whole spy ring 'circuit', as the SOE called it, into helping out. Ten British agents, or 'Bods' as he dubbed them, were scattered throughout the U-Bahn tunnels laying explosive in preparation for the coming battle.

Where Daniel had really come up trumps though, was in pointing out to Major Kowalski that three different tunnels from separate U-Bahn lines, ran under the launch site, one beneath the other. They intersected in two key positions below the southern street. Daniel suggested that if they were to plant a series of explosives in each tunnel, at the point where it crossed beneath the tunnel overhead, then timed each explosion so that the tunnel above would fall into the one below it in succession, they could create a crater deep enough to cause every building to disappear from view in a matter of seconds.

"Right then lads," he said when they had primed all the explosives. "That's us. It's time to make our way back up to the service entrance." Karl and Tex followed Daniel and Roger as they made their way back up. There were four other snipers from the OSS elite corps, and one further SOE 'Bod', waiting for them at the bottom of the shaft.

There was an air of nervous anticipation among the snipers. They were going into a battle situation that would put them in a lot greater jeopardy than they were used to. To take up their positions they had to run the gauntlet of German soldiers on the inner perimeter, behind which they would come out, and any snipers on the roof that Karl didn't pick off with his crossbow. This was not to mention the close combat they might have to face getting to the roofs of the tenement.

In addition to this the snipers were very aware that they were working alongside the two highest-ranking snipers in the US army. Even though Tex could no longer shoot, they still held him in awe. Karl knew only one of the four snipers, a tall man called Masterson who sported a neatly trimmed black beard. He had graduated from Westpoint the year before Karl and Tex. The others had all graduated after Karl began his active service. The youngest, Johnson – a blond, Nordic looking young man in his early twenties – had only been in the field since the middle of last year. The other two, Mailer and Hardy, had also graduated from Westpoint two years ago with that year's joint highest ranking. Mailer, a wiry little tough guy who stood only five foot seven, had since moved ahead in the sniper's ranking, overtaking Hardy, a tall red head with a quarterback's physique. A fact that Karl could see annoyed Hardy no end.

Karl and Tex, followed by the four snipers climbed the metal rungs up to the street. When they reached the top they removed the metal grate and Karl stepped out into the street while the others remained out of sight in the shaft.

Karl quickly found cover behind some fallen masonry and used his binoculars to find the two snipers on the roof of the tenement. The sniper furthest from him was lying behind a chimneystack and Karl would not be able to hit him from where he was currently stationed. However, the man could not see his fellow marksman from where he was stationed. This meant Karl could take out the sniper closest to him without being spotted.

This sniper was not so well hidden as his colleague. He had chosen a good position on the corner of the roof, which afforded him a great view of the terrain below, but in doing so he had made himself too prominent and was an easy target. Using the rudimentary sights of the crossbow, Karl drew a bead on the sniper. This was not easy as he was shooting from an upward angle that was always awkward to accommodate, especially when firing a bolt rather than a bullet.

Once he was certain that he had the shot, Karl released the bolt. It shot upwards and hit the sniper in the throat severing his windpipe so he couldn't cry out. The man started violently and his hand went to the bolt, unable to believe that it had suddenly appeared there as his blood poured into the gutter just beneath him.

Karl came out from behind the fallen masonry and moved to a new position by a pile of discarded sand bags, taking great care not to be seen by any of the soldiers on the inner perimeter. He had a clear shot at the other sniper now. Unfortunately the sniper also had a clear shot at Karl when he spotted him behind the sand bags.

The man levelled his rifle and aimed. Karl did the same with his crossbow. It was a race against time to see who made the shot first. Karl released his crossbow bolt just a fraction sooner. It shot right through the sniper's telescopic sight, pierced his eyeball and embedded itself in his brain. The man's finger was still on the trigger when he died and he jerked involuntarily and let off a shot. It whistled past Karl's and struck the ground right next to him. More importantly it alerted the guards on the inner perimeter, something Karl had been desperate to avoid.

He shifted around to the other side of the sand bags

as three guards raced over. Karl had one crossbow bolt left. He should have had more but in the confusion he couldn't seem to find them. He loaded the bolt, drew back the string and shot the guard on the right straight through the heart. The guard squealed like a stuck pig and looked down at the bolt. Then he fell face first into the dirt.

Karl threw the crossbow aside, pulled out his P-38 and attached the silencer. He took out the second guard with a bullet to the head first time around. The third guard was bobbing and weaving about to make himself much harder to hit. He ducked behind a half demolished wall then turned and ran back to get reinforcements. Karl shot him twice in the back before he could call out for help.

He whistled to the others that the coast was clear and they climbed out of the service entrance. Tex shot off in a different direction. He was not joining the snipers and had a different objective at this point in the mission. Most of the snipers had seen a good deal of what had just happened from where they were. They knew that time was now of the essence if they were to take their positions.

Karl led them over to the one backdoor on that side of the row of buildings. He smashed the heel of his boot into the door but it refused to give. Hardy added his considerable bulk, as did Johnson, but it still refused to shift.

Karl pointed to a window, just above head height to the left of the door. He told Hardy to give him a hand up. Karl put the window through with the butt of his rifle and climbed in. Hardy then helped Mailer, Masterson and Johnson up, then Karl and Johnson reached down and helped Hardy in.

The building smelled of damp and desertion. It had

been gutted and looted like most of the buildings but a few hints that it had once been a home still existed. Torn shreds of floral wallpaper still clung to a few, there were shards of what might once have been the 'good china' and scraps of family photos in among the dirt on the floor.

Karl led the four men up the stairs towards the roof. On the second landing Karl heard a groan coming from a room on their left. He motioned for everyone to be silent. There was another longer groan. Someone had left his post to make use of the lavatory, Karl imagined. Such little luxuries meant everything in wartime. He signalled to the men to standby, counted down from five with his left hand then kicked the door open.

To their complete surprise they saw a Russian private with his trousers round his ankles and an officer of the SS kneeling in front of him. Neither Karl nor the other four men had been expecting this display of international accord. When they saw Karl and the other four, both men started guiltily. The private grabbed his trousers and the SS officer reached for his Luger.

Karl smashed the butt of his rifle into the officer's shoulder before the man could find his weapon. The private made a bolt for the stairs. Hardy caught him in a headlock. The private struggled but Hardy overpowered him and crushed his windpipe, his legs kicked and then he went limp.

The SS officer sprawled back on the floor of the lavatory. Before he could get up Karl brought his rifle butt down hard on the man's face. Karl heard bone and cartilage snap. He smashed the butt repeatedly into the officer's face. An eyeball popped out its socket. The officer's face was mashed to hamburger meat and he lay still. Karl wiped the congealed gore off his rifle butt with an old curtain.

The five of them shared incredulous looks, shook their heads and laughed. "You know, call me an old romantic," said Masterson. "But shouldn't we at least have let them finish first?"

"Maybe you coulda joined 'em if you'd asked," said Mailer. "Two's company but three's allowed."

"There's only one thing of mine any German's gonna be sucking," said Masterson. "And that's a bullet."

"Okay guys," said Karl. "We don't have time for this. We need to be up on that roof."

They tramped up to the attic and found a skylight that they jimmied open. Karl crawled out and the others followed. They found the bodies of the dead snipers, dragged them back to the skylight and dumped them in the attic. Karl gave the other four snipers their positions and the men went and filled them. Each man was carefully hidden from enemy fire and had at least one escape route in the event of being discovered.

Karl took up his position in the middle of the tenement roofs. He was neatly hidden between the crest of the central roof and a large square chimney. He had a perfect view of everything that was taking place in the square.

It had been fairly easy for Karl and the other snipers to get into position because the square was such a hive of activity that there were few people to notice. Kowalski and Max had both kept the square under constant surveillance since the plan of attack had been approved so they would know exactly when to strike. They didn't have to wait long. Even with all the privations of operating in a city under siege, German planning and efficiency were so well honed that the US and the British hardly had time to put their plan into operation.

This was the first moment Karl had had to stop and

simply watch since the go-ahead was given. Through his binoculars, he watched the preparations being made in the square. The technicians were working at a fever pitch to make all the last minute adjustments. The last time Karl had seen the square the lawn in the middle was being dug up and replaced with concrete. Now the concrete had dried and an Abschussplatform, a steel launching table like the one that Karl had seen in the missile silo, was standing in the middle of it.

A Meillerwagen was standing alongside it, and its mechanical arm was raising a primed V-10 rocket into position on the launching table. Two alcohol supply vehicles, a pump and a towed liquid oxygen vehicle were also being manoeuvred into position next to the rocket.

Over on the southeast corner of the square Karl could see Gruppenführer Kammler standing with two troop commanders by the firing control vehicle. The troop commanders were overseeing the preparations under Kammler's watchful eye. Kammler's personal guard stood near by. All ten men wore tense and expectant expressions that made Karl think that Kammler had something planned.

Their tension increased as an armoured car drove into the square from the southwest corner, followed by a large, armour plated truck, flanked on all sides by armed SS soldiers on motorbikes. The armoured car came to a halt. The lead SS soldier dismounted and held the door open. Two bodyguards stepped out followed by a tall, overweight man in an SS General's uniform carrying a large metal case. Karl recognised the man from the photographs Max and Chuck had shown him: SS General Friedrich Helmstadt.

An officer climbed down from the truck, walked up to Helmstadt and made the Nazi salute. Helmstadt acknowledged the salute and gave the officer instructions. The officer returned to the truck. The back of the truck opened and a squadron of heavily armed SS soldiers got out. Helmstadt made his way over to greet Kammler, surrounded by his bodyguards.

The two small crowds of guards around Helmstadt and Kammler parted as Helmstadt arrived at the firing control vehicle. Helmstadt stood seven or eight feet away from Kammler and nodded. Kammler returned the nod a little more graciously. They exchanged greetings in a stiff and formal manner. Both men tried to hide how aware they were of the case Helmstadt was carrying, and how much it meant in this whole power play.

They reminded Karl of two samurai masters before a duel. Each of them weighed up the other, searching for a tiny flaw in their opponent's defences. Neither man gave anything away.

Six soldiers carried a large metal canister out of the back of the armour-plated truck. The canister had a sign on the side to show it contained radioactive material. This was the nuclear warhead. A terrifying new weapon and the harbinger of the age of nuclear warfare.

The moment had arrived. The future history of many nations would be decided by the next few shots Karl would take.

He put down his binoculars and began to track all six men in his sights. He had to make certain they were far enough away from the south side of the square before he struck. He couldn't risk the warhead being too close to the southern row of buildings when they were demolished.

As the six soldiers approached the rocket Karl let out a breath and took aim. From the angle at which he was firing, he would have to shoot straight past the fuel supplies. He couldn't afford to shoot wide. If a single stray bullet hit either the fuel or the canister the results would be disastrous.

Karl fixed the middle soldier on the left hand side of the canister in his cross hairs. There was no margin for error. He let the man walk into the shot, pulled the trigger and took the back of his head off. The man fell. The soldier in front of him stumbled with the extra weight of the canister, as did the soldier in back of him, who was wearing the dead soldier's brains all over his face. Before any of the five remaining soldiers could properly react, Karl took down the middle soldier on the right with another perfect headshot.

This was the signal for the beginning of the offensive. Many things happened at once. Every member of the US and British military went into action.

The other four snipers began firing at select targets, sowing as much confusion and panic as they could. Their shots were important cover for Karl's. They made it impossible for any of the soldiers on the ground to pin point exactly where the shots were coming from.

Karl shot the soldier to the front right of the canister. The other three were forced to place it carefully on the ground and seek cover. He shot two more as they ran bewildered, but lost the last in the general confusion of the square. This was no matter. He had secured his first objective. The warhead was undefended and in the close vicinity of the rocket.

As soon as Karl took his second shot he heard a flare go up behind him. That was Tex. The flare was a signal to the SOE agents, who were waiting by surrounding U-Bahn service entrances to detonate the explosives they had laid.

The first to respond to the sniper fire raking the square were the Russian snipers on the opposite side. Johnson took a bullet in the shoulder. Karl heard his scream. He glanced and over and was relieved to see that the young man was still alive. He traced the direction of the shot back to its source and found the Russian sniper in his sights.

Before Karl could take the shot, a huge tremor shook the ground as the explosives in the lowest tunnel went off. He had to cling to the roof to stop from falling off. Slates rattled free, chimney pots tumbled to the ground below.

Another larger tremor followed it and a third in rapid succession. In the square soldiers were knocked off their feet. Some were struck by falling slates or crushed by masonry.

None of them knew what was going on. None of them expected what happened next.

A giant crater ripped the ground apart beneath the south row. Every building plummeted into the chasm and disappeared from view in a matter of seconds. A mound of rubble and a giant cloud of thick dust appeared where less than a minute ago there had been a row of five-storey houses.

There was the sudden sound of cheering and gunfire. Bullets tore through the thick cloud of dust and five hundred of the fiercest US fighting men followed them.

The American troops charged over the mound and into the square. Major Kowalski stood at the very summit of the mound: a cigar stub in one hand, an MP40 sub-machine gun in the other, firing bullets and orders to the men pouring into the square all around him.

Karl switched his binoculars to the southeast corner, the firing control vehicle had been overturned in the demolition but Helmstadt, Kammler and their men were unhurt. Kammler's men sprung to their feet first. They pulled out their pistols and shot Helmstadt's bodyguards. Then six of them hauled Helmstadt to his feet and frogmarched him towards a building on the east of the square. The other four surrounded Kammler, providing covering fire as they escorted him to the same building.

Kammler was making his move. Karl would have to do something quick to keep the plan on track.

He moved from behind the chimneystack and slid down the roof to the eave. Once his feet touched the thin stone ledge he shuffled along to the eastern corner. Above him on the roof Mailer and Hardy continued to pick off enemy soldiers. Behind him on the ground the soldiers on the perimeter were charging to the defence of the square, unaware they were going to their slaughter.

Karl rounded the northeast corner and nearly lost his footing as the eave disappeared. He had to clamber up the steep roof and crawl along the top.

As a fierce and bloody battle raged, five storeys below, Karl edged his way up to the skylight in the roof of the building where Kammler's men had taken General Helmstadt. He lowered himself down the roof until he was over the skylight then shattered the glass with his boot and dropped into the room below.

The attic was dark and filled with musty boxes covered in mouldering dustsheets. Karl listened carefully. Three floors below him he could hear shouting in German. He lifted the trap door and dropped to the landing below.

Karl could make out the voices more clearly now. One of them he recognised as Kammler's. The other had a thick Munich accent and the unmistakable ring of authority to it. Karl guessed it must be Helmstadt. It was commanding the men not to open the case unless they were ready to face death. Kammler was telling him to be quiet.

Karl crept softly down four flights of stairs following

the sound of the voices. As he came down the last flight he saw the door to the main room on that floor was open. He leant over the banister and peered in.

Five men were standing around Helmstadt. Another was kneeling in front of him turning the tumblers on the case. He was holding a piece of paper with the code written on it. It seems Kammler had made a back up copy after all, just in case.

Kammler was also taking the risk of being present when the case was deactivated. The whole manoeuvre was bold and desperate, but the Nazis were cornered and Kammler had obviously been forced to improvise.

All of the men in the room had their backs to the door. Karl assumed the other four men, who had escorted Kammler into the building, must have been guarding the front door.

Karl pulled out his pistol and strode confidently in to the room. He shot the man kneeling over the case in the back of the head. Before any of the other men could remove their weapons he shot the two men on either side of Kammler. He grabbed Kammler from behind around the throat and put his pistol to the Gruppenführer's temple.

He took two steps back towards the door so he had the other three men fully in his field of vision and told them to drop their weapons. They looked at Kammler who nodded and they all threw a gun to the floor each. "All of them," Karl snapped. "Or you can say good by to your leader here." The men all pulled out another weapon. Two had pistols in their boots, while the other had a knife in his belt. Once they were fully disarmed Karl shot them all, two in the chest, one in the head.

He led Kammler on to the landing with the pistol still at his head. "Where are the other four men?" Karl said.

"Two of them are dead," said Kammler. "The other two

are guarding the bottom of the stairs."

"Call them up."

"So you can shoot them? I don't think so. It's the young American assassin isn't it? The little thorn I can't remove from my side. I recognised your voice, you're Frederic Fairburne's boy." Karl jumped at this and Kammler felt it. His voice took on a sardonic and amused tone. "So I'm right then. I wondered why an American assassin would risk so much to kill me then waste his time quizzing me about a meeting I couldn't even recollect. I racked my brains for a few days and then I recalled what the meeting was about. Once I had done this I worked out Frederic Fairburne had a son who would be about your age. It had to be you. His career ended badly I recall and you, of course, blame me. I am not the one you should look to though. Wouldn't you like to know who is?"

Kammler paused. He was playing with Karl again, trying to lull him into complacency so he could strike. Karl knew this. He was about to speak when he heard a hammer being cocked and felt the barrel of a gun at the back of his head. "Drop your weapon," a voice said.

"You better do as my man tells you." Kammler said.

Two shots rang out and Karl heard the man behind him fall to the floor. He turned towards the doorway and saw General Helmstadt standing there, the metal case in one hand, a smoking Luger in the other. "He was lying about the other three men," said Helmstadt. "They are all dead."

Karl still had his pistol at Kammler's head. "I have information you require," said Kammler. "You once risked everything to get it. I am the only one who can tell you what you want. If you kill me now you will never know." Karl knew this might be his last chance to learn the truth. He also knew that Kammler was not to be trusted. He was simply stalling for time. Time was something that Karl did not have. He pulled the trigger on his pistol. He felt Kammler go rigid as the bullet blew the other side of the General's skull open. Karl felt the man's brains spatter his shoulder and he let go of Kammler's corpse. In that same instant he let go of his last chance to clear his father and himself.

Karl turned to Helmstadt who held up the case. "You know what this is don't you?" he said. Karl nodded. "Then you better get out of my way." Karl stepped to one side and let Helmstadt walk down the stairs and out the front door, knowing full well he was due to kill the man and steal his case in a matter of hours.

CHAPTER TWENTY-FIVE

Karl looked out of a first floor window. Outside in the square the fighting was all but over. Kowalski had captured the rocket and the nuclear warhead. The centre of the square, where the rocket stood, was filled with US soldiers. The surviving German technicians were lying face down with their hands behind their heads. Each of them held at gunpoint by two or more US soldiers.

The square was littered with the bodies of German and Russian soldiers. Under a third of the troops who had been guarding the area were left alive. Those that were, were kneeling in small groups or lying face down surrounded by their American captors.

The only exchange of fire still taking place was on the second floor of a building in the northwest corner. US troops were storming the building and a small handful of Germans were making one last desperate stand. The fighting was heated but ultimately doomed to failure on the German's part.

Helmstadt strode out into the square holding the case in front of him, as though it were a shield. Several US soldiers trained their weapons on him, but were quickly ordered by their officers to stand down. Kowalski's troops had been well briefed about Helmstadt and the case he was carrying.

"I want to speak to your commanding officer," Helmstadt shouted in a broad German accent.

Major Kowalski stepped forward warily. "That would be me."

Helmstadt lowered the case and drew himself up to his full height. He stared down at Kowalski who met his eye without flinching. "As you have stolen my warhead," said

Helmstadt. "I assume you will be aware of what I am carrying."

"Indeed I am," said Kowalski.

"You must also know that if this case gets more than ten feet away from me. Or if, for any reason, my heart stops then the nuclear device it contains will explode." Kowalski nodded without once taking his eyes off Helmstadt. "Imagine," Helmstadt continued. "What would happen if it were to detonate right next to an atomic warhead? It would leave a smouldering crater almost the size of Berlin, do you not think?"

"Something like that," said Kowalski, without giving anything away.

"I am going to go and get into my car," said Helmstadt. "I am going to take my driver and we are going to leave this square. No-one is to hinder me in any way. Is that clear?"

"I'm afraid I can't let you do that," said Kowalski. He was aware of the plan to let Helmstadt escape, but he couldn't make it look too easy.

Helmstadt walked over to Kowalski. He stopped inches away from the Major and placed the case at his feet. Then he turned on his heel and walked away. Sweat broke out on the Major's forehead. Kowalski glanced between the case at his feet and Helmstadt's back. He waited until Helmstadt was about nine feet away then lost his nerve.

"Wait! I understand you're leaving. I think you forgot something on your way out."

Helmstadt stopped walking. He turned slowly and looked down at Kowalski with an imperious sneer of triumph. "So I did," Helmstadt said. "How foolish of me."

Kowalski bent to pick up the case at his feet. "Stop," commanded Helmstadt. "I will retrieve the case." Karl could see that Kowalski did not like being told what to do, but he was also relieved that he didn't have to handle the case.

Helmstadt walked right back to the Major until they were practically toe to toe. He looked down at Kowalski with an arrogant and supercilious expression. Kowalski stared right back, undaunted. Helmstadt bent and picked up the case in a slow and measured manner. Then he turned his back on the Major again and walked over to the mound of rubble at the south of the square, where his armoured car still stood.

Helmstadt walked right at a crowd of US soldiers who were standing between him and his car. They stepped out of his way in a hurry. Helmstadt walked over to the soldier who had his driver at gunpoint. "Stand down and put away your weapon," he ordered. The soldier did as he said without question. Then realising that he had just obeyed an enemy officer he looked over to his NCO, who nodded to him that he had done the right thing.

The driver got to his feet and went and opened the door of the armoured car. Helmstadt climbed in, his driver got into the front seat and started the engine. The car drove across the square to the northeast corner. Everyone got out of its way as quickly as they could. Then Helmstadt was gone.

Karl couldn't help but marvel at the man. He certainly knew how to wield power and there was quite obviously nothing he wouldn't risk in order to gain it. The strain he must be under, carrying the case around, was more than Karl could imagine. The strength of purpose it must take to live every day in the certain knowledge that one tiny slip, or a momentary lapse of attention could ensure not only your death, but the death's of hundreds of thousands around you impressed Karl.

The pressure of living every second of every day in such close proximity to a weapon of such mass destruction would drive most people insane. To Helmstadt it was simply a method of increasing his power and influence over others. Such power did not come cheaply either. He had sentenced many brilliant and dedicated men to long and painful deaths in order to procure it. Yet it hardly seemed to trouble his conscience at all.

This was the man that Karl now found himself up against. In a matter of hours he would find out if he was up to the job.

First he had to go and pick up Yelena. He was still dressed as a member of the SS. So he would be at great risk if he were to go alone into the square. To avoid this he had planned another route out.

Karl went to the back window that looked out on to the terrain surrounding the square. The building had been an apartment block so there was no backdoor, but there was a fire escape. Karl put his head out of the window and checked the area through his binoculars to make sure there were no US troops securing the perimeter that might spot him leaving. The last thing he wanted was to draw some 'friendly fire'. He couldn't see any soldiers so he made his way as quickly and quietly down the fire escape as he could.

At the bottom he heard a whistle. It was Daniel, standing by the northeast corner. He signalled that the coast was clear on his side. Hugging the building, Karl ran quickly over to him. "Sounds like things went with a bang," said Daniel.

"We've captured the rocket and the warhead," said Karl. "Helmstadt got away as planned, but thanks to Kammler that was touch and go for a little while."

"Nothing messy I hope."

"Nothing I couldn't handle. How's the tunnel?"

"It's clear along the route you want to take. There's a bit of structural damage around the bottom of the entrance shaft, but as long as you're careful you shouldn't be putting yourself at too much risk. There's a hell of a lot of subsidence in the other tunnels though, so watch out for any craters. If you fall down one, you could be falling for a long way."

"I'll keep a careful eye out."

"Right, I better be off then," said Daniel. "I've got to go and make my report to your short and angry Major."

"We all have to sooner or later."

"Take care of yourself old chap. I'll have to take you for a drink when this whole business is sewn up."

"I look forward to it," said Karl. The two men shook hands then parted company.

Karl sprinted over to the U-Bahn service entrance and climbed down to the tunnel below.

He came out at a disused station. The safe house where Yelena was being kept was in the basement of a nearby terrace. The terrace itself had been destroyed in one of many bombing raids. The basements had remained intact and quite comfortable though, several had been apartments and a below ground level walkway connected them. The ruined terrace above ground provided ideal camouflage for the safe house below.

Hidden down a tiny road to the side was Karl's transport. Karl went to check on it before calling at the safe house. Under a tarpaulin and behind some metal trash cans he found a jeep. From the way some of the cans were scattered around the road and the way the tarpaulin was lying it looked as though there had been another vehicle left there which had been recently taken.

Karl went back to the terrace and walked down the

steps. He knocked on the door furthest to the right. An agent Karl didn't know answered. The safe house was being manned by operatives from Bern and wasn't under Max's jurisdiction. Isaac was also being kept at the safe house and after promising to find his daughters, then failing to make good on the promise, Karl was not keen to meet him.

Luckily he didn't have to. Isaac had apparently disappeared earlier that day and the other two agents guarding the safe house had gone to find out what might have happened.

The agent who answered the door went to get Yelena and left Karl in a reception room. It was furnished quite comfortably with mismatching pieces of furniture that had probably been salvaged from different houses in the terrace. Karl could hear the agent talking to Yelena. He couldn't make out all the words but his tone was warm and even a little deferential. He referred to Yelena as ma'am. From his accent Karl guessed the man was a Virginian and trying to be every bit the Southern gentleman.

The agent stepped into the room and held the door open for Yelena. "Why thank you Oliver," said Yelena, with a coy but knowing smile. "I shall miss being treated like a proper lady. Karl here could certainly take lessons from you." Oliver blushed and looked at the floor. "Are we ready to go?" she asked.

"Jeep's outside," said Karl and nodded to the street. He turned and walked out without waiting to see if Yelena was following. He was determined to show Yelena that he at least was not susceptible to her allure.

Karl started the engine up and Yelena climbed in beside him. They sat next to each other in silence for about twenty minutes as Karl drove along a series of backstreets so as not to run into any Russian patrols. Hellersdorf, where they were heading, and the surrounding districts of Marzahn and Köpenick had all fallen to the Soviet army and would be hazardous to Karl, dressed as he was.

"Which way are we headed?" he asked, breaking the silence.

"You might want to ask me in a less surly tone," said Yelena.

Karl sighed. "Are we going to have this the whole journey? Are you still sulking because I left you in OSS custody?"

"I'm sulking am I? That is strange. Am I the one refusing to talk? Have I sat behind the wheel with a petulant look on my face the whole journey?"

"What do you mean?"

"I do not think I am the one who is sulking. I think you are the one who is sulking because you have been told to take me along on your boys only adventure."

"That's ridiculous."

"I know it's ridiculous. You are a grown man and yet you insist on acting this way."

"Look," said Karl. "I know what this is all about."

"Do you?"

"Yes. You're just trying to get a rise out of me. To punish me for leaving you behind."

"Of course I am," said Yelena, her voice heavy with sarcasm. "Because I am so hurt that my big brave hero deserted me. All I've done since he left is sit around and pine for him." Karl snorted, unable to think of an answer. For a second he thought he saw a black Sedan in his rear view mirror. This was the second time he thought he saw it, just for the briefest of moments. Surely no one was following him.

"You will need to turn left here," said Yelena as they approached the main road into Marzahn, the district just before Hellesdorf.

"Alright," said Karl. "Maybe it was pretty low of me to slope off and leave you the way I did. I've got a job to do though, and orders to follow. I know you saved my skin on several occasions but I generally do work better alone. I couldn't have taken you with me even I'd wanted to, which frankly I didn't, for the reasons I've outlined all along."

"In spite of what you might believe," replied Yelena. "I do not hold a grudge against you for abandoning me. The only disappointment I felt was at the fact that you are exactly like all other men, which I should have expected. Men have always deserted women to go off to war. It's what they invented it for. So they can turn their back on their responsibilities and go off and kill. War is very addictive to men. It is a fantastic game to them, a game that wives and mothers and sisters only spoil. That is the only reason why your Geneva Convention denies us the right to go and fight ourselves. Without your own women around you can treat the women of other countries as nothing more than the spoils of war."

"Is that right?"

"Yes. That's right."

"And what would you know about it?"

"I know that my countrymen are raping every woman and practically every girl in Berlin. I know they are doing so in what they believe to be revenge for what the Germans did to my countrywomen. But they are not taking revenge for what Germany did to us. They are taking their revenge on womankind as a whole for what we do to them."

"You mean making us take a bath every so often. And stopping us swearing when you're around?"

"Yes. Your reasons are as petty and pathetic as that.

You need to turn left here."

Karl turned the jeep into what had once been a tree lined avenue. "You think you've got the whole of mankind summed up do you?"

"I've known enough men to be able to sum you all up."

"You haven't known me though, have you? Though I might be the only man in Berlin who can say that."

"No, I haven't known you in that sense. And for a while at least I thought that made you different. I have known you a lot more intimately than any of the men who were my lovers. We have killed together, and you are the only man in Berlin of whom I can say that."

"So you think you know me do you?"

"Better than you might imagine. Right again here."

Karl turned off the main street on to a smaller road that wound behind the derelict buildings of what had once been a slum. "I thought at first that your treatment of me was gallantry," said Yelena. "But I was wrong. The only reason you don't want me in the same way every other man wants me, is because can't have me that way. You are impotent. I don't know if you are physically capable or not, but you are certainly emotionally impotent and you have no physical desires. That is why you kill. Because you can't make love and you can't make life. So you spread death instead. It is why you have such an extraordinary talent for it."

They pulled up at a crossroads on the very outskirts of Hellesdorf. Tex was waiting for them. Mounted on one of the motorbikes they'd captured from the SS soldiers escorting Helmstadt. He pulled alongside the jeep. "How's it going there pardner? Nice work in the square." Then he clocked Yelena, broke into a broad grin and turned on all his Texan charm. "So this is the mysterious lady you've been keeping secret. No wonder you've been keeping quiet about her. You didn't tell me she was this good looking. Name's Tex ma'am."

"Yelena," she replied, daintily offering him her hand. "And you flatter me Tex."

Tex kissed her hand gallantly and his grin became even broader. "I'm just telling the truth ma'am," he said. "I hope ol' Karl here has been treating you like a gentleman,"

"More than you might know."

"More fool him," said Tex.

"Indeed," said Yelena. She shot Karl a knowing look. He knew she thought her point had been illustrated.

"Okay," said Karl, taking his annoyance out on Tex. "Put your tongue back in cowboy. Did you get a chance to scout the area?"

Surprised by Karl's tone, Tex didn't make his usual smart comeback. He simply said: "I had a quick look around. There are no patrols for the next couple of blocks. Even still it's best to stay off the beaten track as much as possible. This is dangerous territory for two guys dressed like SS troopers." Karl nodded and said no more. He pulled away and Tex followed him.

Yelena led them away from the main thoroughfares. After a few narrow backstreets she directed Karl completely off the beaten path up a long gravel path. This led to an abandoned breaker's yard. "We're here," she said. Karl put the brakes on and kept the engine running. Tex slowed to a stop at his side.

In the centre of the yard was an open space where trucks had probably parked at one time. Surrounding all but one side of the space were huge piles of rusting automobiles and discarded machine parts. On the remaining side stood a disused six-storey building which might once have been offices and a storehouse.

"We'll hide the jeep and bike round the back of the building," said Karl. "Yelena you'll stay out of sight with the vehicles. Tex you should hide in amongst the junk, until I pick off Helmstadt."

"Already on it. You're gonna find a spot on the sixth floor of that building over there, somewhere in the far corner."

"That'll give me the elevation and the angle I need for the shot," said Karl. "It will also provide me with cover and a safe exit."

Once the vehicles were hidden Tex sprinted off to find a vantage point among a pile of ancient cogs and gears. Karl jogged around to the front of the building and tried the door. It was unlocked. The minute he stepped inside he had the nagging feeling that something was amiss.

Karl walked through a large deserted storeroom and found a flight of stairs. He couldn't see anything that ought to put him on his guard, but his instincts told him to be wary as he made his way up the stairs.

He proceeded cautiously up to the fifth floor. As he put his foot on the first flight up to the next floor he was deafened by the roar of an explosion. The force of the blast knocked him on to his back. The door to the sixth floor blew off its hinges as a huge burst of fire rolled out from inside the room beyond and shattered the windows on the landing. Two men ran out of the doorway screaming and in flames. The first one fell dead just outside the door. The second made it half way down the stairs before he expired.

As the flames and the heat died down, Karl got to his feet. He walked up to the sixth floor and peered through the doorway. He could make out the remains of four other men in the room beyond. Something was very wrong here and Karl wanted to know what was going on.

He ran back down the stairs and out the front of the building. Yelena suddenly bolted out from the side and ran across the open space screaming something in Russian. An automobile appeared from behind a pile of spare parts. Three men got out and began firing. Karl stepped back in to the doorway as the bullets ricocheted right past him.

He moved round to a window in the storeroom and put it through with his rifle butt. Karl pointed his rifle out of the broken window and focused on the men running towards him. He got the first in his crosshairs and fired. The man was too close and running too fast and what should have been a headshot nicked his ear. Karl fired three more times. The first two caught him in the chest but he didn't stop. The last one caught him in the guts and he doubled over and lay still.

The other two men began firing at the window where Karl was. The bullets smashed the glass and it rained down on him. Karl ducked out of sight and changed his position. The man in front was now very close to the building. Karl had one last shot at him before he reached the door. He estimated where the man would be in a couple of seconds, fixed that site in his crosshairs and waited for the man to run into it. The second he was there, Karl fired and the top of the man's head burst open ejecting shards of skull, thick globules of brain and a gallon of blood.

The remaining man was about half way across the open space. He turned and ran back for the cover of the car. Tex stepped out from behind his pile of junk and shot him twice in the stomach just before he reached his vehicle. Neither shot was instantly fatal. Both were intended to incapacitate him so he lived long enough to answer some questions.

Karl left the building and walked over to the car where the wounded man lay slumped. Tex was walking over to the man at the same time. Before either of them could reach him Yelena stepped out from behind the vehicle. She picked up the pistol the man had dropped, placed it to his head and pulled the trigger four times.

Tex came up and grabbed her from behind, pinning her arms to her sides. Yelena spat on the corpse of the man she had just executed and kicked it repeatedly, swearing in Russian, until Tex yanked her away.

Karl slapped Yelena hard across the face as Tex still held her. She calmed down and stared defiantly back. "What the hell is going on here?" He demanded. Yelena said nothing. Karl persisted. "Who the hell are these guys and what the hell were you shouting about?"

"They are agents of the NKVD," Yelena said. "I told them you had a rocket launcher. That you had blown up the agents waiting for you on the top floor and now you were going to turn your weapon on them."

"But why? We didn't have any rocket launcher. We had nothing to do with the explosion."

"I needed to flush them out. To get them to attack you so you would kill them in order to defend yourselves."

Tex let go of Yelena and held his hands up in bewilderment. "Wait a minute," he said. "Do you mind explaining to me just what is going on here? Who is that guy you just shot?"

Yelena took a deep breath. She had the calm demeanour of a woman who has let go of everything she ever lived for and is now resigned to her fate. "That is Comrade Ilyich Velikovsky. The man who killed everyone I ever loved and destroyed my life. He ran the NKVD operations here in Berlin. He was the man responsible for placing double agents and arranging defections to the East. He was supposed to be meeting General Helmstadt here. But first he had planned to capture the two of you. The men on the sixth floor were waiting to take you by surprise. They knew you would choose to take your shot there. They chose the site specially, so that you would only have that one option. Then they would have taken Tex."

"What," said Karl. "He knew we were going to be here?"

"He planned the whole thing," said Yelena. "It was all his idea. The whole thing has been a set up from the very moment I contacted the OSS. Its purpose was to allow Velikovsky to get his hands on the code to Helmstadt's case. When we learned that Kammler had come across it he conceived the whole plot. He couldn't afford to make Helmstadt suspicious by sending a Russian agent to steal the code and he knew I would never have made it out alive with the stolen code all by myself. So I contacted the OSS and suggested to them how they might steal it. Then you came and I made you rescue me. The plan was then to flatter your ego and make you fall in love with me, as so many other men have. So you would want to protect me and keep me close to you. Ironically the OSS sent the only man in Berlin who couldn't fall for my charms."

Tex shot Karl a quizzical look. Karl shook his head to dismiss what Tex might be thinking. "Carry on," said Karl. "I'm listening."

"When you wouldn't fall in love with me I had to find other ways of staying in your company. I wasn't too worried when you abandoned me at first. I knew I still had the location of Helmstadt's defection as a lure to entrap you again, just as Velikovsky had planned. Once he had tortured the code out of you or Tex he would then have disposed of Helmstadt and kept the Nazi's nuclear secrets."

"So you were working for him the whole time?"

"You catch on fast," said Yelena.

"So why did you just shoot him?" asked Tex.

"No-one foresaw that you would send me to the safe house and I had to improvise," said Yelena. "While I was there I saw my chance to take the revenge for which I had been yearning since the death of my family."

"So you planted the bombs," said Karl. "And double crossed Velikovsky in order to kill him."

"I didn't plant the bombs."

"You didn't," said Karl. "Then who did?"

"I did," said a voice behind them. They turned to see Isaac standing over Velikovsky's dead body. "It's strange," he said looking down at Velikovsky's corpse. "I thought I would take more satisfaction in this moment. But I feel... I feel nothing at all."

CHAPTER TWENTY-SIX

"Wait a minute," said Tex. "You planted the explosives?"

"That's right," said Isaac. "I did."

"Why in hell would you want to do that?"

"To do the one thing that everyone has been promising but abjectly failing to do for me," Isaac said.

Isaac reached into Velikovsky's pocket and removed some keys. Then he went around to the trunk of the car and opened it. Lying inside the boot were two young girls. Their arms and feet were tied behind them and their mouths were gagged. They both whimpered as the boot opened.

Even with the neglected condition they were in, Karl recognised instantly who they were. Ruth and Sarah, Isaac's daughters. Karl and Tex helped Isaac lift them from the boot. Tex cut the ropes binding them, Karl removed their gags and Isaac hugged them to him.

The girls burst into tears and so did Isaac. After all this time the three of them could hardly believe they were reunited. They clung desperately to one another, tears rolling down their cheeks, wailing their relief. Isaac kept repeating "Ya tebya lyublyu. Ya tebya lyublyu. Ya tebya lyublyu," over and over. Yelena told them this meant, "I love you" in Russian.

"What in Sam Hill were they doing in the boot of that car?" Tex said.

"They were a gift for General Helmstadt," Yelena told him. "A little sweetener for his defection. When Comrade Velikovsky found out that Helmstadt had certain unique vices he realised he had some leverage with which to arrange his defection. Rather than use this information to blackmail Helmstadt, as many officials would, he instead elected to indulge Helmstadt's vices in order to win the man's trust."

"What vices?" said Karl, who was reminded of the things that Herr Docktor had told him and Tex. "What are you talking about?"

"General Helmstadt takes his fanatical anti-semitism further than even his most zealous colleagues," said Yelena. "He likes to rape, torture and eventually murder pre-pubescent Jewish girls. The Nazi's treatment of the Jews has supplied him with a limitless supply of little girls with which to indulge this sickness. He is addicted to it, and his main worry about defecting was that his supply of victims would be cut off. Velikovsky assured him this would not be the case and that the Soviet Union would be only too happy to accommodate his particular needs. Velikovsky already had Isaac's daughters in his custody so he used them as a sign of good faith to Helmstadt. They were also to be a distraction, to keep Helmstadt occupied while Velikovsky's men extracted the code from you. When I met Isaac at the safe house I told him of this and we began to secretly hatch a plan to double cross Velikovsky, rescue Isaac's daughters and take our revenge on him."

"That's almost too sick to believe," said Tex.

"Just about everything about this war is almost too sick to believe," said Karl.

"If I hadn't seen it with my own eyes..." said Tex and trailed off.

"You see what sort of men you are dealing with," said Yelena. "This is the measure of what they are capable of."

At that moment Helmstadt's armoured car rolled up the little gravel path and pulled into the breaker's yard. The vehicle stopped and Helmstadt and his driver assessed what they saw.

Karl quickly raised his rifle. Before he could let off a shot the driver swung the armoured car around and took off back down the path.

"We've got to head him off," said Karl. "We can't let him get away." He and Tex ran for the jeep and motorbike. They started up the engines and gave chase.

When they got to the bottom of the gravel path, Helmstadt's armoured car had disappeared into the maze of backstreets. Karl and Tex turned off their engines and listened carefully. The unmistakable sound of Helmstadt's car could be heard a street and a half away. Karl started up the jeep again and burned down the back streets at full throttle.

He caught up with Helmstadt's car as it was pulling on to a main thoroughfare. Karl pushed the accelerator to the floor but Helmstadt's vehicle kept a constant distance ahead of him. It seemed unlikely that he could overtake it. The engine in the car was superior to the jeep Karl was driving.

Then Karl began to spot landmarks he had seen before, and recently. It started to dawn on him where he was. It was one of those moments when you suddenly connect one part of a city that you know well with another that you hadn't realised was so close. Then it became obvious to him where Helmstadt was heading.

Tex was riding right behind him. Karl waved for him to pull alongside. "I know where he's going," Karl shouted to Tex. "I also know a way to head him off. You stay on his tail, I'm going to take a detour."

Karl took a left at the next crossroads while Helmstadt and Tex carried straight on. He then took an immediate right. As he made the turn he was sure he caught sight of the black sedan he had seen tailing him earlier. He looked again and couldn't find it though. Although it was strange to see such a vehicle on such deserted streets three times in one day, Karl could not afford to dwell on the issue. He had far more pressing matters to contend with.

He drove as fast as he could down the bombed out streets and up ahead saw the flyover where he had blown up the fuel convoy. It ran straight over the road Helmstadt would have to take if he carried on in the direction he was going. Karl turned up the slip road and rode the top of the flyover. He screamed to a halt on the scorched tarmac, just at the point where the remains of the bridge had collapsed on to the road below. The flyover should give him the elevation he needed to get a good angle on the shot.

Karl anticipated that Helmstadt's driver would spot that the flyover had collapsed and slow down before turning and choosing another route. He would shoot out the tyres as the armoured car slowed then take out the driver. When Helmstadt made for cover he would wound him and let Tex take care of the case. Karl had taken the shorter route so Helmstadt should make an appearance in a matter of minutes.

He scanned the road through his binoculars. He listened carefully and caught the sound of Helmstadt's engine. He couldn't see the vehicle on the road below him though. This was worrying. As the sound of the engine got closer Helmstadt's car still failed to appear.

Too late Karl remembered that the road forked just beyond his line of vision. Helmstadt's driver must have taken the right hand fork. Karl looked over at the road the jeep must be taking. Through a gap in a row of buildings he saw it charging along at high speed. Then it was out of sight, hidden by half ruined houses and other structures. Karl looked to the next gap in the buildings through which he could see the road. There was one just a little further up ahead.

Karl had a clear shot but it had to be 1,185 to 1,200 metres away. That was at the far end of his rifle's range. He could not guarantee firing with pinpoint accuracy at that distance. There were too many factors to take into consideration. Karl knew of only one sniper who had ever fired with certain accuracy at that range. That was Tex and his sniping days were over. If Karl was to make these shots he either needed a lot of luck, or to take the single best shots of his whole career.

Karl took out his rifle and aimed it over the barrel of the jeep. He listened to his heartbeat slow then let out a long measured breath that took all the air out of his lungs. He went into a state of pure concentration. Nothing in the world existed outside of his finger on the trigger, the bullets in his clip and the wheels on the armoured car.

Helmstadt's vehicle drove into view. Karl fired three times at the front and back wheels just to be sure. Both of them burst and the vehicle skidded to a halt, just at the edge of the gap in the buildings. This narrowed Karl's field of vision and gave him only a small space in which to aim at his human target. There would be no margin for error.

The driver got out to check what had happened. Karl set his sites at 1,200 metres. He fired at the driver's chest and nicked his shoulder. He was a fraction off on the crossbar of his sights. He adjusted accordingly and put two in the driver's chest. The man bounced off the armoured car and slid to the ground, leaving a large red smear down the side of the vehicle.

Helmstadt got out of the armoured car on the opposite side, trying to keep the vehicle between himself and Karl's line of fire. Tex hadn't caught up to him so there was still the possibility that he could get away. Karl fired a couple of warning shots to keep Helmstadt from running out of his line of fire and behind the buildings.

The General panicked and made a run for it. This was just the moment Karl had been waiting for. He had a couple of seconds to make the shot. It was simultaneously the most difficult and most important shot of his entire career.

Helmstadt was running across the street and was almost out of the range of Karl's rifle. Karl had to stop him moving without vitally wounding him. At this range it was impossible to guarantee that a freak gust of wind or a slight miscalculation might not mean the bullet would strike inches off target and hit a vital organ.

If that happened then the only way Karl would know about it would be when he woke up in hell. He consoled himself with the thought that the stress of hell wouldn't be any greater than the pressure he was under right now.

He decided to aim for Helmstadt's legs. No easy feat as they were a constantly moving target. He let out his breath once more and a small prayer with it. Maybe God wouldn't care too much for the fate of a killer like Karl, but there were a lot of innocent lives resting on the success of his next shot and perhaps the big guy would look out for them.

Helmstadt's legs were a blur. Even if they were stationery Karl would have had difficulty focusing on them as they were now practically out of the range of both his sights and his weapon. He aimed using pure instinct and sent two bullets into the empty space between him and his target.

For a moment all he heard was the pounding of his

heart. The air rushing past his ears. The sweat dripping from his forehead.

Then Helmstadt appeared to skip like a small child, or a housewife who has been scared by a mouse running over her foot. Blood gushed copiously out of his right leg just above the knee and he keeled over forward and dropped the case.

Karl had made his shot. He breathed in for the first time. He felt light headed and almost giddy with the success. He wanted to burst into tears, laugh his ass off and punch the air all at the same time.

Helmstadt lay flailing on the ground. Now it was over to Tex and the most crucial part of the operation. Karl watched through his binoculars as Tex pulled up on his bike. He dismounted and picked up the case setting it upright so he could look at the tumblers.

Helmstadt was screaming something at Tex. Karl could imagine the threats and warnings that Helmstadt would be issuing. Tex didn't bat an eyelid. He just got on with the job in hand.

Karl switched his focus between Tex slowly turning the tumblers, Helmstadt berating him and the case itself. Karl could just about make out the tiny light on the top of the case turn green then red then green just as Herr Docktor had told them. Then he saw the little row of lights on the side also turn green then red then green in the same sequence. Satisfied that the code had worked, Tex stood up and picked up the case.

Then Karl saw the little row of lights on the side turn red again. This was bad. Something was wrong. The code had not worked and the case was still armed.

What was worse was that Tex hadn't noticed. He just kept walking away from Helmstadt and ignored the General's warnings.

Karl had to warn Tex, to stop him, but how? He was so far away it would be impossible for Karl to call out to him and Tex was seconds away from taking out half of Berlin.

Tex was nearly nine feet away from Helmstadt. A few more steps and the case would detonate. Karl fired a warning shot at Tex's feet. Tex pulled out his pistol and crouched low, trying to see where the shot had come from. Karl realised that Tex had no idea where he was. The shot could have come from anyone.

Tex stood slowly scanning the area and started to walk back to his bike. There was only one way Karl could stop him. He would have to shoot him like he had shot Helmstadt. Tex was even further out of range though. The shot was even more difficult and Karl had even less time.

He drew a bead on Tex, but his finger wavered on the trigger. Karl couldn't guarantee he wouldn't fatally hit Tex. He knew that if the tables were turned then Tex would make the same call, would expect Karl to make this call. That didn't make it any easier.

Tex had saved Karl's life on more occasions than he could count. He had been there for Karl when no-one else had. And now Karl had to shoot him, for the sake of every man, woman and child in Berlin.

Tex was too far out of range for Karl to attempt a leg shot. He had to aim for the body as his best option and hope he didn't do too much damage. He wasn't even sure if he could make the shot, but he was sure that he had to try. Tex was more than nine feet away from Helmstadt when Karl squeezed the trigger.

Tex shuddered and fell forward dropping the case just within the ten foot radius. He hit the ground and lay still. A large pool of blood began to form beneath him.

He was dead. Karl had just killed the best friend he had ever had.

CHAPTER TWENTY-SEVEN

Karl jumped into his jeep and tore over to where Tex and Helmstadt lay. As he made the journey he was positive that he saw the sedan again, but he didn't care. He had more important matters to worry about.

Karl pulled up next to Tex's discarded bike. He climbed out and walked over to the case. "Ah, it is you," said Helmstadt. "The soldier from the square. You have become my guardian angel it seems. Quickly, help me to the car. We need to get away from here before any more of the Americans come."

"I'm afraid I can't do that General," Karl said. "You see I am American." Helmstadt stared at him incredulously the minute Karl began talking in English. Then he went back to swearing and hectoring Karl to leave the case alone.

Karl was studying the tumblers, which showed the right numbers in the sequence when he heard Max's voice. "Alright Karl," Max said. "Stand up and back away from the case." Karl looked up, surprised to see Max at the scene. He was even more surprised to see Max had a gun trained on him.

"Max," Karl said. "What is this all about?"

"Just stand up and back away from the case. And while you're at it take off your rifle and pistol and throw them on the floor."

"I don't understand. What's going on? How did you get here?"

"Just drop your guns. And the two knives you carry. Throw them all on the floor and kick them away from you." Karl did as he was told. "As to how I got here," said Max. "I've been following you since you left the square."

"The black sedan," said Karl. "That was you, but why the gun Max? Is this about the business with my father and the suspicions over whether we're both collaborators?"

"Yes," said Max. "It is."

"But Max, you can't believe them. You of all people should know the accusation isn't true."

"Oh I know the accusation isn't true alright," said Max. "Because I made it." Karl could not believe what he was hearing. He felt like someone had just punched him in the gut. All the strength drained out of him. "But... but why?"

"Two reasons. The first was to save my career. I was all washed up when I got back from working for your father in Berlin. There was a cloud hanging over me and my career was finished. Then the war broke out in Europe. National security became of paramount importance. The Nazis had received certain sensitive documents from your father's office and he had several meetings with high-ranking SS officers that were unaccounted for. I stepped forward, made allegations and suddenly my superiors started to take notice and I started to go places. Your father never knew it was me who accused him and he refused to explain himself. He was protecting me you see. It was perfect. I knew he would. He was always loyal to his staff, even when they betrayed their country."

"Max..." said Karl unable to believe what he was hearing.

"That's right," said Max. "I passed on the documents. I had to you see, they were blackmailing me. I was younger then, more inexperienced. I wasn't prepared for the sexual sophistication of Berlin. I met a beautiful young girl at an official party. She seduced me and before I knew it the Nazis were putting the squeeze on me. Your father found out straight away. I confessed everything.

He arranged a meeting with Kammler and other high-ranking SS officers, did a few trade offs and straightened out the whole thing. Then he sent me home on the next flight."

"He protected you. He looked after you and you betrayed him."

"He betrayed me," Max spat. His eyes were alive with a hatred that Karl had never seen before. "A lesson in sexual politics wasn't the only thing the filthy little siren gave me. I also caught a dose of the clap – gonorrhoea to be precise. I went to your father about that too. He told me to wash it with soap and water and it would go away in a few days. I believed him. As I said I was younger then and more inexperienced. By the time the doctors did get to it there was nothing much left to do. I was infertile. It was your father's fault and I wanted to pay him back for what he'd done to me. The allegations seemed like the perfect way to ruin him as he had ruined me. But it didn't end there. There were further complications. Because the gonorrhoea had been left unchecked for so long, several years later I developed cancer. Cancer in the one place where every man dreads getting it. I had several operations, but none of them worked. I'm dying Karl, I won't see the end of this war and that's all your father's fault. I still owe him payback and I mean to get it by taking away from him the one thing he holds most dear."

"Max. I don't understand."

"Of course you don't. You never did. Following me around all doe eyed, looking to make me the father your own father never was, because he could never tell you just how much his golden boy meant to him. How proud he was of how well you did at Westpoint. If I could take that away from him then I could really get even. So I won your confidence, came on all fatherly and brought you out to Berlin. Fed you any corny old line and you bought it hook, line and sinker. And I thought I was green at your age."

"What are you saying?"

"I'm saying I kept sending you out to die and you kept surviving. That's your real talent: staying alive. Lots of men can kill as well as you can. Few can survive what you've survived. The mission to the Reichstag was a suicide mission. That's why we were all so surprised to see you. I thought I'd finally managed to kill you and then you pop up with that infernal code."

"But you needed the code."

"The code is a fake. We came up with it. It was one of our agents who passed it on to Kammler and he died in the process. We sent you in there to try and kill him and steal it to make it look good, so they wouldn't be suspicious. You weren't supposed to succeed. We wanted Kammler to detonate the case. Before Washington got greedy and wanted to take the missile we planned to destroy it by playing Kammler off against Helmstadt here. We knew he would try and seize the case and defuse it as soon as he could if he had the code. He would have taken out the missile in the explosion and a lot of soon to be hostile Russians in the process, leaving Berlin ours for the taking."

"Wait," said Karl. "That means you must have known about the missile."

"We've known about it for some while. Helmstadt originally intended to come over to our side and point the missile at Moscow. For some reason he had a change of heart at the last minute. What we didn't know were the finer points of the project. Where the missile was being stored and how they intended to fire it from the centre of

Berlin. Once we knew all that we could start planning our counter offensive."

"If you knew the code was a fake, then why did you send me and Tex out here to retrieve the case?"

"To draw Velikovsky out and find what he was playing at. We didn't foresee Yelena and Isaac's double cross though."

"But we could have set the case off."

"That's exactly what we wanted you to do. The boys on the Manhattan Project want to study what happens when someone lets off a nuclear device in a densely populated area. The war with Japan isn't coming to an end and we're going to have to use the bomb on them. We want to find out what might happen before we do."

"But the lives of millions of innocent people... "

"Mean absolutely nothing. They mean nothing to the people we're up against; look at Pearl Harbour, look at Auschwitz. You don't win wars by being nobler than your enemies. You win them by being better at killing. So it's time to create a few atrocities of our own. Starting here. I followed you to watch you finally die. That's all I have left to look forward to. Yet somehow you still managed to cheat me out of it. So it's time for me to sort that out personally. I'm going to finish your mission for you. And this time it's going to end the way it's supposed to."

Max bent down and picked up the case. Karl held out his hands. Helmstadt started shouting violently. "Wait Max," said Karl. "You don't have to!"

"Oh but I do. I'm afraid I have to."

There was the sudden sound of a gunshot. Max dropped the case at his feet and looked down at the hole in his chest. It was pumping out blood by the gallon. He looked up at Karl. "Damn you," Max said, his mouth full of blood. "You're still alive. How in God's name do you do it?" Then he sank to his kneels and fell face first into the dirt.

Karl looked down at the bodies of Max and Tex at his feet. In the last half hour he had lost his only true friend and his surrogate father.

He looked up to see who was responsible and saw Yelena holding a smoking pistol.

CHAPTER TWENTY-EIGHT

"And how exactly did Miss Petronova arrive at the scene?" asked Allen Dulles, OSS Deputy Head and commander of operations in Bern. He had been grilling Karl, in the company of Major Kowalski, for hours.

"She had been following us in Comrade Velikovsky's car sir."

"So let me get this right," Dulles said. "Miss Petronova was following Max Avery who was following you. You were following the late agent Tex Jones who was in turn following General Helmstadt's car?"

"I wasn't following General Helmstadt's car the whole time sir," Karl said. "I did take a detour to cut him off."

"Nevertheless," said Dulles. "It sounds like you had a regular convoy making its way through the streets of Berlin. I'm surprised that no-one mistook you for a parade."

"I'm just telling you the facts as I saw them happen, Sir."

"Yes, and the 'facts as you saw them happen' seem to have rather conveniently benefited you, wouldn't you say Agent Fairburne?"

"I don't know what you're implying sir."

"Of course you don't. Your commanding officer happens to have been a traitor to his country who falsely accused you and your father of treason. He confessed all this to you just before someone else shot him. This completely exonerates you from all of the charges for which you were being investigated, without you having to come up with any tricky burden of proof. Am I supposed to clear you on this slim piece of evidence? Do you think it will neatly tie up the investigation?"

"Investigation be damned," shouted Kowalski, banging his fist on the table. "This man played a key role in capturing that missile and securing the area. He's one of the men responsible for saving hundreds of thousands of American lives and I mean to see that he gets a medal for it if I have to knock down every door in the Pentagon and walk over every official."

"You might have to go through me to do that," said Dulles. "And I have some rather powerful friends."

"Yeah, and I've got some rather powerful weaponry," said Kowalski. "I know which I'd rather have on my side in a fight."

"Indeed," said Dulles. "Speaking of weaponry, what happened to General Helmstadt and his case?"

Karl took a minute to consider his answer, to review the events that followed Max getting shot. He looked around the utilitarian office in the OSS HQ, comfortably situated on neutral Swiss territory. The American flag furled in the corner, the picture of President Roosevelt on the wall and the dull, grey stenographer sitting silently in the corner taking down the whole interview. None of it seemed real to him, not as real as the streets of Berlin. He had been alive there.

The conflicts had been genuine, so had the adrenaline. This tedious head to head with Dulles was not a proper face off. Not like facing down Yelena with a pistol in her hand.

"Put your hands in the air," Yelena said the minute he saw her. "I just saved your life once again, but I won't hesitate to take it if you don't do what I tell you." Karl put his hands in the air.

"Yelena," he said. "What are you planning to do?"

"I'm going to take the case, and don't even think of trying to stop me. It was you who taught me how to kill. I had a very good teacher, but you had a brilliant pupil. Don't think you can take me on and win." Karl took a long, seasoned look at Yelena as an opponent, and realised she was right.

"Come with me," she said and led Karl at gunpoint to Velikovsky's car. She tossed him the keys. "Open the boot," she said. It was filled with handcuffs, shackles, rope and hoods. "These were intended for you and Tex," she said. "Now I have other uses for them."

She made Karl take them and tie Helmstadt up so that he couldn't move. Karl had to gag him first. His endless ranting was becoming unbearable. Yelena was careful to make sure he left both the leg wounds accessible. "I shall need to tend those," she said. "I need him immobile but I shall have to keep him alive during the long drive I have planned."

When Helmstadt was fully secured she directed Karl to carry him to the armoured car and place him inside. "What about the case?" Karl said.

"I'll take care of the case," she told him and picked it up.

It struck Karl that all three people who had handled the case in the past half hour had been shot. And of those, only Helmstadt was still alive. He wondered if Yelena would fare any better.

Karl hoisted Helmstadt onto his shoulders and stumbled with him to the car. Yelena opened the back door and Karl threw Helmstadt across the seat. Then she went around to the back of the vehicle. There were three large gas cans in the trunk of the armoured car. Two were full, the other was empty. She directed Karl to fill the empty can with gas from Velikovsky's automobile and the jeep.

"What happened to Isaac and his girls?" Karl asked as he siphoned off the gas.

"He put the girls in the jeep that he took from the safe house and went to find the agents who were looking for him. He wanted to make sure that he and his girls were properly protected."

"Will he find them?"

"Oh yes," said Yelena. "He knows exactly where they are. That's how he was able to give them the slip so easily. After spending so long in the custody of the Russian secret service we both find your OSS rather amateur to be honest."

"Thanks. You know how to make a man feel good about himself."

"Oh no, it is a good thing. It is one of the main reasons he wants to go and settle in your country. Our country provides complete security for its citizens but at the cost of our individual liberty. One of the main tools it uses to deny us this liberty is the vast secret service. The fact that you don't have as effective an organisation as our NKVD is a good thing for your freedom. You need only be worried when your OSS, or the organisations that succeed it, becomes as ruthless and efficient as our secret service."

"I imagine Isaac will do rather well in the US," said Karl as he shook the last few drops of gas from the tube in Velikovsky's tank. He has a lot of knowledge that will be highly useful to my country and they'll treat him a lot better than your country did."

"I don't doubt that they will," said Yelena as Karl moved over to the jeep and began to drain its tank into the gas canister.

"You will leave me with enough gas to get back won't you? You don't want to leave me stranded in Russian territory dressed like I am."

"You're a very resourceful man," said Yelena. "I'm sure you'll find a way to survive. As your former boss said, just before I shot him, it's what you're good at. You have a talent for it."

"Hmph," Karl grunted. He did not like being reminded of his recent conversation with Max. He was still coming to terms with everything that had been said.

"I'll leave you as much fuel as is left in the tank after you've filled the canister," Yelena said. "I will need a lot of fuel to get to where I'm going."

"Where are you going, if you don't mind me asking?" The gas canister was full. Karl screwed the lid on and put it back in the trunk of the armoured car.

Yelena climbed behind the wheel and put the case on the passenger seat. "To Siberia," she said. She still had her pistol trained on Karl.

"What's in Siberia?" he asked.

"The labour camp where my brother died, and where Isaac's wife and so many other people's loved ones also perished. A bleak little encampment on a remote hill, surrounded by trees and scrubland for hundreds of kilometres. A place of misery and exile that had no place existing at all. It's empty now. They evacuated it after all the inmates and most of the guards were killed in the epidemic. It won't be empty for long though. Soon its gates will open once again and it will be filled with more dissidents, more intellectuals who cannot accept the inevitable march of history and other undesirables. Their souls will be crushed by meaningless work and the ruthlessness of the petty regime. I can't allow that to happen."

"What are you going to do?"

"I'm going to drive there with General Helmstadt and

keep him alive until we arrive," said Yelena. "Then I'm going to take the case and watch one last glorious sunrise from the top of the hillside. When that is done I'm going to fling the case as far from me as I can, down into the camp. All that will be left of the accursed place is a giant crater. What's more, Isaac tells me that the earth all around will be so contaminated by the radiation that it will not be safe to use for at least another hundred years. Hopefully by that time my country will have abandoned the use of such places. Tell your superiors that if they try and stop me, or impede me in any way I will not hesitate to detonate the case. They have been warned."

With that she started up the engine and pulled away. That was the last that Karl saw of Yelena, the case or General Helmstadt. He watched the armoured car for a long time as it drove off into the distance. Such a small vehicle carrying such a great threat.

Karl drove Tex's motorbike back to the breaker's yard where the corpses of Velikovsky and his men still lay. He found a Russian uniform that wasn't too covered with blood or punctured by bullet holes and he put it on. So disguised he had ridden back to Kowalski's camp on the motorbike and reported for his debriefing.

His report went up the chain of command and he found himself in Bern, reporting to Dulles and Kowalski. Repeating his account of the events over and over in minute detail.

Kowalski and Dulles listened carefully to Karl's account of what happened to Helmstadt and his case. They were not pleased about Yelena's warning.

Dulles stood up and nodded to the stenographer that he could stop taking notes now. He told Karl that everything he had said would be investigated. Until his account of the events was properly verified, Karl was restricted to the nearest US army base and he was to make himself constantly available to the Bern OSS office. Dulles said a formal farewell to the Major and then left with the stenographer.

Karl stood and saluted Dulles who just looked at him and then walked out. Kowalski got up and walked over to Karl. "At ease Fairburne," he said. "Don't worry too much about Dulles, he's just got to keep up that front to cover his ass. He's a bureaucrat, not a man of active service. That's the way military intelligence is going these days. Men like the current head, Wild Bill Donovan, the most decorated soldier of the last war you know, they're becoming a thing of the past. Dulles and the men like him, they're the future now. They'll still need men of your talents though. Don't worry about that. They won't throw you to the wolves. You'll be back in active service in no time."

"If I want to go back," said Karl.

"Son," said Kowalski. "You just shot your best friend and watched your commanding officer get killed. So I'll forgive the stupidity of that last remark. Of course you're going back into active service, you're too talented not to."

"Okay. But what have my talents really done to win this war?"

"No man wins a war son. Only nations and political philosophies win wars. Men just survive them. It doesn't matter how well a soldier fights, the best measure of a man under fire is whether he lives through it or not. You lived through a lot. That makes you highly valuable to your country. Surviving is also the best way we can honour our fallen comrades. If some of us don't come home and carry on defending our country then they will have died for nothing."

Karl silently nodded his assent. Kowalski slapped him on the shoulder. "Good man. Now Dulles wants you posted to a US army base for the duration of this investigation does he? Well I have a few little jobs you can take care of. Report to me first thing tomorrow morning."

"Yes sir," said Karl and saluted.

Kowalski returned the salute. "Dismissed," he said, and left.

If Kowalski was right, then at least Karl had honoured fallen comrades like Tex and Gary by living through the last days of Berlin. He had played the game right to the end. He had finished every mission Max had sent him on, and in spite of Max's intentions he had survived. That was the one and only thing that Max had really taught him. That he could survive. He had a talent for it.

THE END

JASPRE BARK writes fiction and comics for grown ups and children. He has written for everyone in British comics, from *2000 AD* through to the *Beano* and *Viz*. He has published one previous novel, *A Fistful of Strontium,* for Black Flame. Prior to this he toured extensively and made numerous radio and TV appearances as a stand up poet. He has also worked as a national film and music journalist and written scripts for short films, radio and stage plays. He has published two books of poetry and was awarded a Fringe First at the Edinburgh Festival in 1999.

Now read a chapter from the first book in
Abaddon's exciting new series...

CHAPTER ONE

On the Origin of Species

The night Alfred Wentwhistle died began just like any other.

The cold orb of the moon shone through the arched windows of the museum, bathing the myriad display cases in its wan blue light, enhancing the blackness of the shadows and giving their time-locked occupants an even more eerie and sinister quality. The electric street lamps on Cromwell Road were a mere flicker of orange beyond the panes of glass.

Alfred Wentwhistle, night watchman at the museum for the last thirty-six years, swept the polished cabinets with the beam of his spotlight, gleaming eyes, hooked beaks and outstretched wings materialising suddenly and momentarily under the harsh white attentions of its searing bulb. The beam's path was a familiar one, the repeated motions of a never-ending ballet rehearsal of strobing light. And the winding path he took through the miles of corridors, halls and galleries was a familiar one too, the same route taken every night for the last thirty years. It was the course his predecessor had taken and taught him when he was a boy of barely sixteen, and when old Shuttleworth had just two months to his retirement, having trod the same path himself for the last fifty-four years.

There was never any need to change the route he took. Night watchman of the Natural History Museum at South Kensington was not a demanding role. Alfred carried his truncheon and torch every night but he had never had need of the former in all his years in the post, and he no longer really needed the latter either. He could have found his way around the galleries on a moonless night in the middle of a blackout with his eyes closed, as he used to like to tell Mrs Wentwhistle with a chuckle. He simply carried the spotlight through force of habit. There had not been one break-in in all his thirty-six years at the museum. And apart from the infrequent change of the odd cabinet here and there or the moving of an artefact every once in a while, the familiar layout of the museum had changed little in any significant way since the arrival of the *Diplodocus carnegii*, ninety-two years before in 1905.

But Alfred Wentwhistle enjoyed his job and it gave him great satisfaction too. He delighted in spending hours amongst the exhibits of stuffed beasts and dinosaur bones. Of course, you could experience the real thing now, with the opening of the Challenger Enclosure at London Zoo in Regent's Park, but there was something timeless and magical about the fossil casts of creatures that amateur archaeologists, who had effectively been the first palaeontologists, had taken to be evidence of the existence of the leviathans of legend such as the dragon or the cyclops.

Every now and then, undisturbed by the presence of the public, Alfred took pleasure from reading the hand-written labels explaining what any particular item was, where it had been collected from, who had recovered it and any other pertinent information the creator of the exhibit had seen fit to share. After thirty-six years there were not many labels that Alfred had not read.

And he took great satisfaction from knowing that he was playing his part to keep secure the nation's – and by extension the Empire's and hence, in effect, the world's – greatest museum of natural history. Even though there had been no challenge to its peaceful guardianship of Mother Nature's myriad treasures since he took up his tenure, Alfred Wentwhistle was there, every night of the year – save Christmas night itself – just in case the museum should ever need him.

Every now and again he would come upon one of the museum's research scientists working late into the night. They would pass pleasantries with him and he with them. They all knew old, reliable Alfred and he knew all of them by name, but nothing much more, and that was how they all liked it. Over the course of thirty-six years, he had seen professors come and go – botanists, zoologists, naturalists and cryptozoologists – but some things stayed the same, like the Waterhouse building itself and its night-time guardian. Alfred knew his place. The scientists were highly intelligent and erudite luminaries of the museum foundation and he was merely a night watchman. It was enough for him that he was allowed to spend hours enjoying the exhibits on display within. Nature's treasurehouse was what they called it; Sir Richard Owen's lasting legacy to the world.

Alfred's slow steady steps inexorably brought him back into the central hall and to the museum entrance, just as they always did. He paused beneath the outstretched head of the skeletal diplodocus to shine his torch on the face of his pocket watch. Five minutes past, just like every other night; regular as clockwork.

He looked up, shining the bright white beam of his torch into the hollow orbits of the giant's eye-sockets. It stared impassively ahead at the entrance to the museum and saw 20,000 visitors pass between its archways practically every day. He heard the tap of metal against metal, caught the glimmer of light on glass flicker at the corner of his eye, and it was then that he realised one of the doors was open.

There was no doubt in his mind that the door had been locked. It was the first thing he did upon coming on duty. Having had the keys handed over to him by George Stimpson, his counterpart during the daylight hours, and bid his colleague farewell, Alfred always locked the main doors to the museum. Should any of the scientists or cataloguers be working late and need to leave after this time, Alfred himself had to let them out and then would always lock the door again after them.

No, there was no doubt in his mind that something was awry this night. Pacing towards the doors he could see by the light of his torch where the lock had been forced.

The sound of breaking glass echoed through the silent halls of the museum from an upper gallery.

There was something most definitely awry. For the first time in thirty-six years, something was wrong. His museum needed him.

Turning from the main doors the portly night watchman jogged across the central hall, his shambling steps marking the full eighty-foot length of the diplodocus to the foot of the main staircase.

Once there he glanced back over his shoulder and up at the grand arch of the first floor staircase, at the other end of the hall over the museum entrance. Above him carved monkeys scampered up the curving arches of the roof into the darkness, amidst the leaf-scrolled iron span-beams. The sound had definitely come from somewhere up there, where the museum staff's private offices were located.

Putting a hand to the polished stone balustrade and taking a deep breath, Alfred Wentwhistle started to take the steps two at a time. At the first landing, where the staircase split beneath the austere bronze-eyed gaze of

Sir Richard Owen, he turned right. Hurrying along the gallery over-looking the central hall and running parallel to it, passed stuffed sloths and the mounted skeletons of prehistoric marine reptiles, brought him to the second flight of stairs.

Here he paused, out of breath and ears straining, as he tried to work out more precisely where the sound had come from. In the comparative quiet of the sleeping museum he heard another sound, like the crash of a table over-turning. The noise had come from somewhere on this floor, away to his right, from somewhere within the western Darwin wing.

Alfred turned into this series of galleries, passing beneath the carved archway that read 'The Ascent of Man'. He quickened his pace again as he came into a moonlit gallery of cases containing wax replicas of man's ancestors. They stood there, frozen in time, in various hunched poses, every kind of hominid from *Australopithecus* to *Homo neanderthalensis*. His sweeping spot-beam shone from bared snarling teeth, glass eyes and the black-edged blades of flint tools.

On any other night, as he had on any one of a hundred other previous visits, Alfred would have paused in this gallery to examine the specimens and their accompanying explanations once again, telling of the evolution of Man from primitive ape. He would have been just as fascinated and amazed as he had been the first time he had read of *The Origin of Species* and learnt of the incredible story of the human race's rise to become the most powerful and widely proliferated species on the Earth, and beyond.

When Charles Darwin had first proposed his hypothesis of the origin of species, natural selection and the survival of the fittest, he had been derided by the greatest scientific minds of his day and denounced as at best a charlatan and at worst a heretic. For he had spoken out against the worldwide Christian Church and its core belief that God had created all life on the planet in its final form from the beginning of time.

And with the re-discovery of the lost worlds hidden within the jungles of the Congo, atop the mesa-plateaus of the South American interior and on lost islands within the Indian Ocean, others – many of them churchmen – had come forward to challenge Darwin's claims again, vociferously supporting the supposition that because dinosaurs and other prehistoric creatures still existed on the Earth in the present day, the idea of one species evolving into another was ludicrous. And the debate still raged in some persistent, unremitting quarters.

But over a hundred years after his death, Darwin had been posthumously exonerated of all accusations of bestial heresy and scientific idiocy to the point where he was practically idolised as the father of the new branch of science of Evolutionary Biology, and had an entire wing of the Natural History Museum dedicated to the advances made since he first proposed his radical ideas in 1859. In fact there were scientists working within that field now, in this very museum; men like Professors Galapagos and Crichton.

On many previous occasions Alfred Wentwhistle had found himself wiling away some time gazing into the faces of his evolutionary ancestors, his reflection in the glass of the cabinets overlaid on top of the pronounced brows and sunken eyes beneath. On such occasions he had wondered upon Darwin's legacy for the human race and what implications such an accepted theory might have for Her Majesty Queen Victoria, in that it presumed that the British monarch was ultimately descended from the apes of ancient aeons past. But there was no time for such musings now. As he hurried passed the exhibits on this occasion, and turned into one of the numerous secondary galleries of the Darwin Wing, he barely even registered the frozen apemen locked within their glass cages.

The familiar smell of camphor and floor polish assailed his nostrils. Moonlight bathed the gallery with its monochrome light from skylights in the ceiling. The place Alfred found himself in now was one in which examples of animals from the orders of mammalia, reptialia and amphibia had been arranged so as to clearly show the evolutionary path Man had followed from the moment his Palaeozoic ancestors had first crawled out of the primeval swamps to the present day when he bestrode the globe like a colossus, the human race covering the Earth and the nearer planets of the solar system with all the persistence and perniciousness of a parasitic plague.

It was off this room that some of the scientists had their private workspaces. A number of doors on either side of the gallery stretching away before him bore the brass name plaques of the great and the good who worked within the museum, busily unravelling the mysteries of Evolution and Nature's – or God's – predestined plan for mankind.

He could hear clear sounds of a struggle now. In the beam of his spotlight fragments of glass glittered on the floor of the gallery before one of the frosted glass-paned doors, looking like a diamond frost on the first morning of winter. The flickering glow of an electric lamp cast its light into the gallery from inside the office before suddenly going out. There was a violent crash of more breaking glass and furniture being overturned.

He would certainly have a dramatic tale to tell Mrs Wentwhistle over his platter of bacon and eggs the next morning at the end of his shift, Alfred suddenly, incongruously, found himself thinking.

As the watchman neared the invaded office he noticed vaporous wisps of smoke or some sort of gas seeping under the door and a new smell – like aniseed, with an unpleasant undertone of gone off meat – made his nose wrinkle and made him instinctively hold back.

The door suddenly burst open, sending more shards of glass spinning into the gallery, clattering against the arrayed display cases. The figure of a man burst out of the office and collided with the aging night watchman. Alfred reeled backwards as the man barged past him. He couldn't stop himself from stumbling into a case containing a family of Neanderthal waxworks posed around an inanimate fire. The torch fell from his hand and its bulb died.

"Here, what do you think you're doing?" Alfred managed, calling after the man as he sprinted from the gallery. He was holding something about the same shape and size as a packing box in his arms. But the thief did not stop, and before Alfred had even managed to regain his balance he was gone, disappearing into the main hall of the Darwin Wing.

Alfred's heart was racing, beating a tattoo of nervous excitement against his ribs. In all his thirty-six years he had never known anything like it. Adrenalin flooding his system, he was about to give chase when something reminded him that the thief had not been alone in the office. Alfred had heard more than one voice raised in anger as he had approached and there had been definite signs of a struggle.

Cautiously, he approached the darkened doorway of the office. The rancid mist was beginning to dissipate. The soles of his boots crunched on the fractured diamonds of glass. He could hear the sound of the thief's feet pounding on the polished floors of the museum as he made his escape. But from inside the pitch black office-cum-laboratory in front of him he could hear a ragged breathing that reminded him of an animal snuffling. Then, suddenly, there was silence.

Alfred took another step forward.

"What the devil?" was all he could manage.

In an explosion of glass and splintering wood something else burst out of the office, ripping the door from its sundered frame as it did so. The night watchman barely had time to yelp out in pain as slivers of glass sliced his face and hands as he raised them to protect himself, before a hulking shadow of solid black muscle was on top of him.

Alfred had a momentary impression of thick, matted hair, a sharp bestial odour – a rank animal smell mixed in with the aniseed and rancid meat – broad shoulders and a blunt-nosed head slung low between them. There was a flash of silver as the moonlight caught something swinging from around the thing's neck.

He had never known anything like it, never in thirty-six years.

And then, teeth bared in an animal scream, its hollering cry deafening in his ears, fists flailing like sledge hammers, the ape-like creature attacked. Feebly Alfred put up his arms to defend himself but there was nothing he could do against the brute animal strength of his attacker.

It grabbed Alfred's head by the hair so violently he could hear as well as feel clumps of it being ripped from his scalp. And then, in one savage action, the enraged beast smashed his skull backwards into the Neanderthal display case. With the second blow the glass of the cabinet shattered and Alfred Wentwhistle's world exploded into dark oblivion.

For more information on this
and other titles visit...

Abaddon Books

Dreams of Inan

A KIND OF PEACE

Andy Boot

Price: £6.99 ★ ISBN: 1-905437-02-1

Price: $7.99 ★ ISBN 13: 978-1-905437-02-3

Price: £6.99 ★ ISBN: 1-905437-03X

Price: $7.99 ★ ISBN 13: 978-1-905437-03-0

THE AFTERBLIGHT CHRONICLES

The CULLED

Simon Spurrier

Price: £6.99 ★ ISBN: 1-905437-01-3

Price: $7.99 ★ ISBN 13: 978-1-905437-01-6